The Passage To Eden

An Historical Perspective Novel

by Ken B. Williams

The Passage To Eden

Published by Ken B. Williams & Associate
Patricia A. Williams

Edited by: Read in Barbados.com

Cover designed by: Kellie Alicia Barker,
CompuPrint, Ltd. Welches Terrace, St. Michael Barbados.

ISBN: 976-8077-18-2

Printed in Trinidad by Saudia Enterprises Limited

This book is dedicated to my wife, the late Adora Elise,
without whose contribution
it could not have come to fruition.

A WORD TO THE READER

This book was born from an idea so rare, that my most intimate friends would doubt its existence in me.

For many years I have been interested in people; and my extensive travels, and association with those I have met of different nationalities have led me to the conclusion that people are people. They differ greatly in many aspects; but fundamentally, they are all alike. Every man is a sinner and every man is a saint; and these traits are expressed to a greater or lesser degree in accordance with our spiritual awareness.

Modern man has declined to an appalling stage .... a stage when vice is accepted and virtue is scoffed at.

In this book I have tried to re-establish a virtue that is almost alien; but I sincerely hope to rekindle its dying embers in this blackened world and light man's way to guide him whence he came.

Ken B. Williams

Ken B. Williams

The Author's Historic Review
On
The Passage To Eden

I was forty-four years of age in 1961 when this photograph was taken, mainly to become part of the decoration on the cover of 'The Passage To Eden' which was written between 1959 and 1962.

However, after an attempted theft of the manuscript, and numerous rejections which amounted to several hundred dollars in postage over the years, I became frustrated and chucked it away in the bookcase until I surrendered to the pleading of my daughter to try for publication once more. By this time the paper was discoloured and the entire work had to be reproduced. This was done word for word, page for page .... identical to the original idea from which the manuscript was born.

But this New, and unfamiliar idea for conscientious living which is pre-scribed in 'The Passage to Eden,' will undoubtedly be again rejected by those persons who continue to uphold the Old idea. So I have decided to be publisher of 'The Passage To Eden' - The **PASSAGE** to be adopted for a fearless journey into the new millennium.

ACKNOWLEDGEMENTS

Mr. Nathaniel (Jonnie) Millar, who sacrificed his Sunday afternoon siesta with his family, to type the first draft of the manuscript back in 1962.

Mrs. O. Merlese Drayton, who endured many sleepless nights in order to proof-read the manuscript.

Mr. Hugh A. Belle (with whom I worked as a seaman), who gored me into writing my first piece of poetry, 'Before I Left Her' in 1949, and afforded me the use of his portable typewriter so that I could present him a finished work. After intense scrutiny he shook his head approvingly and said: "You will one day become a penny ha'penny (three cents) poet."

George and Angela Warner of CompuPrint Limited, Barbados, for their invaluable contribution.

Mrs. Paula Williams-Benjamin, Trinidad, for selecting the printer.

And last, but by no means least, the many persons who searched the daily newspapers for my writings.

PHOTOGRAPHS

Through the courtesy of the Barbados National Trust, I was able to secure photographs of old Barbados from the files of Edward Stoute and Euchard Fitzpatrick's collection.

Henry Fraser, Sean Carrington, Addinton Forde and John Gilmore – who readily gave permission for the use of photographs from their - "A – Z of Barbados Heritage."

Sincere gratitude to Ann Watson Yates – Author of "Bygone Barbados."

From my own collection – The Old Woman's Hovel, The Chattle House and the Stand-Pipe.

My sincere thanks to all those who made this project a success.

On March 8, 1910, the 'S.S. Lavara' crossed the turbulent Atlantic Ocean to enter the calm water of Carlisle Bay where it dropped its heavy anchor, while the earth was slowly taking the sun towards its zenith. The early rising sun fought and had gained supremacy over the thick, dark, moisture-laden clouds which had threatened to obscure its usefulness. Those clouds had now vanished; and the small patches of snow-white clouds drifting swiftly across the deep blue sky were more befitting to the Tropics. The breezes, having travelled the vast expanse of the Atlantic Ocean, were cool and refreshing as they swept the most easterly, and coral-formed island in the Caribbean.

Among the limited number of passengers on board the 'LAVARA' was a very wealthy gentleman. His name was Peter Barrow, who came from Kent; one of the famous farming counties in England. From the open deck of the 'LAVARA,' Mr. Barrow, wearing brown tweed trousers, a cream cotton shirt and brown brogues, was looking through his large binoculars at the island, now bathed in the brilliance of the sun. Until that moment, such beauty was beyond his comprehension.

The greater part of the island was green; with crooked marly roads, which either turned sharply behind tall green trees, swaying sugar canes, or divided the verdant hillside to vanish seemingly into the sky. In places where the sugar cane had been cut, the remaining dry trash presented a light brown tint. In other areas, the newly turned, black soil offered a picturesque contrast to its surrounding mass of green. Against the blue background of the sky tall casuarinas swayed gracefully in the strong wind.

'What a beautiful island,' said Mr. Barrow to himself. Releasing the binoculars, with their leather retaining strap around his neck, they fell to his stomach with a soft thud. 'I think I would like to live there.' He looked around to find that he was alone on the deck. "Hello!" he said, moving swiftly towards the companionway. "They have all left me." With his baggage already set for debarkation, and awaiting the arrival of the immigration authorities, Mr. Barrow went quietly to his cabin and took to the reading of his favourite magazine.

Minutes later, Mr. Barrow stood against the rail watching the boatmen who had willingly offered to convey his luggage down the gangway. When the last piece of his belongings had been safely placed in the small boat below, he went swiftly down the gangway and into the little boat which pulled away immediately afterwards.

The air was pregnant with the odour of the sea. Mr. Barrow watched the boatmen as they rowed strenuously against the strong easterly wind and choppy sea. The wind, breaking the crest of the waves, swept light sprays of salt-water over the boat and into their faces.

"We will be lookin' to take you back to the ship, Sir", said one of the three dark-skinned boatmen. They had almost completed their journey.

"I won't be going back to the ship," Mr. Barrow replied, smiling faintly, "at least, not today."

"You staying here long, Sir?" he went on. "How long?"

"I don't know for sure, but I am looking forward to the day when I will be able to reside permanently."

"I hope you like it here, Sir."

"Thank you."

With the boat secured to a bollard firmly set on the quay, the boatmen hurriedly took the luggage into the Customs and placed it carefully upon a long wooden counter.

Mr. Barrow paid them. They offered thanks, wished him a pleasant stay, took to their boat and shoved off for the side of the 'LAVARA', where they hoped to solicit business from other passengers.

" 'e give you anythin'?" one of the boatmen asked the other.

"Give what? You ever hear of uh Englishman givin' uh tip?"

"I thought 'e was uh Yankee. How you know 'e is English?"

" 'Cause it write on his luggage."

"Oh!"

Mr. Barrow turned and went slowly towards the Customs. He had completed one section of his journey. He suddenly remembered his wife, her tear-stained face as he kissed her goodbye. He heard her sobbing voice as she said, "Oh how I shall miss you."

Elizabeth was the only girl of six children. Until her marriage to Peter Barrow, she had served as a director and a secretary to her father who owned one of France's largest breweries. She resigned from her secretarial post shortly before her wedding; but remained a director, which, along with her shares in the business, earned her a tidy sum annually. She first met Peter during one of his summer visits to the Continent with his parents. He was at that time in his nineteenth year and she, one year his junior. Three years of seasonal visits and numerous letters led to an engagement. Peter's parents attended the banquet, which was held in France. The finest of wines and liqueurs were served. The carouse ended peacefully. Peter had been left to spend the weekend with his fiancée while his parents left for Kent the following day. They had crossed the channel quite safely but lost their lives in a train disaster. The bereaved Peter consoled himself with a short courtship which ended on the eve of his twenty-second birthday.

In the Customs, Mr. Barrow saw a large number of people. They were of different racial origins. His observation led him to the conclusion that they were relatives and friends of those arriving and departing. There was much joyful chatter. There were also many sorrowful whispers.

"May God take care of you," said a woman of African origin to her son who was leaving the island, "and bring you safely back to me."

Tears were streaming down her lean face as she spoke.

"Thank you, Mamma," replied the lad, sniffing softly. "God will take care of me."

Amidst pitiful sobs, a woman of European origin said: "Goodbye my son; take care of yourself."

"I will, mother," the youngster replied bravely. "You do the same."

Scanning the long wooden counter for his luggage, Mr. Barrow saw a tall, fair-skinned customs officer awaiting him. He hastened to unlock his bags for inspection. After a casual search, the officer initialed the bags.

"How far is the train station from here?" Mr. Barrow asked him.

"Just across the street, Sir," he replied, pointing. "One of these men will take your luggage on his cart for you."

"Thank you .... By the way, can I get any other kind of transportation to Beachmount Hotel?"

"Sure, but you wouldn't be able to take your luggage along. The truth is, Sir, the train wouldn't take you to the hotel, but there is a station somewhere in the vicinity .... I think it is called Bushy Park .... I'm not quite sure, but you can ask at the train office. Is there any one at the hotel expecting you?"

"Yes."

"In that case, you can phone and let them know you are coming and ask them to send some conveyance to the station."

"I think that is a splendid idea," he said cheerfully. Mr. Barrow got all the information about his trip to the hotel from the short, light-skinned clerk who sold him the ticket; and finding himself with time on hand he asked: "Will my luggage be safe here? I want to take a look around the city."

"Certainly," replied the clerk. "Go right ahead."

Walking slowly along, Mr. Barrow was startled by a woman's high-pitched voice which shrieked: "Mau-bee! Mau-bee!" Looking in the direction whence the voice came, he saw a short, fat, dark-skinned woman. On her head was a tall, green-painted pail. Near the bottom and to the front of the pail protruded a tiny brass tap. "Who want me?" she went on. "I cool and sweet." Over her left arm swayed a small galvanised bucket. It contained a quantity of water, four tin cups and the two halves of a yellow lime. "Taste me .... taste me .... I cool and sweet .... taste me."

From a large two-masted schooner in the inner basin, great quantities of lumber were being unloaded and piled upon the wharf.

"Give me uh mauby," called one of the men engaged with the lumber. His black face was drenched with perspiration. "I hope it cold."

Mauby Vendor

"You better know yuh place," the vendor returned heatedly. "I been sellin' mauby for 'ears and 'ears, and anybody who know me would tell you I does sell good mauby!"

From the bucket she took a tin cup. Holding it with one hand, she released the tap with the other and the golden liquid came forth. It struck the bottom of the tin cup producing a high-sounding note which died away as the quantity increased.

"Come, take yuh mauby," said the vendor, "and give me muh cent."

The man received his mauby and paid in return. After he drank some he said: "This mauby really taste good."

"I glad."

Mr. Barrow observed that the mauby had a close resemblance to beer, in that it had the same frothy head. He wondered how it tasted, and promised himself to try it some day.

It was a pair of lines sunk to the surface of the dusty white road that started Mr. Barrow's trend of thought in another direction. He wondered if the locomotive passed through the city; but his curiosity did not last long. Only a short distance away, at what appeared to be the terminus, he saw two vehicles stationed upon the lines. Drawing near, he discovered that they were open cars. To the uprights which maintained stability between base and roof, long adjustable seats were affixed. The only enclosed sections were at the front and back. A pair of horses were attached to each car by means of a leather harness.

"Anything today, Mistress?" asked a vendor. She was slim and dark. On her head was a tray. It was covered with a clean white cloth which protected the commodity she offered for sale from the dust of the streets frequently aroused by gusty winds.

"Anything Mistress?" she repeated. "Nuts? Sugar cakes?" Balancing the tray on one hand, she uncovered a portion of

Tram Car

the tray's contents with the other. "Nuts? ... One or two?" she asked, extending a quantity of nuts in a small paper bag to the veil-faced lady who was approaching. "One?"

"One," replied the lady, coming to a halt to make her purchase. "Please put in another bag, two sugar-cakes .... one red, one white, two comfits .... one round, one pipe, and two nut-cakes."

"That would be eight cents, Ma'am," said the young vendor. Returning sixteen cents change with, "Thank you, Ma'am .... get home safe."

"Thank you," replied the lady. Moving towards the car, she met Mr. Barrow who lifted his hat ever so slightly as they passed.

"What time does this tram leave?" she asked the light-skinned conductor who sat on the rear seat. He blinked his red eyes sleepily. He pulled at a silver chain across his fat abdomen and a silver case toppled out of his pocket. Snapping the case open, he said. "In five minutes time, lady."

"Thank you," she said stepping into the car. "That affords me a little rest."

"You are very welcome," said the conductor. With eyes half closed, his head bowed slowly.

"Well I never see more," said a fat dark-skinned woman with a tray on her head. "You are nothin' but a thief.

"What did I steal from you?" asked the accused in astonishment.

"You stole the sale you just made," the fat woman replied heatedly, "you know damn well that lady always buys from me."

"Wait," said the slim, dark girl, standing with feet astride and hands akimbo, "you think de res' of us come in de tram stan' fuh we health?" She shifted her head ever so slightly to balance the tray. "You was sellin' somebody," she went on, "and I make de sale. What wrong with dat?"

"You young people won' learn to respect big experience people."

"I see how you feel 'bout this thing," the girl replied coldly. "Only big experience people must live? Well I goin' tell you something, when I come in this stand I intends to sell Toot-moon-back-I-lah, and who don't like it can lump it."

"You go 'long, soul," the fat woman said angrily, "you going reap uh okra crop." (Means she will die early).

"That suit you."

The two vendors turned about face and went their separate ways singing. 'Quite a pleasant way to settle a dispute,' Mr. Barrow thought to himself.

With the formality of his country, Mr. Barrow addressing a policeman said: "Good day, officer." He wore a white tunic, white helmet, black boots, and black pants with red stripes along the side-seams. A puzzled look crept into his large black eyes. He was astonished. To his mind, he was not an 'officer.' In Barbados, he was called a policeman or police constable.

"Good .... good day, Sir," he stammered, "what can I do for you?"

Suspended across the street was a rope. It was about waist high. As a sign of danger, a piece of red cloth was tied in the centre of the rope. Beyond the rope, four men were stripped to their waists, their black sweating bodies glistening in the sunlight.

"What's going on over there?" asked Mr. Barrow concernedly. "Is there going to be a fight?"

"No, Sir," replied the policeman more steadily than formerly. "They are preparing to swing the bridge."

"Why?"

"To allow that schooner with its tall masts to pass out," replied the policeman. He pointed to the schooner. On board, the men were hard at work releasing the sail in preparation to leave; but when Mr. Barrow returned his gaze to the bridge,

The Chamberlain Bridge

Trafalgar Square

The Careenage

he was astonished at the method employed. Attached to some bollard-like structure were two cranks, which the men were turning slowly and laboriously to remove the bridge not more than a fraction of an inch at a time.

"Antiquated," said Mr. Barrow, shaking his head negatively.

"I beg your pardon, Sir,"

"The system is obsolete."

The policeman was not quite certain what Mr. Barrow meant, but he agreed.

"What is the name of the bridge?" asked Mr. Barrow.

The policeman could not remember. Playing for time to recollect his thoughts, he removed his helmet to dry his perspiring brow.

"The Chamberlain Bridge," he said finally, "but it is usually called the Swing Bridge." He replaced his helmet, and for the first time, Mr. Barrow saw that it bore a small metal number similar to that on his collar. "The other," the policeman went on, pointing in a south-easterly direction, "is the Victoria Bridge; but few people call it so. It is mostly referred to as the Old Bridge."

"The Chamberlain Bridge, the Victoria Bridge," said Mr. Barrow, as though trying to commit them to memory. "I'll be moving a little further on," he added. "I am having a tour of your city."

"I'm delighted," replied the policeman, "I certainly hope you like it."

"I trust so. Good day."

"Good day, Sir."

Mr. Barrow walked in a northerly direction. With his back towards the bridge, the massive, rough, moss-coloured walls of the Public Buildings loomed straight before him. In its high tower, the large dial of a clock announced the hour. Looking into the yard through tall green-painted iron rails which formed protection against intruders when the gates were closed at night, Mr. Barrow saw a discarded war cannon of obsolete design and a large black car parked in the shade of a big evergreen tree. People, too were moving freely about and in and out of the two gates. 'Move on, Peter Barrow,' he said to himself, 'if you want to see more.'

Set on a pedestal in the centre where five streets met, was a lofty, bronze-coloured statue which Mr. Barrow did not recognise as he approached it from the back. However, as he viewed it from the front he soon observed that it was the statue of Lord Nelson. Having read the inscription at its base, Mr. Barrow bowed and said a silent prayer in honour of the brave British admiral who was killed in action in the Battle of Trafalgar.

The air about the vicinity was foul. Standing before the statue, Mr. Barrow looked around to ascertain the cause. To his right, in the shade of a huge evergreen tree, whose bulky trunk and lengthy branches resembled an umbrella of gigantic size, stood four weather-beaten cabs. Attached to each cab was a horse, whose long life and inadequate feeding had deprived it of the ability to hold its head well up. It was easy to recognise the owners of these cabs. They lingered nearby, their appearance not unlike that of their animals. About the horse's feet were small piles of manure and little pools of dark, yellow urine. The greater portion of the urine had trickled zigzaggedly across the street leaving it stained in many places.

'What a hideous sight in the heart of the city?' said Mr. Barrow to himself. 'It smells awful.'

"A cab, Sir?" asked one of the men in a low, feeble voice.

"No, thank you," replied Mr. Barrow, and passed on.

There was a hive of activity along the upper end of the wharf. Many two-wheeled pushcarts came in rapid succession dumping large bags of sugar which were stacked in huge lighters and conveyed to an anchored ship in the harbour. Mr. Barrow watched with much interest the system and ease with which the men worked.

Preceding Mr. Barrow by some fifty yards staggered a tall, black shabbily-dressed man who supported his faulty steps by the use of a crooked, knotty stick. His bare feet, and the soiled bandage about his right ankle bore evidence of an old sore. His head, shaded from the burning tropical sun by a black, broad-rimmed Wilson hat, whose identity would have been disclaimed by its designer. His trousers, which could have been black at one time, now bronze-coloured, dusty, and so worn out that it twisted easily around his slim long legs as he struggled along. The dingy white shirt he wore was buttoned close to the throat while the long sleeves dangled independently.

A little boy came running down the street. His head and feet were bare. He was whistling softly as he passed Mr. Barrow, who noticed that through his dirty, knee-length khaki trousers and khaki shirt, circles of black skin was showing. Nearing the old man, the boy quickened his pace. Then, simultaneous with the sweeping stroke of his left foot at the old man's stick he shouted: "Monkey!" His high-pitched voice was a deafening shriek that broke the silence. The old man stumbled forward. His stick fell. His hat toppled off. A long steam of saliva tinged by tobacco escaped his half-opened mouth and mingled with the unruly black bristles about his chin. The boy kicked the stick hard along the ground. Then at some distance he picked it up and faced the old man defiantly, shouting "Monkey! Monkey!"

Wordlessly the old man retrieved his hat. He placed it gently on the top of his big head. The muscles of his lean jaws hardened as he ground his gums. His eyes glared red with rage.

Drying his mouth and chin on the back of a shaky hand, he straightened to challenge his assailant.

"God damn you," the old man swore. His voice was gruff and thunderous.

"M o n k e y! M o n k e y!" the boy taunted, jumping high in the air brandishing the stick above his head.

"Bashart Allie want you to call out de goods in de store."

"Does your mother want me to advertise her merchandise too?" he retorted.

"Me mother don't sell nothin', Monkey," returned the boy, backing away from the old man who was advancing. "Me mother don't sell."

"No?" roared the old man. "She don't sell for you to know."

"Give the man his stick," Mr. Barrow whispered softly as he passed the boy. "He is old, you know."

"He a'int so old, Sir," replied the boy in an undertone. "He does play old to get cents and pennies from people, Sir."

"Never mind, son," said Mr. Barrow sympathetically. "Give him his stick."

The boy obediently placed the stick upon the ground; and shoving it vigorously, sent it skidding in the direction of the old man. "There is your stick, Monkey," he said. "Don't let nobody take it from you again."

"If I ever get within arm' length o' you," thundered the old man. "I goin' break you up and swing de gallows for you."

"Monkey! Monkey!" he continued shouting, his shrieking voice fading as he receded into a narrow alley and vanished.

Looking across the Careenage to one of the lighters en route to the ship, Mr. Barrow was confronted with a scene that seemed absolutely incredible. As though to clear his vision he rubbed his eyes. With an open hand, he formed a hood over his brow. 'Am I seeing right?' he questioned himself. In the process of propelling the laden lighter which was submerged to mere inches above the water, four men were walking unheedingly back and forth on its narrow gunwhale in order to effect the precise movements their tremendously long and stout oars required. "Well, of all the crazy things I've seen, this one beats all!" Mr. Barrow muttered.

The road widened to a cluster of evergreen trees. To the left of them appeared the colossal stone building which housed, among other offices, that of the cable office. So occupied in the activities of the city, it did not occur to Mr. Barrow that he should have sent his wife a cable. He hastened up the steps.

"How-do-you-do," he said to the first lady he approached behind the long counter.

"Good day," she replied, looking up from the book in which she was writing. Ruffled blonde hair fell above the nape of her long neck. Her gray eyes were kind and searching when they met his. "What can I do for you, Sir?"

"I would like to send a cable," he replied, resting against the counter.

"That way, Sir," she indicated. "The gentleman at the extreme end."

"Thank you, lady," said he, bowing slightly.

"You are welcome."

The slow rhythmic click of Mr. Barrow's heels upon the wooden floor attracted the gentleman at work. He looked up. "What can I do for you, Sir?" he asked in a crisp polite manner.

"I would like to send a cable to England."

"Give me the name of the person to whom you are sending it," said the clerk, reaching for a pad and pencil.

Mr. Barrow observed that he had a disfigurement of the left arm. It was short and underdeveloped.

"Mrs. Peter S. Barrow, Winslow Gate, Avonton Street, Kent, England."

"Now the message," said the clerk smiling warmly. "It has got to be brief or it will cost you a lot."

• • •

Mr. Barrow thought wordlessly. He rested an elbow on the counter and in the palm of his right hand, he placed his chin. "Arrived safe and well," he began slowly, "after a pleasant trip. Love. Peter."

"That is excellent," said the clerk, scribbling across his pad, "Did you think of it before?"

"No."

"Taking my training into consideration, I couldn't have done better. I'll fix this and return." He tore the message from the pad, took the pound Mr. Barrow offered and disappeared behind a door.

When the clerk returned some minutes later, he found Mr. Barrow thumbing through the Daily Advocate, which he had bought on the way.

"Your change Sir," said the clerk. "Your message will be off in no time."

"Thank you."

In an effort to evoke a conversation the clerk said: "I think you would do well in my job; with your short messages and things of that sort."

"I guess so," replied Mr. Barrow. He took the change and slipped it into his pocket. "As a youngster I was very good at short story and précis writing," he went on. "At least that is what was said."

"What kind of stories did you write?"

"Philosophical fiction."

"Philosophical fiction?" the clerk asked puzzled. "I don't get it."

"A philosopher teaches. I don't …. can't for that matter; but I make my characters teach …. demonstrate to be more exact. You see, most adults resent the very implication of being dictated to. My method is more palatable."

"You seem to have quite a practical approach to writing. Why didn't you stick to it?"

"That is a long story. My grandfather had a very big farm in Kent. Upon his death, my father the only child, inherited the farm. As a young man, I wanted to write, but my father insisted that I studied agriculture. I was extremely successful in the field; that being so, I felt I had lost nothing."

"Were you the only child?"

"Yes .... and that made it easy for my father to concentrate his rigid influence upon me."

"It is a pity."

"What is?" asked Mr. Barrow in surprise.

"It is a pity you didn't take up writing. I think the world is in dire need of authors of your kind."

"I can agree with you in the latter," said Mr. Barrow thoughtfully; "especially on the subject of religion." Somewhere in the building, a clock struck three. "What the devil!" he exclaimed, glancing at his watch to see if it coincided. "I haven't much time left. I have to catch the train, but I'll tell you something before I go. Seeing it from where I am, the Christian religion as practised in the Western world has failed. The failure is largely due to the mass deception by the religious leaders. Many people in their quest for something spiritual have shifted from one religious group to another and another only to be deceived by their leaders. Many people are still perturbed as to what, or whom religion represents. Failing to find anything which they can truly conceive as spiritual, these bewildered individuals turn to things material, and finally become self-centred. We are told that religious leaders are chosen by God, but that is a hoax. I .... "

"What is a hoax?" interrupted the clerk.

"That talk about religious leaders being chosen by God."

"Don't you believe it?"

"Who could?" asked Mr. Barrow. "No one in their right mind would."

"Are you serious?"

Mr. Barrow's nod answered the question. Breaking the silence that followed, he asked, "Do you really believe that religious leaders are chosen by God?" His words came slowly.

"Yes," replied the clerk, "I most decidedly do."

"Then God has also failed."

The clerk's mouth fell open. His eyes bulged. He backed away from the counter on which he was resting. His hands hung limp at his side. A bewildered look on his chubby face.

"D...do...do you know that is blasphemy?" he stammered. He was barely audible.

"Blasphemy what!" snapped Mr. Barrow. "If religious leaders are failures and they are chosen by God," he continued, "is it not conclusive then, that God has failed in His choice?"

The clerk's face twisted ever so slightly. A yearning look for a greater understanding of such knowledge stole slowly into his brown squinting eyes.

"Thank God I'm not a materialist, nor am I self-centred," continued Mr. Barrow. "There are others like myself .... I know. I know too, that God does exist, and that He has not failed man. But man being free to choose, has polluted religion and caused many to doubt its reality."

After a pause during which Mr. Barrow dried his brow with a handkerchief which matched his tie, he added: "To my mind, it would be futile to ask these self-centred characters to serve a God who has already deceived them. They would laugh us to scorn."

"But you can't leave things the way they are, they would go from bad to worse," said the clerk, when he finally found his voice. "Man knows that there is a God to serve."

"If it is necessary."

"H...h...how do you mean if it is necessary?" stammered the clerk, after a brief interval of silence. "Don't you think it is?"

"I wonder."

"You are a strange man," said the clerk timidly. "You know there is a God .... you serve Him ... I believe ..... "

"Yes."

"And you still don't think it is necessary for other people to know of Him. What is necessary?"

"I think we should learn to serve man first," said Mr. Barrow, as he retrieved his coat from the counter where he had rested it. " '*If a man say, I love God, and hateth his brother, he is a liar: for he that loveth not his brother whom he hath seen, how can he love God whom he hath not seen. And this commandment have we from him, that he who loveth God love his brother also.*' " Mr. Barrow quoted. John 1-4-20. He looked at his watch. "Our greatest need is to remind these self-centred individuals that the man next door is his brother. Help them to realise that they have a brotherly duty to all men; with no regard for the colour of his skin, the capacity or capability of his work, the size of his home, and least of all for the language he speaks. When we shall have achieved this," he continued, shaking his head sadly, "we could then rest assured that they would be well on the road whence they came."

"I am sorry you have to leave so soon," said the clerk. "I find you very stimulating. I should like to meet you again; how long do you expect to remain on the island?"

"Well...if I can find a small estate to purchase, I may remain permanently."

"Is that so?" asked the clerk enthusiastically. "Then I may be able to assist you."

"How is that?" Mr. Barrow asked eagerly.

"My uncle is contemplating selling a portion of his estate."

"In which parish is it situated?"

"St. Philip. Would you be interested?"

"I could be."

Beachmount Hotel

"Where are you staying?"

"At Beachmount Hotel."

"Oh! that's only a stone's throw from the estate."

"Is that so?"

"Sure. I have a suggestion, if you'll like it."

"Let me hear it."

The clerk stood erect. His ink-soiled fingers played idly with the long knot of his colourful fly tie. "Monday will be a holiday," said he, "and I'll be free; if you wish, my uncle and I could drive over to the hotel and take you to the estate."

"Not a bad idea," said Mr. Barrow, smiling pleasantly. "You are very kind."

"While that may be true," returned the young clerk, "it could be viewed from the other side ... business."

"You are a smart boy," said Mr. Barrow, extending his hand through the small opening in the cage, "I am Peter Barrow."

"I am Wilfred Skinner ... it is a pleasure meeting you, Mr. Barrow, you are very interesting."

"Thank you ... it is nice meeting you also, or I might have had some difficulty finding someone with a lot for sale," he said smiling. They shook hands once more and parted.

The receding sun was shining brilliantly out of a cloudless sky when Mr. Barrow walked onto the chalky-white street. Unaccustomed to the blinding glare, he squinted through half-closed eyes to wend his way about the city, thronged with horse and ass-drawn carts.

The Government's gigantic locomotive was at the station when Mr. Barrow arrived; but to him it was no more than one of those small engines used in England for coupling coaches and luggage vans. He wondered if it was capable of conveying the long line attached to it.

"Your baggage has already been placed in the front coach,

Sir," said the clerk who had sold him the ticket. "It will be leaving soon."

"Thank you," replied Mr. Barrow. "That was rather nice of you."

"Don't mention it."

A small number of passengers were going out from the station and into the two coaches attached to the locomotive. Mr. Barrow joined them and took a seat. It was hard and dusty, and there was the odour of cinder about the coach.

"All aboard!" shouted the tall dark-skinned conductor. "All aboard." He made a sign to the driver. The whistle sounded loudly and the engine crept slowly forward, discharging thick black smoke and tiny fragments of charred cinder out of its tall chimney.

Guided by its winding parallel lines, the locomotive slid gently out of the station yard to wend its way over a short bridge which was suspended across a slowly trickling stream, muddy rivers and busy thoroughfares .... through clustering trees and fields of swaying sugar cane .... across the vast expanse of the countryside and finally to its destination at Belleplaine in St. Andrew.

Attracted by the loud voices of children shouting, Mr. Barrow caught a fleeting glance of a football game in progress. "Is that a park?" he asked the passenger who was sitting across from him.

"Park?" the passenger repeated, eyeing him questioningly, "it is a school .... Combermere School."

"I am Peter Barrow," he extended his hand. The gentleman took it. "Pleased to know you .... I am Derick Lewis."

"What type of school is it?"

"It is one of the Government's secondary schools," he replied, in a more friendly tone than previously. "We have Government

25

elementary and Government secondary schools." He removed his white helmet, and the rush of wind ruffled his sleek, reddish hair. He was wearing all white. Mr. Barrow wondered about the nature of his work.

"Although maintained by the Government," he went on, "the Government does not appoint teachers without the recommendation of the minister who presides over the schools ... the elementary schools."

"I think that system is a good breeding ground for hypocrisy," said Mr. Barrow, breathing deeply.

"How?" Mr. Lewis asked in surprise.

"Well," returned Mr. Barrow thoughtfully, not wanting to sound offensive, but to be conscientious nevertheless, "an individual may play ball with the priest for the loaves and fishes."

"I'm afraid I don't understand you, Mr ...."

"Barrow."

"Mr. Barrow."

Mr. Barrow had a very clever way of saying things in order to evoke the question he wanted. He didn't seem to be telling you anything, but replying instead. Such a method often dissolved resentment. He appeared to be unique in this respect.

"Suppose after school a youngster found difficulty in getting the job of his choice," he began, smiling, "it would be easy to resort to the Church, take part in its activities and find favour in the eyes of the priest."

Mr. Lewis bowed his head understandingly. The train whistle sounded periodically.

"He would be giving nothing honest to the Church," he added, "and little to the school to which he is appointed ... appointed, probably at the dismissal of a more honourable and conscientious worker, who did not find it equally convenient as his successor (not to mention the ulterior motive) to attend Church and all its activities."

Combermere School

"Kingston!" shouted the conductor, entering the coach, "First stop, Kingston." He disappeared through the other door.

The train came to a halt amidst a cluster of leafy, mahogany trees. There was no station; only a platform devoid of human life. Journeying there, the train had crossed one horrid smelling river ... through vastly congested areas and across four busy thoroughfares which were momentarily obstructed by railed, white-painted gates, one of which was thronged with children. Mr. Barrow concluded that there was a girl school in the near vicinity.

Frightened by the sudden blast of the whistle, birds in the trees suddenly took to their wings with frightful chirpings, only to settle again as quickly, and as peacefully. Disturbed like the birds, a bull, tied on an open lot across from the platform, broke loose, scampered away and vanished in a thicket. The train plodded onwards.

"That is an elementary school," said Mr. Lewis, pointing in a southerly direction. "It is Belmont School, a Methodist school."

It was a gray-painted wooden building with an adequate number of windows and doors, which were still open. A limited number of girls still lingered idly about its grounds.

"Dominated by the Methodist priest, eh?" asked Mr. Barrow, shaking his blonde head negatively.

"Yes. You are not very much in favour of that system are you?"

"Suppose you used to worship in a Methodist church and there was a vacancy at a Methodist school," asked Mr. Lewis ponderously, "how would you like it if you were overlooked and some youngster from an Anglo Catholic Church was appointed?"

"My mother told me a..."

"Rouen station!" shouted the conductor, making his rounds. "Rouen station!"

"You were saying," said Mr. Lewis, when the train got on its way, "Something about your mother."

"Oh! yes. She once told me a tale about two children a girl and a boy. One day the boy had two apples and he gave his sister one. She raised hell. 'That is the thing I can't understand about you,' she raved. 'Mama has repeatedly told us that when we have anything to give away we should give the best.' 'All right, sis,' the boy replied calmly, 'if these apples were yours what would you have done?' 'I would have given you the better of the two,' she replied proudly. 'Then there is no need to make a fuss,' he replied in his usual calm manner. 'I have it'."

Breaking the laughter that ensued, Mr. Lewis said: "I like your sense of humour, but I think your analogy is very irrelevant."

"Really!" Nodding was affirmation of his statement.

"Mr. Lewis, if you want to see that it is not irrelevant," Mr. Barrow began, making a gesture with his hands, "erase the thought of religion .... then you will see that you have to choose one .... of two applicants for the vacancy."

As though in a daze, Mr. Lewis sat looking straight out of the window.

"Tickets, please," requested the conductor, "next stop Bulkeley."

Awakened by the conductor's shouting, Mr. Lewis snapped open his brown leather case and produced his ticket. His destination was Bulkeley. Mr. Barrow fumbled in the pocket of his coat and brought forth his ticket.

"We have got to be very cautious in our approach," Mr. Barrow said finally, "even in things religious .... religion has a way of playing tricks."

"I have learnt a great deal from you in the few minutes we had together," said Mr. Lewis, preparing to leave. "I should like to meet you again."

Like a thoughtful mother who is ever mindful of her children's frailty and the warmth they require against the chill of night, the receding sun had spread a warm, golden blanket over the island, ... her final act of kindness before disappearing beyond the far western horizon.

When the train arrived at Bushy Park, the station of Mr. Barrow's destination, a shabby-looking double-buggy and a matching shabbily-clothed coachman awaited his arrival. The coachman, a short, dark-skinned man with a thick mustache that was already beginning to gray, promptly took the luggage from the coach and arranged it upon the buggy. Making use of a piece of rope to secure the luggage, he asked: "Did you have a nice trip, Sir?" His voice was gruff .... more gruff than would normally be expected from a man so small in stature. "I hope you like it here," he added.

"Thank you. Were you at the station long?"

"You mean waiting for you, Sir?"

"Yes."

The coachman replied that he got there only a few minutes before the train stopped. Adding that it was his job to take passengers to and from the station when it was necessary. He had been in the job for many years now. He first used to work for Mr. Mayson's father. At that time, Mr. Mayson was just a small boy. He had not even begun school yet. "Mr. Mayson is a nice man," he went on, after a short interval. "He is nice to me. I hear the other servants say he is no good but I can't say so. See this trousers and shirt," he went on, stopping for a moment during the act of lacing the luggage to tug on the over-sized garments he was wearing, "Mr. Mayson gave me these.

You think I could say he is bad?"

Mr. Barrow was thoughtful.

"You think I could?"

"I guess not."

"Oh."

The road to the hotel was long and rugged; winding here and there through fields of swaying sugar cane, canes whose tops had already been removed but not yet cut down; or fields where the canes had been taken away to the mill. Silhouetted in the waning afterglow of the already sunken sun was a large oval topped object.

"What is that?" asked Mr. Barrow, pointing across an open field.

"Oh! that is nothing to be afraid of, Sir," replied the coachman, assuming that the question was a frightful one. "That is only a trash heap, Sir."

"Trash heap?" repeated Mr. Barrow in surprise. "How did they get it piled so high?"

"The cane cutters and the cane headers pile it up, Sir," he replied, astonished at so simple a question. "They carry up bundle after bundle until they get it big, Sir."

"I see," said Mr. Barrow, nodding. "But who is the header?"

"The header is the woman who carries the canes to the truck, Sir."

"Oh!" said Mr. Barrow. "You have taught me a great deal."

"I'm glad to teach you, Sir."

Mr. Barrow's reply was a short laugh.

Out from the slowly enveloping dusk loomed the massive structure of the hotel which was not unfamiliar to Mr. Barrow who had seen many pictures of its exterior, and of its colourful interior which was already lit and emitting the congeniality of the management through its many large open windows.

• • •

Alighting from the buggy in the glowing light that came down the pathway through an open door, Mr. Barrow thrust his hands deep into the pockets of his trousers.

"I am glad to be here," he said.

"I hope you like the place, Sir," said the coachman, as he untied the luggage. "Mr. Mayson is a nice man."

After the usual formalities which no boarder has ever been able to elude, Mr. Barrow was ushered to his single accommodation by a well-mannered, dark-skinned bell-boy whose uniform was amazingly clean. Placing the luggage in a convenient section of the room, but at the same time out of the way, he said: "Dinner will be served at seven; will you be down, Sir?" His voice was soft and polite. Mr. Barrow looked at his watch. It did not permit him time for a shower and a change of clothing.

"No," he replied, "but can I have something sent up?"

"Why certainly, Sir," replied the boy, anxious to serve.

He took an order for tea and sandwiches, promised to return shortly and disappeared behind the door which he closed gently. Alone, and unaccustomed to the heat of the tropics and the bumpy ride by train and buggy, Mr. Barrow slumped down on a reclining chair exhausted and longing for complete relaxation.

In response to a soft knock on the door sometime later Mr. Barrow said: "Come in."

He was still reclining when the boy returned with a small tray, its contents neatly covered with a clean, white, pink-bordered napkin. Placing the tray upon the table and setting the chair in order, he turned around and said: "I am on duty tonight, Sir .... if there is anything you need just press the button and I'll be glad to help you, Sir."

"Thank you."

• • •

Instructed by the bell-boy as to the location of the bath, Mr. Barrow then took a quick shower. He dressed himself in a colourful suit of pajamas, ate his supper and was rummaging in one of his suitcases which he had casually tossed upon the bed when there was a soft knock on the door and the boy appeared in answer to the bell.

"Did you call, Sir?" he asked politely, barely forcing his round head through the small opening he made.

"Yes," replied Mr. Barrow without looking up. "Take away the tray please."

In a small collapsable frame on the table was a picture of a beautiful woman. The boy eyed it slyly. He extended a sincere wish for a pleasant night's rest and left in his usual calm manner.

My Dearest Liz, (Mr. Barrow wrote that night)

I hope you are as well as I am. The trip was a pleasant one. The weather was fine throughout, with little or no excitement. Among the few passengers on board, a man and his wife were going to B.G. The lady said her father, the last of her parents, had died recently and left to her his estate; so they were going there to reside permanently. They were a very pleasant couple, and since I was travelling alone, I envied them

Barbados is the most beautiful island in all the world; (smile, although by all appearances poor), the people seem friendly and happy. I was astonished at the large number of horse and ass-drawn carts about the city. I saw a truck loaded with puncheons of syrup and drawn by a team of six mules. There was a little, dark-skinned boy riding one of the foremost mules. It was amazing to see him riding without stirrups.

The system of transportation is deplorable. A train, which passes through six of the island's eleven parishes, a few small buses, the tram-cars, each of which is drawn by a pair of sturdy mules and is restricted only to the parish of St. Michael; buggies, cabs and only a comparatively small number of bicycles. The greater portion of the population walk. I am told that many people have lived to the ripe age of eighty or ninety and have never seen the City of Bridgetown. I met a youngster at the cable office and we got to talking. He told me that his uncle has a section of his estate for sale. He promised to tell his uncle that I am interested and they will call for me at the hotel and take me to see it. If I like it and the price is attractive I shall buy, hoping it does not displease you. I will write you regularly and let you know how things are progressing. Give my kind regards to family and friends. Take care of yourself and may the Lord bless and keep you till we meet again.

I am,

Your true and loving husband,

Pete

Tense with hopeful anticipation of the day, Mr. Barrow arose from bed when the first grey streaks of dawn were appearing. He took a shower, dressed in a semi-tropical trousers and shirt; then taking special care to see that the rest of his attire was well co-ordinated, even though he omitted the coat, he set out from the hotel to view the surrounding scenery.

Outside, the breezes were cooling and gentle, but there were occasional gusts which brought with them the fragrances of roses, the odour of dry earth and the strange freshness of the Atlantic Ocean.

On the eastern side of the hotel, the land had taken on a gradual sloping effect until it reached the sea some distance away. Enriched by the golden rays of a half-emerged sun, and the foaming waves sparkled orange as they rolled on and on towards shore until at last they kissed the awaiting white lips of the sand with hushed soothing sounds.

"Mr. Barrow, this is my uncle," said the clerk from the cable office, when they met shortly after breakfast. "Mr. Barrow, Mr. Skinner." They shook hands firmly.

"I am pleased to meet you," they said in unison.

"Wilfred has told me about you. He thinks you are very interesting ..... "

"Interested in the estate you have for sale," interrupted Mr. Barrow, laughing heartily.

"Don't tell me what I should say, please, Mr. Barrow. I am old enough to know what is good for me."

They all laughed. Mr. Barrow and Mr. Skinner were of the same age group. Mr. Barrow looked younger, but the answer to that could probably be attributed to the climate of his country. On the other hand, Mr. Skinner certainly looked well. He was thirty-five years of age; tall, broad shouldered and sun-tanned; he seemed to be in a state of good health.

"See what I told you?" said Wilfred, laughing, childishly, "Mr. Barrow has a strange sense of humour."

Stimulated by the first meeting and renewed by the possibility of becoming a neighbour to Mr. Barrow filled Wilfred with joy and light-heartedness. Of course, he was young enough to be light-hearted. He was only twenty-two years old. He was tall and lean with gold-coloured hair.

"Wilfred thinks a lot of you."

"You shouldn't take him too seriously," returned Mr. Barrow jokingly. Winking at Wilfred he added: "He is still very young, you know."

"Yes," said Mr.Skinner, "but he is a chip from the block."

They were standing in the yard of the hotel chatting

under a rising sun when the horse neighed and shook his harness vigorously. The unexpected noise reminded them of the important business they had ahead.

"What are we waiting for?" asked Mr. Skinner, with the flippancy of an excursionist, "let's get going." The three of them climbed into the double buggy. Mr. Skinner took the reins.

The estate was located only a short distance away from the hotel. The road was crooked and dusty. Much of the dust rose from time to time and cleaved to the cane blades, the leaves of pigeon-pea trees and the short, but thickly-grown grass along the narrow, shallow gutters.

When the buggy came to a halt in a road that divided a cluster of huge tall trees, to the right of which the land had fallen away suddenly into a valley, Mr. Skinner said: "Well Mr. Barrow, you can better see from here the parcel of land I have to offer." His voice was slightly more serious. They left the buggy; and walking between the huge trees which formed a magnificent shade, they came to the brink of a precipice.

"That is my home down there," he continued. "The parcel of land I have for sale stretches from ..." He indicated, quoted the number of acres, the approximate cost, the number of labourers assigned to that section of the estate who would continue to work, but under his management, and the date when it was most likely for him to have complete possession. "If it wasn't for your attire," he concluded, "we could ride around the lot."

"It is true they are not riding gear," Mr. Barrow returned, "but I don't think they will tear."

Here and there in the far distance, large four-point mills, standing like sentinels, turned slowly extracting the juice from the canes to become sugar, syrup, and fancy molasses, one of the island's staple products. Black men, women, and children

36

of different ages in various fields, executed tasks to which they were assigned. Here and there along the way, teams of oxen or mules conveyed canes to, or returned from the mill-yards. Taking it all in, "This is very picturesque," said Mr. Barrow, as he turned away.

"I've seen it all my years," returned Mr. Skinner, "for me, it has lost its attraction."

Mr. Skinner was greeted by a barking, black bitch which ran playfully about the horse's feet as he walked slowly into a yard cluttered with fowls, turkeys, ducks, guinea-birds and geese. Darting swiftly about in search of new thrills, the bitch drove the fearful birds in every direction of the yard.

"Flossy!" shouted Wilfred, jumping down from the buggy before it actually stopped. "Flossy!"

"Come here, Joseph," shouted Mr. Skinner, tossing the reins across the horse's back and patting its sturdy neck. "Hurry!"

A thin black lad whose head and feet were bare emerged from a long, subdivided stable which formed shelter for many horses, mules, cows, sheep and goats.

"Yes, Sir," replied the lad, running swiftly across the yard which was, for the greater part shaded by a huge mahogany tree. "I'm comin', Sir."

Joseph's garments were smelly. They had a mixed odour common to the wide variety of animals with which he dealt.

"Harness three horses for riding," ordered Mr. Skinner. "I'm in a hurry."

"Yes, Sir," replied the lad, removing the harness from the horse attached to the buggy.

A fat black, middle-aged woman appeared at the kitchen door. She was undoubtedly the cook. The soiled marks about her dingy white apron indicated the length of her hands and the height of the kitchen table. A faded headtie adorned her big head. "Mary, the master has company," she said to the house maid, "go and open the front door."

"My wife and son are out for the day," said Skinner, entering the door which was released by a thin black maid who bared milk-white teeth to offer a welcoming smile and a formal "Good day." To which the gentlemen reciprocated.

"Make yourself at home," said Mr. Skinner, extending his hand as he entered the living room, "sit anywhere .... "I'll be back in a minute."

Mr. Barrow sat on a cane-bottomed bentwood chair. A big black, Persian cat jumped down from a nearby chair, trod noiselessly across the pine floor and onto Mr. Barrow's lap where he curled slowly into a knot and fell asleep. Wilfred excused himself and went into an adjoining room.

"You are accepted as one of the family already," said Mr. Skinner, standing before Mr. Barrow with a small tray containing three glasses of lemonade, "even by the animals .... have one .... lemonade is good for this weather, but there is a scarcity of ice in this part of town." They laughed.

"Thank you," said Mr. Barrow, taking one of the glasses.

Re-entering the room and taking a glass, Wilfred said, "I can never get enough of this stuff."

"It is not so bad at all," said Mr. Barrow. He shook his glass ever so slightly and the floating bits of ice made soft tinkling music.

They scarcely got to talking when the maid appeared at the door and announced that the horses were prepared.

"Already?" asked Mr. Barrow in surprise. "You have an efficient boy .... I think he did it very quickly."

"Efficient or not," Mr. Skinner growled, "treat them alike and you will get the best of them."

"But that isn't nice," Mr. Barrow interjected. "How can you

treat a good person badly?"

"You'll learn .... if you stick around long enough."
Wilfred drained his glass and they all left the house.

"You take the grey mare," said Mr. Skinner, as they advanced towards the three waiting horses in the shade, "I'll take the black one." Tapping Wilfred on the shoulder he added: " The third we'll leave for you."

As soon as Mr. Skinner slipped his feet into the stirrups the mare shot down the path and disappeared around a clump of trees leaving a thin white cloud of dust which vanished with time.

"Your Uncle is a good rider."

"He wouldn't ride anything less active," Wilfred returned, shaking his head slowly. "I suppose it gives vent to his domineering character."

"Did you say domineering?" Mr. Barrow asked, looking at Wilfred's face as the animals walked quietly side by side.

"Yes .... he is master of his home and all that dwell therein. As for the workers, he..."

"Has he had many falls in your time?" interrupted Mr. Barrow. He didn't want to learn that way. It was not his policy to prejudice people or things. To him it was honourable to prove all things, and that was his motto.

"Not in my time," Wilfred replied after a pause, "he told me the first horse he rode as a young man floored him .... once only .... since then he defies them."

"I think he is wonderful."

"That was child's play," Wilfred laughed, shaking his reins to urge the horse more swiftly. "You should have seen him trying to mount the day she came. All work came to a standstill. Ellin begged him not to ride the wild beast."

"Who is Ellin?" Mr. Barrow queried cautiously.

"His wife .... she is the only person who can put the twitch on him."

"Do you mean she rides that horse?"

"No, she puts uncle in his place, but of course it takes a lot to do that. I think he has implanted much of his tyrannical character in his son."

They rode in silence. Only the swish-swash from the horse's tail, the thumping from their hooves and the chirping of the birds on the wing were heard.

"Uncle is all ears for wild horses. When they become quiet, he hates them. Do you think he would ride one of these? No," he answered himself.

The black mare came galloping up the road. Her groins, neck and mouth were lathered and she was breathing gaspingly.

"See .... see what I .... told you about the black produce of Barbados?" Mr. Skinner said brokenly. He was gasping for breath, perspiration dripping from his pointed nose. "If you ever make love to one of these black women," he continued, breathing more freely, "you never want to stop."

"Mr. Skinner! we have a youngster in our midst," Mr. Barrow remarked. He was surprised at the tone of his voice. "I'm sorry," he added.

"Be sorry for nothing," Mr. Skinner returned. "He'll learn if he sticks around long enough."

Wilfred lashed his horse and rode off.

"See," said Mr. Barrow indicating. "You have embarrassed the lad."

"Never mind him," he returned, dismissing it with a stroke of his hand. "I like to make love to them anyway."

"Mr. Skinner, don't you think that is personal and should be kept to yourself?"

"Could be," he admitted, running his long fingers through his sleek goldish hair, "but I seldom get the chance to talk about it."

"Why, you scarcely know me?"

"I guess so, but something tells me you are a good sort."

After a pause he added: "I suppose the black women I've had are responsible for my vigour."

"Did your wife ever get to know?"

"Man we fought like dogs one night after the servants were gone. She near ...."

"Did you say fought?" Mr. Barrow interrupted.

Surprised, Mr. Skinner looked at him. They stared at each other silently.

"Are you implying that you and your wife have never fought?" Mr. Skinner asked, a puzzled look on his sun-tanned face.

"Never."

"I hope you wouldn't be offended, but I think your life must be pretty dull."

"Not in the least."

"Well, I like a little excitement once in a while," he shrugged his broad shoulders. "And I like my black women also, and nobody is going to stop me."

During the silence that followed Mr. Skinner lengthened the straps of his stirrups. He always rode with short stirrups until the animal was somewhat subdued. Breaking the silence, he said: "It was a housemaid we had that caused the fight. She was a smooth black, with the prettiest pair of legs one could hope to see. She had no necessity for the use of brassieres. Her bust was firm and pointed. I used to make ..."

"Do you know anything about fidelity?" Mr. Barrow interrupted.

"That is only a word."

"Why do you think so?"

"Because at some time or other we are all guilty of breaking it."

"I think you have something there," Mr. Barrow laughed. "But would you say promiscuity is only a word?"

"I'm not that bad, really, although I must confess that I like my stuff."

• • •

The acute silence which fell upon the workers in the field when Mr. Skinner arrived on the scene was astonishing to Mr. Barrow. He immediately remembered what Wilfred told him only minutes ago, but he tried to dismiss it by saying: "They are working like mad."

His reply was a mere grunt which God alone could have interpreted, and probably he himself. Wilfred, who was still in the saddle and talking to the labourers as they worked, became aware of the abrupt silence. He looked back to see his uncle and Mr. Barrow approaching. Turning his horse he quickly joined them.

"This will form the division between our lands," Mr. Skinner said, at the grassy entrance of a path where three parallel lanes came into view. The middle lane was produced by the pounding hoofs of oxen, while those on either side were gorged by the wheels of heavily laden carts, which conveyed the canes. Following the winding passage amidst full grown canes, the trio suddenly saw before them an old, vine-covered mill-wall. Here, the parallel lanes veered to the left, and farther on they met east of the mill-wall.

"There is a lovely bunch of bananas over there," said Wilfred, pointing to a cluster of banana trees, which, until recently, had been obscured by tall canes. "I saw them when I went near the workers."

"Do you like bananas?" asked Mr. Skinner.

"I love them," Mr. Barrow replied greedily. "We don't get many of them in England, you know."

"In that case we'll have them cut and kept for Mr. Barrow .... don't forget, Wilfred."

"I wouldn't."

"Oh! how kind of you," Mr. Barrow replied.

When they had completed their tour of the site and were

refreshed by a tasty lunch which Mr. Skinner instructed his cook to prepare, Mr. Barrow said: "Well .... until today I thought all the talk I heard about cou-cou and flying fish was an exaggeration."

"You did, eh?" asked Mr. Skinner, a look of contentment on his face. "And what do you think of it now?"

The three were sitting in the living room. They were completely relaxed. Mr. Barrow, with the cat curled on his lap, removed his tie and released the button at his throat. Mr. Skinner, who seemed intent on filling the room with smoke from his bent-stemmed pipe, was baulked by the frequent gust of wind which entered the opened windows.

Wilfred set the gramophone to work. It was playing: "When my brown turn me down." The record had a fall and sustained a crack which ticked loudly, breaking the sweet rhythm of the music. The needle suddenly refused to glide smoothly on. It jarred against a tiny cavity on the faulty record, which kept repeating three notes in a particular bar. Wilfred hurried from his seat to stop the machine; but the cat crossed his path; and trying to avoid crushing her he stumbled and fell while the record continued its monotonous tune. He scrambled to his feet as quickly as possible and stopped the machine. They all laughed.

"That record should be thrown away," said Mr. Skinner. Then, turning to Mr. Barrow he asked: "Now that you have tasted cou-cou what do you think about it?"
After a moment's thought he replied: "I think I shall remain silent or I may join the band of exaggerators." Smiling, he added: "It is excellent."

"I'm glad you've found it so."

In approximately three days time the remainder of the canes would have been harvested, the deal made legal and Mr. Barrow would have completed possession of the lot. The thought of it filled him with joy. He spent the greater part of the day in the company of Mr. Skinner and Wilfred whom he found very entertaining. Mr. Skinner was a bit vulgar during his conversation, but Mr. Barrow concluded, that was probably his way; and since they were so hospitable on the first occasion, he decided that it was only manly to be tolerant. Wilfred on the other hand was mostly silent. He blushed and turned his face from his uncle's jokes, but laughed warmly at those given by Mr. Barrow which were kept suitable to the young Wilfred.

"A gentleman and his teen-aged daughters were once travelling on a train," Wilfred began timidly, "in the same compartment was a young man who appeared to be in his early twenties. When they had travelled a great distance in silence, the gentleman took from his small suitcase two magazines.

'You don't mind sharing one, do you?' he asked politely, extending one of the magazines to the young man who sat quietly with his handsome, chubby face turned towards the window ever since he entered the coach.

"I don't read," the young man snapped, resuming his gaze at the window.

After a while the gentleman took from his breast pocket a silver cigarette-case. He flipped it open and asked the young man: 'You don't mind sharing one of my cigarettes?'

"I don't smoke," the young man returned snortingly.
Minutes later, as the train slid slowly into the station, the gentleman said: 'Well .... this is where we part .... you don't mind meeting my daughters, I'm sure.'
Staring astonishingly, the young man replied calmly: " I don't cohabit."
Wilfred's joke had produced a considerable amount of laughter, but when Mr. Barrow's and Mr. Skinner's had subsided, Wilfred, who was sitting on a bentwood rocking chair, had buried his face in his hands, and was still laughing heartily with his high-

pitched voice.

"That has tickled him alright," said Mr. Skinner.

"It sure has," Mr. Barrow agreed.

Returning to the hotel while the reddish glow of the sunset still lingered in the west, Mr. Barrow said: "Despite the fact that business was involved, today has turned out to be one of the most enjoyable and memorable days of my life."

"I'm glad to hear that," replied Mr. Skinner, slapping the reins of the horse's back to urge him up a slight incline.

"I enjoyed your company very much," said Wilfred.

"Thank you," replied Mr. Barrow, "much of the credit goes to you, if I remember correctly."

"Well," said Wilfred, tossing his head side-ways, "I guess so."

"I'm awfully sorry that I didn't meet Mrs. Skinner."

"Oh! you'll meet her," said Mr. Skinner. "There is plenty of time ahead."

"Better times," chimed Wilfred.

"Let's hope," Mr. Barrow returned. "Right now I'm dog tired. I am not accustomed to this weather, you know."

"You soon will be," said Wilfred.

"I know, because I like it here."

The hotel was aglow when the buggy came to a halt at its slightly elevated drive-in. The breeze was warm and friendly, and the aroma of delicious foods stole through the open windows and doors to establish such cooking as was unique to him, and unchallenged by any chef in the near vicinity. As Mr. Barrow stepped down from the buggy, he stretched and said: "Oh! boy, when I hit the hay tonight I'm going to sleep as soundly as a kitten."

"Do you purr like a kitten too?" Wilfred asked teasingly.

"I really don't purr like a kitten," he laughed, " but I do a little purring all right."

He expressed his gratitude for the kindness they showered upon him and wished them a safe ride as the buggy turned homewards. They returned thanks and rode off.

Tired as Mr. Barrow was, he found it difficult to fall asleep. Turning restlessly on the soft, snow-white linens, his thoughts flashed with the swiftness of lightning into the past, the present, and the future. One thing seemed to linger a little longer in his mind and it kept repeating itself. It was the rebuff he suffered during the day. He could still hear himself replying defensively when Mr. Skinner said: "Never you do that again."

"Why, I haven't done anything so wrong," he had replied meekly. "I only told the workers they had a nice crop."

"That is none of their business," Mr. Skinner snapped. "Never let these black bitches know what they are capable or worthy of."

"Every man knows his ability," Mr. Barrow said calmly, "and what he is worth."

"That may be so in England," Mr. Skinner said, "not among these illiterate bastards we have here in Barbados."
After a pause Mr. Barrow asked pleadingly: "Will you please tell me why a man shouldn't know his worth?"

"Because he will want it," was the abrupt reply.

"I see," Mr. Barrow said, nodding his head understandingly, "and don't you think he should have it?"

"No .... if he did, our profits would be less. We must always make them feel that we can do without them ..... that they don't deserve what they are given, that business is a failure, but only because we realise that they have no other way of getting food we try to keep the crop going. They must be kept in a state where they will always feel inferior."

"Do you think that is fair?" Mr. Barrow asked sympathetically, "to a human being like...."

"Mr. Barrow," Wilfred interrupted, "you don't seem to understand. In England all of the people are white."

"White, yes, but they are only people," Mr. Barrow replied sadly. "Have you forgotten our first discussion at the cable office?"

"Not at all, Mr. Barrow, but this is different."

"Well, I guess I'll have to accept it the way it is done here," Mr. Barrow said resignedly.

"The sooner you do that, the better," Mr. Skinner said.

'There will be another time and another place,' Mr. Barrow said to himself, and finally succumbed to slumber.

During the three days preceding completion of the possession of the estate, Mr. Barrow was not idle. Instructed by Mr. Skinner, he located a competent contractor and submitted the blueprint he had of an English designed house. When its proper location on the lot was decided upon, excavation for the foundation was immediately started.

Seven days had already expired since Mr. Barrow's arrival on the island. In reply to his cable, he received one thanking him for his thoughtfulness, and wishing him success and the best of health. On receipt of the cable, he thought of the kindness in the choice of his wife's words. He was happy to have such a wife. He knew that transportation was slow, and except he was fortunate to have caught a boat going direct to England, there was no likelihood of her receiving his mail within another week or so. That grieved him. He could not wait for a reply, so he wrote:

My Dearest Liz,

I am well and I hope you are the same. I have purchased the small estate I told you about in my first letter. Judging from its present crop, the soil appears to be quite fertile. Minor preparations for construction of the house you chose are now going on. As things improve, I'll let you know. I could now write a history on life in Barbados. The vast majority of white people live luxuriously, but the hardship under which the blacks exist is deplorable. The members of two Houses are responsible for the island's Parliamentary procedure. All of the members of the Legislative Council, which is sometimes called the Upper House are white and the members of the House of Assembly or Lower House are predominantly white. These two houses work together and pass legislation to suit themselves and their white brothers. One reason why the House of Representatives is dominated by the white is due to the fact that the financial requirements are set far beyond the reaches of the average coloured person who would gladly offer himself as a candidate. The second reason is this; only a small portion of the coloured population possesses the qualification to vote.

Can you imagine that under no circumstances is a farm labourer permitted to work for an estate other than the one on whose land he resides? Well that is a fact, and many labourers, due to the scarcity of work, have served prison terms for the violation of this unjust law. These workers are miserably poor. They are paid only when they work and not even during sickness.

Domestic servants are even worse. They are expected to get to work at six o'clock in the morning, and few of them can escape the gates of their masters before eight or nine in the night, which is under normal circumstances; but when there is a party, midnight may be considered early; and then having to walk all the way home will serve as no excuse for being late the following morning. The penalty for being late, which is left solely to the consideration of the employer, may be dismissal, or part of their already small earnings deducted. This category of worker has to be on the job every day except one half day one Sunday per month. Don't ask me how they get along with their own domestic affairs; I don't know, and no one even seems to think of it .... including these unfortunate creatures who seem to accept their fate peacefully.

Another group of hard working people are the attendants in

48

groceries, especially those in some of the big business places in the city. The official working hours are from 6 a.m. until 10 p.m. But on Saturdays, it is not infrequent when they are forced to work until 2.30 a.m. The wages these three groups of workers earn are amazingly low, and they get no vacation whatsoever.

The machinery and other appliances in most of the sugar-producing factories are steam driven, but here and there in the remote parts of the island, the old windmill still does the grinding.

I could go on and write pages and pages on the island; but I'll leave some for the next time. Give my kind regards to all inquiring family and friends. Take care of yourself, and may God bless and keep you till we meet again.

Your true and loving husband,

Pete, till the end of time.

Most of the few good artisans had sought employment in one section or another of the industry. This hindered progress on Mr. Barrow's house-building project; but when the crop ended, the contractor was easily able to obtain all the assistance he wanted; and soon a vast improvement was evident. Every day after breakfast at the hotel, Mr. Barrow went to the site. He was enthused by the ease, skill and workmanship exercised on the house, which was taking shape rapidly.

"Why don't you suggest to Mr. Barrow that he should stay here?" said Mrs. Skinner in a warm, friendly voice. They were sitting to table taking lunch. "In the first place it would cost him less," she went on, "and he wouldn't have to be running to and fro every day."

"Suggest is a mild term," replied Mr. Skinner, eyeing Mr. Barrow, who, with indifference to the conversation continued to partake of his lunch. "I would have to bind him hand and foot if I must keep him here."

"You don't mean you have asked him before?" she asked in surprise.

"Yes."

Breaking the short silence Mr. Barrow asked: "Don't you think you are kind enough as it is?" He looked at her, and for the first time, he noticed that her eyes were green and inviting. Her long, blonde hair was combed away from her forehead and tied with a pink bow of ribbon at the back of her small head.

"What is your excuse?" she smiled, "I haven't heard it yet."

"When I left home I told my wife that I would be staying at the hotel," he began. "It may seem cowardly, but I wouldn't want to write and tell her that I've left ... you know how women are," he pointed a challenging finger at her. "Before long she'll be thinking all sorts of things, and probably start accusing me ...."

"I think you are right," she replied, "but all this up and down is doing you no good. Your skin is blistered and you have lost weight."

"I told him the same," said Mr. Skinner.

"I know that I'm blistered," Mr. Barrow agreed, "but the weight .... well I'm not quite sure. One thing I know, I feel fine."

"You have already had two months of this jaunting," said Mrs. Skinner. "How much more have you got to take?"

"Well ...," he smiled, "with the number of people employed, the contractor says he should be able to complete the house in about four months."

"I guess we can do nothing," she addressed her husband, "but accept his excuse."

"I guess not," he replied.

The electrician and his men who were installing the dynamo and light fittings, the engineer and his men who were constructing the windmill and pump for the distribution of water and those engaged in the construction of the house, all under the sole supervision of the contractor, were working harmoniously for a speedy completion. But the weather did not remain sunny and conducive to outdoor work. The rains descended in torrents, strong winds blew and the thunder and lightning was sometimes terrific. It was not infrequent that no work at all could be done. Mr. Barrow never left the hotel during these periods; he devoted his time to reading or writing long letters to his wife and friends. In response to his early letters, he had received some cheerful replies from his wife, which seemed to add warmth to the chill of the day.

• • •

My Dearest Liz,

I am almost dying to have your graceful figure adorn our new home which will be completed in another four weeks. I have checked with the shipping agents here and was informed that if you book passage by 'LAVARA' early next month you will be sure to arrive in Barbados during the last week of the month. This I'm sure, will afford you ample time to make any minor changes to the painting you desire. Book soon and don't miss the ship. Give my kind regards to family and friends.

I remain,

Your true and loving husband,

Pete, till the end of time.

"Please don't think me officious, Mr. Barrow," pleaded Mrs. Skinner one evening when he was preparing to return to the hotel, "the house is almost finished and I have not heard you say anything about your wife joining you .... is she?"

"Of course she is joining me," he replied. "I wanted to

surprise you, but it is me who got the surprise. She should be arriving by the 'LAVARA' this Friday, but .... "

"Do you mean the day after tomorrow?" she interrupted.

"Yes. I got a cable yesterday evening stating that she missed her booking, but she will be due in two weeks."

"Oh! that's lovely."

With the construction work completed and all of the workers gone, Mrs. Skinner volunteered to supervise the scrubbing of the floors and the cleaning of the glass windows. She had assured Mr. Barrow that job was not much of a man's, and she would just love to assume the responsibility. Since his arrival, she had done so little to establish her appreciation for him as a neighbour, and now he wanted to deny her so simple a request. After much persuasion on her part, he succumbed to her request.

Inspecting the floors and windows a few days later Mrs. Skinner said: "So the wife will soon be here, eh?"

"Yes," Mr. Barrow replied cautiously, "if she doesn't miss her booking again."

"She hardly will," said Mrs. Skinner, "when she comes she'll find her home spick-and-span."

"Thanks to you," Mr. Barrow said.

"But what about the furniture," she queried thoughtfully. "Have you placed an order to have them made?"

"When the wife comes she will decide on the kind of furniture she wants. I have never ...."

"You don't mind if I ask a very personal question," interrupted Mr. Skinner, "do you?"

"Not at all," he replied, "as a matter of fact I am glad the question is personnal, because when we shall have become neighbours, I too, have some very personal questions to ask."

"Good," said Mr. Skinner smiling. They were standing on the steps on the easterly side of the house and the strong wind was playing with their hair and garments. "Do you make many decisions," he went on, " in and around your home?"

"How can you ask the gentleman such a question?" Mrs. Skinner snapped. "That is none of your concern."

"What decisions do you make, Mr. Barrow?" he repeated, ignoring his wife whose cheeks had grown red with embarrassment.

"Those that are manly," was the calm reply.

"I like your way out of the situation," said Mr. Skinner laughing.

"Thank you," Mr. Barrow bowed, "but that is not a way out; it is a fact. If my wife should choose the furniture and I disapprove a certain item from the set, I say so. Is that not a manly decision?"

"Thank you, Mr. Barrow," said Mrs. Skinner, glad that her husband had been slapped in the face. "He thinks all men are like himself."

A few days later Mr. Barrow stepped hurriedly up the gangway of the 'S.S. LATHENA' and into a pair of out stretched arms.

"Oh! Liz," he whispered close to her ear, "I've missed you so badly." Maddened with desire, he embraced her lovingly as the aroma of her favourite perfume assailed his nostrils.

"I....I....I've missed you too, Pete," she faltered.
He shoved her off and took hold of her shoulders. He looked into her pretty face. "Is something wrong?" he asked concernedly.

"Wrong? .... What could be wrong?" she lied, "except to be apart so long."

He took her in his arms again and kissed her peach-coloured cheeks.

"You've been sunbathing recently, I notice." He looked her over once more.

Railway Terminus

"All through the trip," she replied, shaking her small head gracefully. "It was just heavenly."

"I'm glad you had a nice trip. Have you checked with the immigration officers already?"

"Yes."

"Then, what are we waiting for?" He signalled to the boatman, who raced up the gangway and took the luggage, while Mr. Barrow and his wife followed him into the small boat which pulled away as soon as they were all settled.

"You rememba he?" asked the skipper of the row boat. They had safely deposited the passengers and their luggage on the wharf and were returning to the side of the 'LATHENA' in search of another job.

"No," replied the second.

"I think I see he face before," said the third.

"He is the Englishman we bring shore a few months ago," said the skipper.

"Oh! yes," chanted the other two.

"Well a woman does turn a man head," said the skipper, "she got 'e head so giddy dat 'e overpay me."

"Don't say so," said the second, "maybe 'e give you extra fuh a tip."

"Tip?" returned the skipper, "can't you see 'e like 'e lost."

"You talking foolishness," said the second, "she is 'e wife."

Passengers were already going out from the train station and into the waiting coaches when Mr. Barrow and his wife rushed into the station yard. Having purchased the tickets earlier, Mr. Barrow's greatest difficulty was to get the luggage into the coach; but one of the yard men seeing his dilemma hastened to his assistance.

"We've barely made it," said Mr. Barrow, dashing through the door of the coach with the last piece of luggage as the locomotive blasted its departure signal.

Slave Hut

"Yes," she replied smiling, "we have."

"I was more fortunate than you," he said resting a fond hand on her knee as the train chugged off. "The day I came I had time to walk around the city."

"I'll see it some other time," she returned, placing her hand on his.

As the locomotive sped through the beautiful rays of a crimson sinking sun, Mr. Barrow took special care to point out and name the places of interest along the way. He had learned them while making his frequent visits to the city during the past months. "You have certainly learned a lot about the place since you've been here," she teased.

"Thank you," he replied smiling faintly, "the island and its people are equally interesting."

They continued to speak of the absence and the way they missed each other and what they hoped for in the future. She was sitting very close to him. She rested her head against his shoulder and whispered in his ear: "This coach is rocking like bloody hell .... but I like it .... mostly because you are next to me."

"Oh! Liz," he returned, placing his cheek against her soft, jet-black hair, "you say the sweetest things to me."

"I'm very glad you think so." She reached up and brushed her lips ever so slightly across his.

At Bushy Park station, Mr. Barrow and his wife were met by a coachman who immediately went to work with the luggage. He began in his usual talkative manner telling about his boss and his kindness, the beauty of the island, sea-eggs, see-moss and flying-fish. But telling was not all; he wanted to know about Mrs. Barrow's trip. How many days had she spent at sea, if she had come alone and why she had not brought the children. Mr. Barrow, accustomed to the coachman and his insatiable desire to reveal the secrets of his own private life and to query the privacy of others, took the responsibility to answer for his wife who stood aside, wide-eyed with wonder.

"Can't she speak for herself?" demanded the coachman.

"She can," replied Mr. Barrow, thoughtful of the words that he should choose next, "but she has had a long trip and is very tired."

"She didn't look so tired when she disembarked from the train," he threw back, "with her mouth flying all over the place."

"I'm sorry if you think so," said Mrs. Barrow apologetically, "but I am really very tired."

Mr. Barrow was absolutely astonished at the simplicity of the coachman who wanted to know all the facts.

Even the comforting arms of Mr. Barrow failed to promote sleep for his wife who turned restlessly amidst the strange surroundings of the hotel room; but when she did, she slept soundly until she was awakened by him for their early morning expedition, which they had previously arranged. Moving around as noiselessly as possible in the dimly lit hotel, they got dressed and sneaked quietly outside where they met the yard-watch who said: "You are up early, Sir, are you going some place special?" He coughed long and hard. Dressed as he was in shabby old clothes, hat and stick, he presented a strange looking picture.

"I am going down to my house," Mr. Barrow answered politely. "I want to be there before dawn."

"All right, Sir," returned the yard-watch. He coughed again and his body shook convulsively. His face was dark and weather-beaten, but his eyes shone brightly. Bathed in the silvery light of the moon, Mr. Barrow and his wife walked hand in hand like young lovers until they came to the house. Inserting the key, he asked: "Should I take you over the threshold?"

"I see no reason why you shouldn't," she replied, running her fingers through his hair as he bent forward. He lifted her in his arms and in the darkness of the closed house lit only by a shaft of moonlight through the half-opened door, his lips found hers.

THE PASSAGE TO EDEN

PART TWO

A gust of breeze rushed through the trees just as the sun came peeping out of the water .... a token that a new day was born to this rural village and all the sunny world. Birds in the trees awakened by the breeze chirped tunes of prayer as they flipped from bough to bough .... it was good to be alive. The sun came slowly over the hill stretching its golden rays like hands farther and farther down the hill and through the trees assuring more and more birds of the new day and of their duty to join their neighbours in chirping prayers, a way of thanking God for life and nature's goodness; and like an obedient child stirred by the loving hand of its mother, so responded the birds in the trees to the groping hands of the sun's rays. Down, down, still farther down, until the air was filled with tunes of various birds .... one happy family in accord.

At the foot of the hill stood two formidable stone buildings, whose lands were divided by low, green hedges. Like the birds, the occupants of these buildings were stirred by the rays of the sun, but they were less active in response .... night's slumber still rested heavily upon them and no sign of life could be seen from outside. But farther along the foot of the hill, some distance away, life was evident among the less fortunate souls who lived in small slave huts. Others, built from flimsy box-boards and bits of tin, these huts formed shelter for man and some of his earthly possessions .... a dog, a few fowls, sheep or goat, but never all of them; for in this world of huts much poverty existed. Huts could be seen over a wide area, and much activity as well. The atmosphere was hazy with smoke rising steadily from improvised hearths which were situated at short distances aback of the huts. Morning meals were being prepared.

To effect as much work as possible and to avoid the burning noonday sun, many of the young men had already left the village. Having tied their trousers legs about the ankles to avoid the intrusion of centipedes and other vermin, they had gone to the field to dig cane holes.

Although the sugar industry provided employment for a variety of skilled and unskilled workers, many of the villagers did not work in the industry. There were a few half-baked artisans and domestic servants among them.

"Mornin,' Irine," said Dorothy, knocking loudly on the wooden door, "you ain' goin' wake up this mornin'?" The muffled sound of a yawn came from within the closed house.

"Irine!" she shouted again, "why de hell you don' wake up?"

A latch snapped and the window opened slowly on its creaky rusty hinges. "What happen with you dis mornin'?"

Irine held open the window with one hand and rubbed her tired eyes with the other. Then, spitting a steam of saliva from her big mouth, she replied, "Chile, I en shut me eye' till jus' now. David was sick in de night. 'E had de cuttin' in 'e belly." She went on to explain how David had been ill with a slight pain in his stomach. The pain got worse and then he started to vomit. "Chile, I din know what to do," she added. "Then I get some fine salt an' burn' kerosene oil an' rub 'e navel an' 'e went sleep. All night I had 'e head in my lap. I en sleep a wink."

"Wait! and Samuel didn't help you with 'e?" asked Dorothy.

"Who, Samuel?" asked Irine in a tone of disgust. "It is weeks since Samuel las' sleep in this hut."

Dorothy's mouth fell open. A bewildered look crept slowly into her large, black eyes. "Irine Goddard," she whispered, "that is true?"

Irine's quick nod answered. It was incredible that Irine should have withheld any secret from her. Not after the many years of unbroken friendship. They had so often shared their joys and sorrows. They had even revealed to each other intimacy of their sex life. Could it be true? Yes, it was. But it was also true that Irine was married to Samuel Goddard. She made a vow to him and God was her witness, and only He was to determine what she should endure. He was to be her sole adviser and defender in this matter.

"Bu...but...but Irine," she stammered, "why you din tell me 'bout this before?"

" 'Cause I din want no advice from you."

Dorothy backed away. Her palm struck her proud bosom with a soft thud. Her eyes bulged. "So you don' trus' me no more?" she asked. Her voice was barely audible. "You don' trus' me?" she repeated.

Irine told her that she did not in any way distrust her .... that she had always treasured and appreciated her sound advice, but this case was different .... different in a great many ways. It was not a case in which she had only herself to please, she had to think of David, her little son who was already asking questions and to whom she was forced to lie. He too, had to be considered. "I will tell you 'bout it one o' these days," she concluded sadly. "I hope you will understan' ... I goin' an' boil some tea .... don' be vex."

Dorothy returned home to find that the fire had died beneath the black skillet in which she left water to boil for the preparation of tea. As she rekindled the fire by placing a lighted match to a few sticks of dried sugar cane, she was stirred with sympathy as she thought of Irine's unhappy state. The reasons Irine had offered for such secrecy were quite logical; but after much consideration, Dorothy was astonished at finding herself incapable of deciding whether Irine was wrong or right to keep her secret. Finding herself utterly perturbed, she dismissed it by saying: "Maybe I would understan' it when she tell me everythin'."

Squatting before the fire with her dress tucked in between her thighs, Irine was not aware that she was crying until the first tear fell onto her slim, dark leg, and trickled off to the ground. She was almost numb with grief, and the realisation of it made her shiver. Why was she crying? Was it due to the illness of her child? No. Was she crying because her husband had deserted her? No. All men have been deserters at one time or another. But a woman was expected to be honest even in the face of desertion. It was honourable for a woman to maintain her respect; and Irine was determined to do so. But in the face of such logic, she was still crying. Why? Because she was a deceiver. She had deceived the only true friend she had.

She heard her own voice saying: 'cause I don't want no advice from you.' Those words were like a dagger to her heart. Why couldn't she have said: "Cause I didn't want no advice." That would have meant that she wanted no advice from anyone. She rose slowly to her feet and entered the hut.

As a token that the crop was approaching its end, each animal participating in the sugar industry was adorned with flowers. During these days the workers would sing and make merry. Five or more months of continuous strenuous labour were slowly coming to an end. But the day the crop actually ended, the factory's steam whistle was blown. Filling the air with its long, mournful blast; people far and near knew that this blast was the last.

When the reaping of the canes came to an end, the villagers went immediately into the fields and gathered all those canes that were accidentally left behind. These canes were by this time half dried; so they took them home and stacked them to dry about their fire hearths of piled stones, and burnt from the stack as they required. When a field was to be supplied with new cane plants, the old stumps were uprooted. These were collected by the villagers and kept for the same purpose as the dried canes. The gathering was not always plentiful; and these poor villagers discovered a good substitute for firewood. When the cows' excreta hardened into little moulds where it had fallen from the animals, it was gleaned, stowed away to be dried, and burnt to cook their meals.

With a very sacrificial attitude on behalf of the shrewd factory owner, each worker was awarded as a symbol of appreciation for the good work done, a quantity of syrup. To them, this was the greatest of all acts of benevolence; and since they were led to believe that syrup was a very expensive commodity, they regarded the management as extremely generous. These poor workers kept their gifts in large, earthen-ware jars to use for the same purpose as they would use sugar.

• • •

In response to a soft knock on the door Vera asked: "Who dat?"

"Me, Olga."

"Open."

Olga opened the door and found Vera sitting at her small table. On the table before her was a large tin cup. The bold printed words on it said: "Quick Cooking Quaker Oats," and from its contents a stream of vapour rose steadily upwards.

"How you manage to drink your tea so hot?" asked Olga, advancing towards the table. Looking into the cup she added: "and it so black."

"I like it so," replied Vera, releasing the first button of her blouse to reveal smooth, black skin and the V formed by her full, firm bust. "I like it so 'cause it keep muh colour."

"Don' stop," Olga teased, her brown eyes shining with curiosity. "Unbutton more."

In an instant, all the buttons were released and a pair of voluptuous busts with black circles around the nipples bounced forward.

"Wuh-loss!" exclaimed Olga, retreating a step or two, "too much for me."

"Den why you ask me to show you? 'cause you foolish?"

Ignoring her, Olga said: "Auntie ask you to sen' some sweetenin' fuh she."

"You aunt think I does keep sweetenin' fuh she?" asked Vera, getting up from the table and going towards the jar which was on three bricks in the corner of the hut.

Olga told her that her aunt did not think she kept sweetening or anything for her, but she wanted a little so she sen' for it. Vera admitted that she had little use for it since she didn't like sweet things. Nearing the end of the crop, she had often found it necessary to give away what she had in order to make room for her fresh supply. "You can get some any time you want," she said, resting the container Olga brought on the table. It shook ever so slightly and a little of the syrup was spilt.

"Why you full it so full for?" asked Olga. "You don' see it throw 'way?"

"Don' mind that," said Vera, taking both of Olga's small hands in hers. "You know why I would give you anythin' you want?"

"No," she replied calmly, looking into a pair of seductive black eyes.

" 'Cause I like you." She lifted Olga's hands and placed the cold palms against her cheeks. "I did like you from de first day you move in dis neighbourhood," she went on. "Although so much time past I still think I see your pretty brown skin an' long brown hair." The buttons were still released; and with her hands held thus, the blouse had fallen apart and two pointed busts protruded. Olga fastened her eyes upon them. Observing Olga's gaze Vera asked: "You want to touch them?"

Olga was embarrassed. She hung her head in shame.

"No," she replied, struggling to free herself.

"Come, touch them," Vera urged. "You is a silly girl." She tugged vigorously. Olga lunged forward and her hand struck soft flesh.

"Oh!" exclaimed Vera, cupping her injured breast and squirming with pain.

"I sorry," said Olga, resting a timid hand on Vera's shoulder. "I din mean to do it." Vera sat on a box. She continued to whimper.

"I sorry, Vera," she said softly, putting a comforting arm around her broad shoulders, "I really sorry."

"It is my fault," Vera returned angrily, "I is a fool .... go an' give your aunt de sweetenin'."

Olga shot upright. Her hands hanging at her sides; a pitiful look on her pretty, brown face.

"You don' got to look so sorry for me," said Vera. "Take de sweetenin' an'go."

Olga turned slowly and took the tin cup of syrup from the table. At the door she said: "Vera, please, forgive me."

Vera liked plenty of tea. She usually drank it hot. Looking into the cup, she discovered that it contained only a small portion. She did not want it. Time was fleeing and she had to clean her little home before going to work on the farm. She got up and started. Suddenly she heard a voice. It was Olga's. Slumping down on the box before the table, Vera rested her head there.

"You still vex wid me?" Olga asked, entering and closing the door after her.

Vera looked up. "Why you come back so quick?"

Kneeling on the white earth which formed flooring for the hut, Olga extended a kind hand and touched her leg. "To see if I can do anythin' to help," she answered. "It still hurtin'?"

"Yes," she replied. She added that when a woman was dealt such a severe blow on her breast it could cause damage to its tissue which could eventually develop into a growth ... in that case the bust may have to be removed .... that was not the worst .... it could lead to cancer.

"Cancer?" asked Olga. "What is cancer?"

"Cancer," Vera whispered, covering her face with her hands, "dat would mean a lot o' pain .... an' certain death."

The act was performed with the efficiency of an expert dramatist. A frightened Olga sprang to her feet. Her eyes bulging. Her long fingers covered her small mouth.

"Oh! Vera, is dat true?"

Vera nodded.

"You want me rub it with some oil?" Olga asked.

With her face still hidden Vera said: "Yes .... look on de shelf you see some in a phial."

• • •

Throwing a few drops in the palm of her hand, Olga, driven by fear and sympathy stretched out a timid hand to touch the soft flesh, which quivered at the touch. As Olga continued her slow caressing, Vera closed her eyes. She rested her head against the side of the hut and soft sighs emitted her half-opened mouth.

"It hurting so bad?" asked Olga, her tears preparing to fall.

"Ru....ru....rub," Vera whispered. Minutes later she shivered, stretched and said: "It feel little better .... go to de pond an' fetch a pail o' water, please."

Olga hurried for the pail and left. "Auntie," she shouted as she passed her hut, "I goin' to fetch some water for Vera."

'I got hell to get she brin' water for me,' her aunt said to herself, 'but she would brin' for everybody else.'

Kneeling beside the bed where her sick child slept, Irine prayed: "Almighty God, I come before you once more to thank you for the light of another day and for sparing the life of my child. For these an' other blessin' which my eyes is too weak to see, I thank you." She continued to pray for the peace of mankind, good understanding with her neighbours; but especially the situation with Dorothy and for the return of her husband. "Not in my time, Lord," she concluded, "but in Your own precious time an' when it seem' best." Rising from beside the bed, she brushed the white marl from her knees. She felt relieved; as though her burden was gone. She started to sing a hymn of praise. Her singing was heard, and other voices joined, the refrain filling the air with sweet music.

Awakened by the singing, David found that tea was already prepared. Irine told him that he was not going to school; but he was to remain at home and keep out of the sun. She had boiled some cornmeal porridge and left it in the skillet; he could use it with some biscuits from the tin. "We don't got much work in de farm to-day," she finished, "I will get home early an' cook."

•••

Irine was an ardent believer in the power of God. She went to the meeting hall regularly and found great comfort reading the Psalms in her Prayer Book. Shortly after her marriage to Samuel, he used to accompany her, but as time went by he became less interested and finally stopped. He even tried to dissuade her; but to no avail. He sank rapidly into the evils of the world. He drank, smoked and even gambled.

Returning from the meeting hall one night she saw Samuel in a heated argument with one of the men from the gambling ring. They were advancing towards each other in preparation to fight. They removed their shirts, and two dark, muscular bodies glistened in the flowing red flame of the torch which stood a short distance away. Leaving her group, she rushed between them pleading with Samuel to join her and go home. But the drunken Samuel swore and shoved her away so furiously that she fell. She sustained a cut on her elbow. Her dress got torn. When her friends rebuked him because he ill-treated his wife in public, he abused them all.

The hazy atmosphere about the village was slowly disappearing. Most of the fires were already extinguished. In some places, preparation of the morning meals had come to an end.

During the season's torrential rains, large quantities of water toppled madly down the rugged hillside, gorging its way to rest peacefully over a wide area to the northern side of the huts where it formed a pond. The water was a saviour to the villagers. They depended on it for washing and bathing; and since they had no floors to scrub, they watered their limited number of domestic animals. Filling her pail, Olga turned homewards.

•••

Resounding clearly through the village was the peal from the bell in the estate yard. It was a means of summoning workers to their jobs. Children, who because of their parents' low earnings, were forced to absent themselves from school before the scheduled school-leaving age of fourteen years, and work on the farms for their parents' unscrupulous masters. These children were referred to as 'The Third Gang.' Their job seldom differed from picking grass and weeds; but the pittance they earned assisted ever so slightly in the financial upkeep of the homes to which these children belonged.

Once more the village became a hive of activity. It was the second time in a very short period. Emerging swiftly from their huts were men, women, girls and boys. With a few exceptions, agricultural instruments such as forks, hoes and grass scythes foretold the type of job these workers were assigned. Leaving the village, parents and guardians issued final warnings to those they left behind.

When Olga returned with the pail of water the village was almost deserted. There were only a few housewives, the very young, the very old, and those left to go to school. Even the birds seemed to have conformed to this stay-at-home theory. There was only an occasional chirp, whistle and coo, and a fleeting glimpse of a food-gatherer as it passed hurriedly on the wing. Amidst the dying embers on the hearth, Olga found her tea. Her aunt had left it there to keep warm. Drinking it and eating some biscuits, her thoughts drifted into the field to where she supposed Vera was working. Working probably under the most painful condition–a condition for which she was responsible. She hated herself.

Three little girls were bathing together on a pile of stones. Each girl had her own pail of water and a milk can with which she dipped the water.

"Where Pearl this mornin'?" asked the smallest girl.

"She en goin' school?"

"She say so," replied the second.

"She don' bathe with we now," said the third.

"Why?" asked the first.

"You didn't go school las' week or you would o' know," replied the second.

"What happen?" asked the first. "Tell me."

"Not me," said the second. "You tell she."

"Not me, soul," said the third. "When I tell she, she may tell she mother and she mother may tell mine an' then I get licks."

"Oh!" said the first, "I wouldn't do that."

"Promise," chimed the other two.

"I promise."

"Pearl mother tell she don' bathe wid we," said the third in an undertone, " 'cause she gettin' too big .... you notice how she stomach growin'.... like two little apples?"

"No," replied the first. "I en notice."

"An' under she arm," said the second.

"Apples growin' under she arm' too?" asked the first.

"You don' look at she?" asked the second.

"Yes," replied the first, "but I didn't see nothin' wrong with she."

"You silly old goose," said the third, "you en see under she arm' got...."

"Listen! you children," Olga shouted from a distance, "if you all don't hurry you will be late for school."

The three girls quickly threw the remainder of water over their skinny, dark bodies and ran to their respective homes to get dressed.

Children on their way to school (whose session began at ten o'clock with a luncheon interval from one to two) heard the blast from the heavily laden locomotive en route to the city and hurried to place pins and nails on the lines to be crushed into tiny, toy knives.

Overlooking a steep, shrubby precipice, below which a curved road declined gradually, was the old, gray-washed stone-building which served as the school house. A long flight of weedy steps led to its arched entrance and bell tower. Hanging from the inner walls of the school room were a few badly arranged pictures. In the middle, and along the eastern end of the room was the platform from which the Headmaster dictated to teachers and children alike. He was a disciplinarian of no mean order, and demanded that each child brought his penny for school fees.

A small stone building at the southeasterly end of the land which marked the school boundary, was an obnoxious smelling toilet. Its dingy white walls bore sketches of birds, beasts, fishes and even human beings. There were, too, bold handwritings accusing pupils of normal and abnormal sex practices. One section of the toilet was reserved for the Headmaster and teachers. The other section contained two large buckets which served as a urinal and a pit. These utensils had to be emptied regularly. A thin, black middle-aged man was assigned to the job.

The hours sped by; and the sun, rising majestically towards its apex, was shining down on this beautiful Caribbean island with its tropical splendour and glamour, moderate temperature and cool refreshing breezes from across the briny Atlantic Ocean, whose waters seemed to play hide and seek among the rocks and along the white, sandy beaches .... amidst the green weeds, around the tall, bending coconut trees whose green heads seemed to bow in welcome to the next oncoming wave.

It was eleven o'clock. The workers knew by the ringing

of the bell that it was time for breakfast, which took various forms. Some had breakfast brought to them, some took it to the job, some went home, and others hurried to their estate's yard to purchase or credit from a woman who sold there.

"Ah!" said a little dark-skinned boy, "she comin'."

All eyes were suddenly turned towards the entrance of the yard as the tall, black woman appeared.

"Thank God," she said breathlessly. Placing the bench she carried on the ground, in the shade of the huge mahogany tree, she added: "Somebody give me a lift."

"Give you a lift," chided the tall, black man who assisted her in taking the large bamboo basket from her head and placing it gently on the bench, "You betta try an' get here early."

The woman ignored him. She untied the corners of a white cloth to reveal the contents of her basket.

"What you got today?" asked Dorothy advancing.

"I got fish cake', and muffin, and bread," the vendor replied.

"I want four piece o' fish and four muffins," said Dorothy.

"What you goin' do with all o' this?" asked the vendor.

"That is none o' you business," Dorothy retorted, "all you got to do is sell."

"All right, soul," said the vendor. She took a sharp pointed stick and stuck four muffins and four fish cakes and placed them in a piece of light brown paper and gave the parcel to Dorothy. Taking the parcel Dorothy asked: "What you holdin' your hand for?"

"Money," replied the vendor.

"Where you think I get money from this day o' the week?" asked Dorothy. "You think today is Monde'?"

"Wha' you tell me jus' now?" asked the vendor. "You en tell me all I got to do is sell?"

"Dat suit you," she replied laughing.

Surrounding the vendor, other workers called noisily for their share.

"Give me uh chance," shouted the vendor, covering her ears to shut out the noise. "One at uh time."

"One at uh time hell," said a woman's voice. "You en know yuh come late?"

"You win, soul," the vendor replied submissively, "but uh beg yuh fur uh chance."

"Where you been?" asked Dorothy, running to meet Irine as she came hurriedly up the back entrance to the yard. "I was lookin' for you."

"I went home to see how David is," she replied breathlessly.

"Here, take dis," said Dorothy, extending the parcel. "I goin' brin' uh swank for you …. sit down there," she indicated a protruding root along the tree-lined path. "I will be back jus' now."

Tears crept slowly into Irine's eyes when she opened the oil-stained parcel. She winked hard to hold back the tears that were ready to fall. Dorothy was approaching. She told her that Martha had come late with the breakfast, and before all was sold out she had taken those and kept for her. "De malicious old bitch want to know wha' I want wid so much," she concluded.

"It was very nice of you," said Irine warmly, "but will I ever get you to stop cursin'?"

"Suppose so," she replied casually.

While Irine ate the muffins and fish, and drank the mixture of syrup and water, she told Dorothy how she had gone home and found David in a feverish condition. He had not tasted the porridge that was left for him. She had soaked the child's head, back and chest with bay rum, and tied some oil leaves on his head. "Uh tell 'e stay in bed 'till uh come home," she concluded.

Dorothy asked her if she didn't think the child could be suffering with worms; they could be very troublesome. She remembered quite well when she was a little girl how her mother used to squeeze the juice from the leaves of the coffee bush in a spoon, put a little salt with it and give her to drink, and a small piece of cod fish to eat after. This medicine was given first thing for nine mornings and on the tenth a dose of castor oil. "Why you don' try an' see if dat would help?"

"Uh mus' try it from tomorrow mornin'," Irine agreed, "an' see if it would help."

The sun was nearing its zenith. Awaiting the ringing of the bell which would indicate that they should return to their jobs, workers sat making talk wherever shade was available about the yard.

"Come on! come on!" shouted Clifford, waving his long hands madly about. "Don' sit down 'pun yuh back-side' an' wait fuh de bell knock. Get back to de job so dat when de bell knock yuh will be ready to start work."

"But look at Clifford," said Dorothy to Irine, "dat big-mout', broad-nose bitch jus' get de job as driver two weeks uh go an' 'e start makin' it harder fuh we' an' 'e only get de job 'cause Thomas dead."

"Don' swear!" Irine snapped.

"Don' swear?" Dorothy returned angrily. "Man he got me so damn vex uh could fight. Suppose de Massah was to give 'e uh hut an' make 'e overseer, it would be hell wid we."

"That is true," Irine agreed, shaking her head sadly. "Uh wonder wuh happen wid we coloured people. They seem to got some curse."

"Curse?" said Dorothy coldly. "Um is de bad mind we got fuh one 'nother."

"Ssssh, 'e will hear you."

"Uh don' give uh damn," said Dorothy. "Las' week 'e did de same as we."

The bell sounded almost simultaneously with Clifford's repeated order to get back to work. There was a sudden stir and they all strode from their places of rest and into the burning rays of the sun.

"Black people does make white people bad," said Dorothy, "before long de manager goin' want we go back to work before de bell knock."

Thomas was the former driver. He had sustained a puncture in his foot while supervising the distribution of animal manure in a field of growing yams. Three days later the manager saw him limping painfully across the yard and inquired of his condition. Learning the facts, the manager ordered Thomas home immediately. He had protested strongly. He said that it would soon be all right; but the manager insisted, and Thomas was driven home in a donkey cart. He was put to bed and cared for by his devoted wife: but six hours later she was a widow. It was incredible; and the manager disbelieved the rumour which had spread like a forest fire.

Thomas failed to take the necessary caution against the nail puncture. His relatives grieved the loss of him, but only a comparatively small number of workers spoke sadly about the incident. He had been the worst driver the estate had in many years. He meddled with, and took so many people's private affairs to the manager, that there was little wonder he became the despised individual that he was. But, harnessing their feelings of hatred for the deceased, they extended words of sympathy to his relatives.

That night the villagers came from far and near to the hut of the deceased to keep 'a wake' in traditional fashion. Only the intervals during which biscuits, cod fish, rum and steaming black coffee was served broke the nightlong singing of hymns. Taking into consideration the size of the hut, they contented themselves with a brief stay in order to give room to newcomers who continued to arrive until dawn.

• • •

The owner of the estate sent a wreath to be placed on Thomas' coffin. This indicated a token of sympathy, and the villagers marvelled at such kindness.

Two sturdy, brown horses were attached to a somber black hearse which stood at the door of the hut awaiting the insertion of the coffin which contained Thomas' body. Busying himself with the horses' harness, the tall, slim, dark-skinned coachman was humming tunelessly and unconcernedly to himself.

The villagers turned out in large numbers to attend the funeral. Except for a comparatively small number of middle-aged women who wore black, all of the younger women were clothed in white. As for the men whose serge differed vastly in shades, their suits were terribly wrinkled. There was only one carriage, in which the immediate relatives of the deceased travelled.

Thomas' body was laid to rest while the sun was sinking in the west. Nine days later there was a repeat performance of nightlong eating, drinking and singing.

"De thin' that hurt me mos' is this," Dorothy went on, "de driver would break we neck with work for de Massah an' 'e don' give a shit 'bout 'e."

"That is true," said Irine, "but they go on doin' it all the time. I wonder if Clifford en see how short God cut off the other one?"

"I goin' see you after work," said Dorothy, breaking off and entering the field in which she was working until breakfast hour.

"All right."

The children were released from school. They had completed the first working session of the day. This was the period for eating, drinking, fighting, playing, laughing, crying and ridicule. This was the period which many children feared. Children, whose poverty-stricken parents could afford them no more than a stewed or roasted sweet potato, a few muffins or a cent with which to buy biscuits and sugar, bread and fish or sweets as the child desired. These children were not the worst off. Other children depended upon thrift, a sense of humour, or their educational ability, and the skill to secretly tutor their more materially fortunate brothers who were less academically called while still at school.

Olga, who had returned from the pond much too late to join the others at work engaged herself at home with washing and mending. Overpowered by the quiet of the hut, she lay across the bed and fell asleep. Awakened by the wild shouting of children, Olga rushed to the window only to discover that they were returning from school. She was surprised she had slept so long. Before going to bed, she had washed the container in which the drinking water was kept, and since there was none in the hut and time for cooking was approaching, she hastened for the pail and hurried off to the pond which was some distance away.

The sun turned crimson in the west. The bell in the estate yard sounded and the labourers were journeying wearily homewards. It would still be a few hours before shop attendants and domestic servants returned to their huts. The birds, too, were returning to their nests, and as the sun sank deeper and deeper and the sky grew darker more and more bats were appearing in their erratic flight.

Night fell, and in the village, numerous glowing fires began flickering in the dense inky blackness accompanied by the chirping of crickets. As the minutes ticked slowly by and the smoke steadily rose on high, the aroma of freshly-cooked food fought to permeate and establish its sweetness in the cool of the night's air.

"Irine!"

"Yes, Dorothy .... look me roun' here in de back." She was squatting and washing the enamel plate from which she had eaten, and the skillet in which she had cooked, by the light of the fire. She told Dorothy that she did not wait for her after work because she had to hurry home to see how David was. She cooked and ate; but she had boiled some Quaker Oats for David who was feeling a great deal better. "I jus' heatin' some water to sponge off David an' let 'e go sleep .... what you cook?"

"I had a piece a punkin dey from yestada' an' I cook it with li'l rice .... I didn't even make no sauce; I put salt fish, lard-oil, onion an' a piece a pig-head an' let everythin' cook up in one .... chile, it did sweet enough."

"That is true, sometimes I does feel to eat a li'l piece a rice like dat. When I did comin' in I meet de man with fish; I take two from 'e 'til pay day and steam them down 'pon a yam an' a potato .... let we go in," she concluded, collecting her utensils.

"Wait! you got dis place san' off pretty enough," said Dorothy as she entered the hut.

"You brin' in marl lately?"

"Not me," Irine replied, putting the things away, "David."

"Well I tell you, 'e do a good job .... 'e got in here fire bright. I wanted to brin' in some since las' week but I can' find time."

Entering the chamber which was formed only by the sewing together of light-brown coarse sacks, Dorothy asked:

"How you feelin' now, David?"

"Much better, thanks," he replied weakly.

"But why yuh don' lay down?"

"No," Irine answered, "I tell 'e don' lay down 'till de slops settle in 'e stomach."

"Oh! dat is right."

• • •

When Irine thought the supper was sufficiently digested, she made sure that David was perfectly clean by sponging him off before putting him to bed; then, turning to Dorothy she said: "I now 'member I en got no sugar fuh mornin' .... wait here 'till uh run at de shop an' come back."

In response to a soft knock on the door Vera asked: "Who is it?" She was sitting at her table mending by the light of her lamp. It was only a substitute, but it provided light. It was a small glass jar. It was half-filled with kerosene oil. Through the metal screw cover a small metal funnel was placed, and from the oil up through the funnel a piece of flannel was tightly rolled and lit.

"Me," replied a soft voice.

"Me who?" she asked, still keeping her eyes on what she was doing.

"Me Olga," was the reply.

"Oh! I din catch de voice," said Vera. "Put yuh han' over de door an' unlatch it an' come in."

Olga walked in and stood in the centre of the small room. "Auntie sen' me out at Gran-ma," she said, 'an' uh now get back .... yuh can' see de lamp too high?"

"I en notice dat," Vera replied, tugging the knotted thread through the material. "Uh tryin' to finish this. Uh hate to men', but I so damn poor."

"Who isn't in dis village?" she asked. "I was doin' some today but I fall 'sleep before I finish." She sat on a box at the table.

"Be careful!" said Vera warningly, "that box shaky."

"All right," she replied. She searched amidst her long, brown hair for a hairpin. Finding it, she inserted it into the thin, red flame of the lamp and forced the wick lower. The soot reduced and the light as well.

"Not too low," Vera warned, "or I won' be able to see."

• • •

Olga told her that when she was returning from her grandmother she saw Samuel and Gladys. They were having an argument. They were standing in the dark shade of the bread-and-cheese trees. He was accusing her of having an affair with another man. She was denying; but he was insisting that it was true because a good friend of his told him. He must have struck her. She was crying. She said that he had her stomach hurting. She said that if he doesn't stop beating her she is going to leave him and he would have to go back to his wife.

"Who is he wife?" Vera asked.

"Irine .... you don' know Irine Goddard?"

"Ooooh!" said Vera surprised. "You mean Samuel Goddard!"

She told Olga that Samuel was no good. He was never any good; at least she heard her mother say so. She didn't understand how Irine ever met up with him. Of course, her parents didn't want her to have anything to do with him, but he had improved his conduct and started going to the mission hall. "I suppose Irine thought he had changed, but people don't change just like that. He likes to beat women. It is only now-a-days that he don't beat Irine. Before you came to live in this village, he used to beat Irine real bad. As for Gladys, I am surprise at she. She was Irine's good friend. "Chile, I goin' tell you somethin'," she concluded, "I don' want no good friend."

"I thought me an' you was goin' to be good friends?" Olga asked.

Vera looked up from her mending. Their eyes met. After a moment's silence, she said:

"Do you know what you saying?" Her voice was like music.

David fell asleep. Dorothy extinguished the light in the chamber and was sitting in the outer room humming softly when the door opened and Irine appeared. There was blood on her mouth and on the front of her dress which was torn from the throat to the waist. A portion of her vest was also torn, and one saggy bust was protruding. Her hair was in disarray.

"Oh God!" Dorothy exclaimed, rushing to her side, "what is the matter with you?"

Irine burst into tears. Her frail body swayed as though she would fall, but Dorothy supported her and led her to a seat.

"Who did this to you?" she asked tenderly.

"Sa....Sam....Samuel," she sobbed, adding that while on her way to the shop she heard voices arguing in the distance. When she got near she noticed that it was Gladys and Samuel. She said nothing. Returning from the shop Samuel pounced upon her as soon as she got abreast of them. He took the parcel from her and crushed it under his feet. He then beat her. " 'e say that I always peepin' and dodgin' behin' he," she wailed, "but that en true. 'e swear 'e goin' kill me. Oh Lord! Dorothy, an' I en do that man nothin'."

"Dis is advantage," Dorothy protested angrily. "He only do this to you 'cause 'e know you quiet. If you was to take up somethin' an' burst loose 'e face 'e would stop this blasted foolishness. Look what uh state 'e got you in now. I goin' get some water an' give you a warm water bath." She hurried out of the room, made a fire and sat a large P.Y. Butter skillet of water to warm.

Olga told Vera that due to the incident which occurred between them during the early hours of the morning she had been very thoughtful all day. She wondered if the breast was painful and if it had prevented her from working. Vera admitted that the breast was painful, but not enough to stop her from her daily activity. She had not told any one about what happened since she wanted it to be kept a secret between them. Olga confessed that she was on the verge of asking her aunt's advice on the matter, but on second thought she decided not to do so. It was a good thing she had not told her aunt. Vera told her that she was really very angry this morning, but after she showed such kindness her anger turned to sympathy.

During the conversation Vera scarcely looked up from her mending. It was painful to Olga who was longing to look into her friend's eyes. "Yuh goin' let me rub it for you tonight?" she asked pleadingly, reaching out a tender hand and touching Vera's bare knee, "before you go to bed?"

Vera stopped her mending. She rested both hands in her lap. She looked up. Their eyes met. They stared at each other silently.

"You want to?" Vera asked modestly. Olga nodded slowly. Vera folded the material. She placed it aside. Then, running her fingers through Olga's long brown hair and forcing her head backwards to look into her brown eyes she said: "You is very kin' .... I goin' an' bathe up my face an' hand' an' then let yuh attend to me."

When the water was hot Dorothy threw it into Irine's wallaba tub and added cold water until the required temperature was reached. She took the tub and its contents into the room. She told Irine to take the lamp into the inner chamber and remove her clothes while she opened two windows.

"When you bathe in hot water in the hut," said Dorothy, "you mus' open de windows so that you won't catch a draf'." Taking a piece of cloth, Dorothy soaked it in the hot water and administered it to Irine who whimpered and squirmed at its contact against her bruised body. "It will keep you from feelin' stiff in de mornin'," said Dorothy, when she completed her task. "If you had li'l Epson salts uh would give you uh dose .... you en got none?"

"No."

"I got li'l home," she said going through the door. "Uh goin' for it an' come back."

Minutes later, Dorothy returned with a small parcel in her hand. "You shouldn't mix salts in uh tot," she said, "you got uh cup?"

"Yes," replied Irine, "look in de box under de table you see uh tea-bowl."

Dorothy threw some of the crystal flakes into the cup. She added a little water and stirred until the flakes were dissolved. "They say you shouldn't drink salts at night," she said, as she offered Irine the cup, "it too col' for the heart, but dis mix with warm water. It would scatter de bruise blood that bitch put in your skin."

"Thank you."

"Lie down li'l bit let it settle in yuh stomach."

"All right."

Dorothy was standing in the centre of the dimly-lit room when Samuel rushed in and charged upon her with two cuffs and a kick which sent her sprawling onto the floor. It was Irine's screaming in the inner room which told him that he had missed his target. Astonished, he remained where he had delivered his final blow. With feet astride and mouth agape, he stared wide-eyed with wonder. His hands hung limply at his side.

"Oh God!" Irine shouted frightfully, "Look trouble tonight."

Scrambling to her feet, Dorothy's outstretched hand found a bottle. Rising with it, she hurled it through the air. It struck Samuel on the forehead, fell to the floor and smashed. Samuel staggered back a few paces. Then, covering his forehead with his hand, he rushed through the door shouting: "Oh God! uh cut, uh cut, uh cut."

Unlike man, ruler of the earth, the birds were resting

peacefully in the trees that loomed with defiance into the black night, illuminated only by the numerous twinkling stars above. They chirped their prayer of thankfulness for the day's offering, and, in appreciation for their thoughtfulness, they received all the peace and tranquillity of the night. The breeze was blowing cool, gentle and friendly; and only the leaves of the flimsiest of boughs shivered in the coolness of the night air.

Many as these huts were, the area they occupied was comparatively small. It was little wonder that the occupants of the huts knew so much about each other business.

"Wh....wh....wha' happen, Mama?" David stammered frightfully, "wha' happen?"

"You father just rush in here an' start to beat up Dorothy."

"Why?"

" 'Cause 'e take she for me."

"Oh," he said sleepily.

A large crowd had already gathered outside the hut when Samuel ran through the door. He did not look to see who was there. With one hand covering the wound, he hurried into the night and vanished.

"Look 'e wash in blood," said one from the curious crowd.

"Irine mus' be chop 'e."

"She right. He always beatin' de woman for nothin' at all."

"Dat is true .... but she should not chop 'e."

Since it was still early and many children had not yet gone to bed, there were a few girls and boys amidst the inquisitive group of men and women.

"You know wha' happen?" one woman whispered to another.

"No."

"Samuel beat Irine out en de road jus' now."

"How you know?"

"She lef' Dorothy in de house wid David an' went to de

shop to buy sugar, when she was coming back Samuel beat she."

"But how you know?"

"I hear she tellin' Dorothy."

"What he beat her for?"

"He an' Gladys was out de road talkin' an' Irine mus' be drop remarks."

"Not Irine, I would swear she en drop no remarks."

"Anyhow, 'e come in an' start beatin' she again an' she must be chop 'e."

"If that did happen to me," a man was saying, "you think I would run an' holla?....man I would turn an rain some licks in she tail."

"Oh you only talkin' big talk," a woman interrupted, "when you wife ready, you does got to keep quiet."

"You talkin' shit, woman."

"I know, all the men 'roun' hay tonight is big bullies jus' because what happen to Samuel en happen to them."

The incident between Samuel and Dorothy had disturbed her no more than if she, in an attempt to drive a fowl from the hut had stumbled over a box and broken an empty bottle. Taking the dried brambles of the whitehead bush which Irine substituted for a broom, Dorothy swept the room. She took special care to brush deep into the marly earth with the hope of removing all the splinters of the broken bottle which were likely to play havoc with the occupants' bare feet. She swept the stuff in a little heap in one corner of the hut. She rested the broom on top of the stuff, and brushed her hands together. 'Dat is finish', she said to herself.

All murmuring ceased when Dorothy stepped through the door.

"Miss Goddard .... Miss Irine ..... Irine," a number of voices called.

"De body en Miss Goddard," she replied boldly. "It is me Dorothy."

"Wha' happen wid Irine?"

In the dark, Dorothy could not observe any one. "Irine all right," she replied, "but dat madman she got for a husban' come in day an' give me two cuff' an' uh kick .... he play 'e worser than anybody else, but I show 'e 'e en worse than me."

"Where Miss Irine?"

"She inside," Dorothy replied. "I live wid uh man there," she went on, "an' he could not do that to me an' think I would take that. Man de only way I would take that is if uh did lef' my hand in my mudda."

"I did hear Irine voice an' uh thought it did she."

"She holla out when Samuel hit me."

"Oh! uh know uh did hear she voice."

A small fire burned brilliantly in the night. Samuel was preparing a little warm water. He begged Gladys' assistance but she refused; saying that he had beaten her only a short while ago. She was glad that some one had found the mark .... it served him right.

When Samuel finished washing the wound on his forehead, he took the flaming torch which served as a lamp and scanned the roof of the hut in search of spider's web. Finding some, he forced it into the cut, bandaged his head and crawled quietly into bed beside Gladys who moved away as far as possible from him.

There was no light in the hut when Vera arrived at the door.

"Gladys gone to bed before uh get here to find out what happen between she and Samuel," she said.

"You drag me up here to malicious in de people business?"

Olga threw back.

"The two of them must be doing dixy in bed."

"You would never know, 'cause you don't got no man."

"But I got you," she locked the fingers of her left hand with those of Olga's right hand.

"Because you do that thing to me the other night, you got me?"

Leaving the regular pathway, Vera moved towards her familiar opening amidst the thickly-grown, vine-covered bushes. "Lower your head," she whispered. It was cosy behind the vines, lit by the pale colour of a new-moon. Vera found the trunk of a fallen tree, took a seat, gently guided Olga to sit on her knees and proceeded to unfasten the buttons of Olga's blouse. Expert fingers curled and uncurled around Olga's naked breast. Olga squirmed and sighed with ecstasy. "Ooooh! V .. V.. V.. Vera ...." The jabbering stopped when firm lips smothered hers in a lingering kiss, which was rudely disturbed by the noisy barking of a dog giving chase to a cat through the bushes. At Olga's request before parting, Vera promised to let her fondle her breasts the following night.

The shop-attendants and domestic servants returned to their respective huts. Along the way they received and participated in their share of gossip about the day's happenings in the village. They retired to bed. Dorothy apologised to Irine for inflicting a wound on Samuel. She made it clear that if Andrew treated her in that manner she would have done the same. She wished her a pleasant night's rest and went home to Andrew and bed. "Hey, Irine, did Samuel ever say anythin' to you 'bout what happen that night between me an' 'e?" asked Dorothy one day while they were weeding in the same field.

"No."

"After all dese weeks 'e never say nothin'?"

"Never .... when 'e come dey an' 'e ask me anythin' uh would answer; or if I got to ask 'e anything, but we don' talk. 'e talk wid 'e chile."

"An' 'e don' got nothing to do with you?"

"No .... 'e don' sleep at me."

"An' why you don' get uh man?"

"Me?" she asked, slapping her bosom with her left palm. "I don' want no man."

"But you still young .... if he don' got you yuh can get somebody."

"No. I married to he an' dat is dat."

"Well uh goin' tell you somethin', I en promisin' no man that. You must be got me in your mind 'bout what happen that night?"

"No, 'e used to beat me too bad .... let Gladys get some now."

"But how 'e ever get to know she?"

Irine told her that she could never forget that day. It was the year when Mr. St. Hill at Bushy Park entered that black, long-legged Alpine for the races. Everybody said that the goat was too big to be allowed to compete, but Mr. St. Hill argued that his goat was within the age limit. It had won every race it entered. Its leather halter and belly-band through which a long rein was looped had been beautifully adorned with twisted red and yellow ribbons. Its runner had been a long-legged dark-skinned youngster who used to work at Bushy Park. He had worn a colourful cap and shirt and short white pants. He carried a long, slender tamarind whist near the end of which a piece of ribbon was tied. Since the goat and its runner were so colourful in their attire, they were very conspicuous.

When Dorothy recalled all of this, Irine went on to say that she had not seen Gladys since they were children, when they worked as pond grass pickers at Pool estate in St. John. They had been the best of friends during those years. There were days when they spent long hours picking lice from each other heads and chiggers from their painful toes. This they used to do alternately. But circumstances changed, when their parents moved to different locations. They had wept bitterly, and their parents laughed at them. Until the day at the races they had not seen each other.

People were lined on both sides of the allotted track awaiting one of the events which was just about ready to get on its way when Irine heard her name called. She looked in the direction whence the sound came. It was Gladys. Tugging a man at her side, she came running across just as soon as the goats and their jockeys went speeding down the track. Neither of them bothered about which goat had won; but it was the Alpine goat.

Amidst all the shouting and laughing and jumping which followed the event, an introduction proved that they were both recently married. She was then living among the tenantry at Colleton factory where she and her husband were working. They had come to visit a friend nearby who invited them to the sports. Over drinks, rum for the men and aerated from marble-stoppered bottles for the women in a nearby shop, they discussed the friendship of their childhood. When the partying ended and the evening shadows fell, they said goodbye and expressed the hope of seeing each other in the very near future.

"But how you find out that somethin' was goin' on between them?" asked Dorothy, glad for the opportunity to say something. Irine made no reply. She stopped her weeding. She straightened up, breathed deeply and sighed just as a huge shadow crept towards her, caused by a thick, dark passing cloud which covered the sun. The long silence which followed was acute. Dorothy watched her curiously. She wondered whether the sigh was an expression of exhaustion from the emotional distress. She was soon relieved of her question.

"I feel as light as a feather," said Irine, releasing her hoe which fell to the ground. She stretched her hands twice over her head and straight before her. "I feel happy too," she added; "As happy as if I did find money."

"The talkin' must be good for you."

"You think so?" she asked, as she retrieved the hoe.

"Could be."

"Then I goin' talk more."

She went on to say that she and Gladys had not met again until the next sports event on the same ground. The champion from St. John had challenged the champion from St. Philip to a stick-licking competition. Gladys and her husband were then living and working at Bushy Park. Since the date fixed for the competition had been a bank holiday and most of the stick-licking fans from the two parishes were free from work, a mammoth crowd attended. Supporting their champion, fans eagerly offered bets of money, drinks or personal belongings to any opponents. It had been a horrible day .... the worst in the history of stick-licking. The decision given by the judges had been unjust to the minds of the fans who demanded that the bets be called off. Some had done so while others refused and a number of fights ensued. Running frightfully to and fro, many innocent people had been injured by the shower of bricks, bottles and stones thrown by piqued men and women. That evening they parted without saying goodbye.

"But how you find out that somethin' was goin' on between he an' she?" Dorothy asked again.

She told her that their husbands used to take them to pay alternate visits at least once every month; but when she became pregnant and could not go, Gladys used to come. She used to come every week after David was born. At first her husband would bring her; then he stopped, and when she came, Samuel would take her home. It was not long before she started coming three times a week. "I hate to say this," she went on after a pause, "but one night 'e take she home an' didn't come back 'til late, an' next mornin' I notice that 'e underwear was dirty. When I ask him 'bout it he come to fight. I didn't long had the baby an' I was not able to take no licks so I kept muh mout' shut. Little by little it went from bad to worse; now 'e don't sleep here at all."

"An' what become of her husband?" Dorothy asked concernedly.

"She race 'e way. She say 'e too slow with de bed work; she like to do that often."

They laughed heartily.

"An' to think she did your best friend," said Dorothy, shaking her head sadly.

"Well, chile," said Irine shrugging her shoulders, "that is the way life goes."

Samuel Goddard was the village barber, but it was not infrequent when parents were seen cutting their children's hair. The shade of a large ackee tree aback of his hut served as his salon. When Sunday came, since that was the most convenient day, all of the men and boys who required his services would gather under the tree and await their turn. He was usually kept busy from dawn until dusk. He would seat his patron on a box, spread a clean, white cloth about his shoulders and start to work with scissors and comb.

When the hair was cut to the patron's satisfaction, Samuel would break a bottle and substitute a piece of glass for a razor. To use this type of razor required great skill; and seldom was the occasion when a patron left the salon with the smallest of nicks.

Like an established barber in any busy commercial area,

Samuel was occasionally confronted with the difficulty of keeping order in his salon. Exposed to public view as it was, he developed a policy that each patron was entitled to the respect of the other, even though he acquired the bad habit of swearing. For this he was often ridiculed. Patrons in a hurry provided another source of trouble. There was always some fellow who wanted Samuel to deprive another of his chance because he had to attend a harvest, service-of-song, cantata or a singing. Sometimes Samuel was very sympathetic to their situation, and he would ask permission to be allowed to handle that patron who was so hard-pressed for time; but if he had a few drinks, he would abuse the offender.

Cutting hair was only a sideline for Samuel, he was employed as an engine-driver; as such he was among the best paid workers in the factory; and although the meagre fee for hairdressing was eight cents and four cents, for men and boys respectively, he could make himself quite a few extra shillings in addition to his weekly earnings. His money and the way he spent it in a little hall just outside the village where dances were held every Saturday night made him very popular; especially among the women. Women used to fight over him, and men would beat their women when they suspected them of having a love affair with him.

"Wait! you still livin'?" Samuel asked one evening just as he entered the door of his hut.

"Yes," replied Dorothy. "You send somebody to kill me?" She looked at him. The old scar was there on his forehead. She remembered the whole incident; and for the first time since that horrible night she felt sympathetic towards him.

"God forbid, soul," he replied. Then turning to Irine he said: "Dat woman don' speak to me, you know."

"I can say so too," said Dorothy. "He does meet me 'long de road an' 'e don' say nothin'. "What I mus' say?"

"De two uh you will make out that," said Irine, as she went

about her housework. "All two uh you want de Lord."

Opening the parcel in his hand Samuel said: "Uh jus' went down by de bay an' uh friend give me three shell' uh sea-egg', you want one?"

"Yes", replied Dorothy, accepting the extended gift. "I en taste none since de season start. I like to eat them raw but not Andrew. Uh goin' home now an' fry up this for me an' he."

"You goin' give Andrew some in truth?"

"How you mean?" asked Dorothy in surprise. "If I got uh biscuit cake he mus' get piece; but 'e can' play no ass with me."

"You en such uh bad woman after all," said Samuel, looking her over.

"You en such uh bad man either," she returned, smiling at him, "only you got de wrong woman .... you should had uh woman like me .... uh would beat sense in your head. Samuel, when you goin' change?" asked Dorothy after a pause.

"He will never change," interrupted Irine, "never."

"Change how?" he asked, looking at Irine. "Uh don' look out for my home?"

"Yes; but that en all," replied Dorothy. "You does spend uh lot uh foolish money. Look! Andrew does make uh few kites an' sell, an' when Easter gone an' kites stop selling', 'e could show near every cent 'e work for out de kites, an' he does go to dances too; but you mus' go to every one. You en know de women only want you for your money? No, you playin' parish ram. You en see you gettin' uh big son to work for?"

"Me an' Andrew is two different people," said Samuel. "If he like to work an' brin' all 'e money an' put in you lap, dat is he business. I does work for mine an' uh mus' spend some."

"But not all .... an' more besides, uh man place is in 'e house wid 'e wife. I would get married to Andrew too, but I en takin' no man ring yet, 'cause uh en goin' stan' for no foolishness."

A very strange relationship developed from the incident

which occurred between Vera and Olga. After supper every evening she would clean up the utensils, make herself tidy and then rush over at Vera where they would sit and talk until time for them to drift quietly into bed.

"I think my aunt like you uh lot," said Olga one night while they were sitting together eating peanuts. She liked nuts very much. Vera knew it, and every Saturday after she got paid and went to the shop to purchase her weekly groceries, she would buy a portion for her. This delighted Olga, and it had a reciprocal effect.

"Why you say dat?" Vera asked, placing some of the nuts she had shelled in Olga's hand.

"You don't know I can crack my own nuts?" asked Olga. It was on another occasion when she repeated that question. "You make me feel like I is a li'l girl," she added.

"You is .... my li'l girl; but that is nothin' to do with what I ask you. Why you think your aunt like me?"

" 'Cause she don' quarrel when I come at you."

"You mean she does quarrel when you go at somebody else?"

"She don' let me go. When we firs' move in dis neighbourhood she tell me that I must speak to everybody, but I must keep to myself."

"So you turn out disobedient to your aunt?"

"No."

"Then what you doin' here?"

" 'Cause I obedient. If Auntie sen' me to you for a pinch a salt, a dus' a flour, a scale of soap or two black-pepper I got to come, aint?"

"Yes"

"Well dat is obedient."

"Yes, but what she sen' you for now?" Olga was silent.

"But how you and your aunt come to move out here?" Vera went on.

Olga told her that her aunt's husband was always in trouble for stealing. She had threatened to leave him if he did not stop it, and one day while she was at work two policemen went to her home and searched for stolen articles. They were found, and that same night she left him and came to live with her parents. One Sunday her mother had gone to the mission hall and left her with her aunt to prepare dinner. While helping, she developed a headache and lay across the bed to rest. She must have fallen asleep. She did not hear her father come in; but their voices woke her.

"Take your hand off me!" Auntie said. Her voice was just above a whisper. She didn't seem as though she wanted anyone outside to hear.

"Uh did long waitin' for dis chance," Daddy said in an undertone. "From de first night you come to live here."

"Take your han' off me!" Auntie repeated. "You think I would live wid muh sister husban'? Man you mus' be drunk. You think I din notice how you did always tryin' to get up to me? I en want no man .... an' if I want a man I en want muh sister man. What she would think of me?"

"But she won' know."

"Know or know not, I en doin' it."

"If you don' let me got you," he said warningly, "you goin' got to leave here."

"An' what you would tell Sylvia is de cause?"

"Uh would tell she you ask me to live wid you."

"You would do dat?"

"Be Chris' uh would!"

Olga told Vera that when she turned suddenly on the mattress which was recently stuffed with dried grass, it made a noise. She stretched and yawned aloud. Her aunt called and inquired of her feelings. She told her that she felt much better and would be out in a minute; but she did not move immediately. She wanted to give her father time to get out of the hut if he wanted to. She did not want them to know that she had heard. When she finally looked out of the window, her father was sitting under a breadfruit tree which was aback of the hut. His face was twisted with ire. Three evenings later she came in from the pond to hear a terrible quarrel in progress. Just as she got to the door her aunt said: "Ah! look Olga hay. If she din sleeping she would tell de truth."

She told them all she had heard. Her father said she was a liar, and that neither her aunt nor she could sleep in his hut that night. They had to sleep at two friends for one week until they came here.

"So you know de whole story now," Olga concluded.

"But uh did ask you before," said Vera. "Why you din tell me?"

"You don' walk 'bout an' tell people you jus' know uh few days ago your business."

"So yuh know me long enough to tell me yuh business now?"

"Yes, an' besides that, you is my bes' friend."

When they climbed secretly into bed a few minutes later, Olga said: "You en see more paper want pastin' up on these boards?"

"Why?"

"So that nobody can' stand outside an' see what we do in bed."

Led by Dorothy, Irine followed the narrow, winding track amidst short, sun-scorched grass and weeds to the hut. It was little more than a hovel, dangerously tilted to the west as though an easterly gale had blown it off its low props. So dangerous was its position, that the rusty pieces of tin which patched the roof must have been placed there long ago. Along the side and part of its roof, a green vine had firmly laced itself. Its fruit, many of which varied in size, resembled the cucumber. Some of them dry, showed signs of decay; and through their porous bodies, smooth, black seeds protruded. Why should a vine be so green in this area was beyond Irine's comprehension. She looked searchingly. Securely set in the earth near the door, the root of the vine and the grass in the near vicinity was also green; evident, then, that the quantity of water dispensed about the area was responsible for the green condition of the vine and grass. But whether the water had been discharged there for the benefit of the vine or for convenience, she did not know.

"Where you goin'?" she whispered.

"Ssssss," replied Dorothy, covering her own lips with an index finger.

"Silence out day," came a voice from within the hovel, "an' don't make no signs."

Irine, nearing the door stopped abruptly. Her heart was pounding frightfully. The voice was undoubtedly a man's. It was incredible that anyone could live in such a place. While her heart pounded, her thoughts questioned a number of reasons why Dorothy had brought her there; but no logical answer came.

"So....som....somebody live there?"

"I say no whisperin' out there; open the door an' come in." Irine was sure no one from within could have heard her whisper. Dorothy slowly opened the door. It swung noiselessly on three pieces of India rubber which substituted for hinges. Irine followed her in, and the door closed after them.

Inside, Irine made a sudden gasp. Her mouth fell open and her black eyes seemed to pop from their deep sockets at the sight before her. She was confounded. White fine marl covered the floor of the room; and the moisture of the neatly, pasted, multicoloured paper on the wide-creased boards indicated recent workmanship. The room, was divided by a screen of coarse bags which had been hand stitched with cord; and

Old Woman's Hovel

although there were no hanging pictures, the colourful paper gave the room a homely atmosphere.

A beaded black cloth was tied about the small head and fell to the narrow shoulders of the crouched individual who sat backing the only door in the structure. Dorothy tiptoed and sat on one of the three vacant boxes around the table. Irine followed cautiously and took a seat; her heart pounding fearfully.

On the dark blue paper-covered table, there was a large Bible. Through it, a strip of narrow, black ribbon marked the pages. Placed diagonally across the Bible was a key; and on either side a shining gold ring. At the upper end of the Bible there was a glass half-filled with crystal clear water, and a deck of cards next to it. Gazing steadily into the small enamel bowl of light-blue water, the crouched figure said in a low, husky whisper; "I know why you come to me .... you want my help .... people never come to me except for help .... I don' know you, but I can see .... I see a big race meetin' ... old friends shakin' hands .... what is this now? .... Oh! this is stick-lickin' and friends meet again, but there is big danger; bricks, bottles an' stones .... ah! this is nice; I see friend visit friend." There was a long pause.

"I don' like what I see," said the crouched figure in a more serious tone. "I see friend makin' love to friend wife an' living at friend wife .... that is bad; an' I will stop it. That woman is a dirty-handed woman .... she is tryin' to kill you to get husban,' but that will never happen. I will protect you against that wicked woman an' you will get husban' back an' will be happy."

During the long silence that followed, Irine stared into the lean, dark face of the figure who sat before her. She could not determine whether the figure before her was male or female.

The headtie was so arranged that only a small portion of the face was exposed to view. Perched on the figure's broad, flat nose was a pair of silver framed spectacles, behind which, shifty, black eyes continued to peer into the bowl. 'Is this a woman?' Irine wondered. But she suddenly remembered the tone of the voice before they entered, and the odour of tobacco while the figure spoke. 'It mus' be a man,' she concluded.

Except for the buzzing of the busy nectar gathering bees who frequented the flowers on the vine-covered roof, all was silent. Then the mysterious figure spoke again.

"Put a cent an' an eight-cent piece in this bowl. Next Friday, bring five shillings an' a black fowl .... remember, the fowl must be all black. We start work next Friday at twelve o'clock."

Dorothy's fingers stole through her kinky, black hair and produced a small parcel. She opened the paper, slipped the coins into the bowl and left the hovel. Irine followed at her heels. They walked a great distance in silence. Irine was perturbed. She felt weak, and cold; and the brilliant sun seemed inadequate to warm her delicate body. She shuddered in disgust. "How long you been goin' at that place?" she asked meekly.

Dorothy told her that when she was a little girl she had gone there many times with her mother and grandmother. They are both dead; but what the old woman told them had come to pass. Andrew did not believe in the things she said, but one day she told him that he would get promotion soon; and two days later he got it.

"You carry him there too?" Irine asked pitifully.

"Yes."

"But Dorothy .... you does go to that woman an' still go to meetin'?"

"Nothing wrong with that," Dorothy snapped. "If she can tell me somethin' about the future to put me on muh guard, I en see nothin' wrong with dat."

"You serious?"

"Yes, I is."

Irine quoted the First Commandment. She told Dorothy that she cannot visit this woman and believe the things she says and at the same time serve God sincerely. "When you have confidence in Him and His power you don't need to look into the future; He will take care of it."

Breaking the long silence which accompanied them as they journeyed homeward, Irine told Dorothy that she felt remorseful, and considered herself a deceiver ever since that day when she so clumsily revealed her innermost secret about Samuel's desertion .... she was awaiting a convenient opportunity to ask for pardon; now she discovered that there was no need to ask pardon; she was equally guilty of secrecy, and guilty of a far more grievous sin in the sight of God.

"Irine that en nothin'," Dorothy protested. "I can pray an' ask God to forgive me after."

"But He is not to be treated so," she said. She stopped in her tracks. She extended her arms appealingly.

"Dorothy, what you would do to a child that keep on doin' de same thin' over an' over askin' pardon every time?"

She made no reply. She was thoughtful. All was silent, except for the soft trod of their naked feet on the hard dry earth, the rustling of the wind through the cane blades, and an occasional moo from a cow in the distance. Nearing home Irine said: "You didn't answer my question."

"I would beat it," Dorothy replied.

"That is what God goin' do to you," she said, as she turned off the road towards her home. "He goin' beat you with many stripes .... 'cause you know."

Because the rainfalls were brief and far between, the leaves

Stand-Pipe

on the trees were few and the earth was cracked in many places. Numerous patches of smoke-grey clouds had drifted reluctantly across the sky all day long. All eyes looked hopefully to the clouds. The rain was badly needed. None came, but the cloud-gazers were not despaired even when the sun disappeared. The wind sprung up and dark, moisture-laden clouds were appearing.

"Auntie, I goin' over at Vera," said Olga, going through the door.

"Girl, you en see de rain drizzlin'?" she asked pleasantly. Their resemblance was so close that she could be easily accepted as Olga's mother. "Chile, why you don' let God rain fall on the ground," she went on. "You en see de earth want it? Uh wish when you get over there the rain start an' fall 'till morning." Looking back as she ran, Olga shouted: "Then you won' got to worry, yuh would know where I would be."

"That girl!"

"Vera! Vera!" shouted Olga from a distance, "Open!" The door flew open and she ran in.

"But look at you," said Vera, eyeing her carefully. "Runnin' through the rain just to get here."

"Oh! Vera, don' say it that way," she pleaded. "You don' want me?"

"Yes, but wet de way you is .... suppose yuh get sick? Take off that wet dress."

She promptly obeyed and handed it to Vera who hung it over the bag screen to dry. "That is better," said Vera, looking her over once more. She saw her small, firm breasts bulging beneath the thin garment she was wearing. She fixed her gaze. Embarrassed, Olga folded her arms to hide them.

"What you hidin'?" asked Vera, "you en see I got two big ones .... look move your hand!" She took hold of Olga and tried to unfold her arms. They struggled about the room laughing as they resisted each other. Exhausted, Olga gave up the struggle. Her arms were pinned to her sides. During the struggle, a strap from her petticoat got broken. She did not notice.

"You playin' so careful," Vera went on teasingly, "an' look." She indicated with her chin. One naked breast popped into view as Olga looked at the indicated spot.

"Oh! no, Vera," she protested, renewing her struggle, "that en fair .... you is uh exvantage-taker."

"Dem li'l monkey things you got an' play you hidin'," said Vera, releasing her arms, "suppose you had some like mine."

"Mine would get like yours one o' dese days," she said fixing the broken strap with a pin.

"Not them."

Olga was prepared to leave, but she was stopped by a heavy shower of rain. "Auntie tell me dat de rain goin' catch me here."

"An' what you tell she?" Vera asked.

"I tell she, she won' got to worry 'cause she would know where I would be."

"Why not sleep then?"

Olga was glad for the opportunity, and while the rain continued to fall and the earth absorbed its gift, two nude bodies revelled in an unconventional act of love. Unconventional as it was, for them, it was a night of ecstasy; and the new day found Olga not only lavishly loved, but convinced that she was also an accomplished lover.

When Friday came and Dorothy failed to persuade Irine that she should accompany her to the hovel of the old woman, she decided to go alone. Although she journeyed there alone on many occasions, today it seemed burdensome. She bought a fowl from one of her neighbours. Among her own fowls, there was none entirely black. The old woman had insisted that the fowl should be black and reasonably young. There was some special significance attached to the blood; and if the fowl was old, the progress derived from the blood would be slow, and less effective. Binding the feet of the fowl with a piece of string, Dorothy placed it in a suitable cabbage-palm basket and took off.

Walking along the narrow, winding track, Dorothy was thoughtful of Irine and her reluctance to see for herself. "This old woman can get Samuel stay home with you," she told Irine a few days ago. "You en see Andrew don' go nowhere."

"Dorothy," she said in a motherly tone, "you wastin' your time. My trus' is in God, and nothin' like that can change me."

"Your trus' in God is nothin' to do with this," Dorothy argued. "This is for here on earth; this is to protect you from de unfairness people does do to you. Irine don' be a fool!"

"If this old woman can do such good things for other people," Irine said, "why she don' get she old shack repair?"

"Maybe she en got no money," Dorothy replied.

"If she got all o' this power," Irine said, "she should be able to make people come an' repair it for nothin'."

"What you don' understand is this," Dorothy said, "she can only do things for other people."

"But, Dorothy, who power is stronger?" Irine asked, "God or this old woman?"

"God," Dorothy answered.

"Then serve Him," Irine advised, as she turned away, "serve Him in spirit an' in truth."

There was whispering in the hovel when Dorothy arrived. She would have liked to see the visitor, but she did not want to be seen. For fear of the latter, she sneaked noiselessly to the back of the shack. Only a short distance away there was a tall, branchy, sugar apple tree. She went there for the little shade it offered from the burning noonday sun. Beneath the tree was littered with black feathers. 'This is de old woman slaughter-market,' Dorothy said to herself. 'Lord! it smell too bad.'

When the departing figure emerged beyond the shack,

Dorothy slumped into obscurity and waited contentedly amidst the mire. There was one thing uppermost in her mind .... her journey into the unknown.

"Where your friend?" asked the old woman, when Dorothy seated herself at the table. "She didn't come?"

"N....n....no," Dorothy stammered bashfully, avoiding the old woman's reddish, searching eyes. "She didn't come."

"Why?" asked the old woman. "Did you forget to tell me anythin' about her private life."

"No .... all o' de things you say is true, but that en make she believe."

"There mus' be somethin' you din tell me," the old woman raged. "I can do nothin' to help people except I get them to have trus' in me." The silence that followed was embarrassing. Dorothy wanted to say something, but she didn't know what. Then the old woman said: "I will stretch out muh han' in wrath against she." She indicated with outstretched arms. Her tone was serious. It frightened Dorothy. She did not expect such an expression.

"No .... no, please," she pleaded, with head, hands and eyes. "Do it to me instead. She is a good woman. She don' deserve it. She didn't come an' I still brin' de fowl."

Struggling nervously, she took the fowl from the basket.

"Here, take it," she went on, "but please don' do nothin' to hurt she."

"So you don' want me hurt dis frien' o' yours, eh?" asked the old woman, leaning across the table. "Well, I will be nice to she fuh you sake. But what she think, she think I can really do my business?" Dorothy was hesitant. She looked to the ground. "No," she replied faintly, preparing to leave, "she believe in God."

Watching Dorothy's receding figure, the old woman said to herself: 'If we din have people like she livin' in dis worl', how I would get young fowl to eat now that I en got many teet'? People like me mus' live by people like she. I like she frien'; she is a wise woman with strong character.'

THE PASSAGE TO EDEN

PART THREE

A gust of breeze rushed through the trees just as the sun came peeping out of the water ... a token that a new day was born to this rural village and all the sunny world. Birds in the trees awakened by the breeze chirped tunes of prayer as they flipped from bough to bough .... it was good to be alive. The sun came slowly over the hill stretching its golden rays like hands farther and farther down the hill and through the trees assuring more and more birds of the new day and of their duty to join their neighbours in chirping prayers; a way of thanking God for life and nature's goodness; and like an obedient child stirred by the loving hand of its mother, so responded the birds in the trees to the groping hands of the sun's rays. Down, down, still farther down, until the air was filled with tunes of various birds .... one happy family in accord.

At the foot of the hill stood two formidable stone buildings, whose lands were divided by low, green hedges. Like the birds, the occupants of these buildings were stirred by the rays of the sun, but they were less active in response .... night's slumber still rested heavily upon them and no sign of life could be seen from outside.

Erupting many hours later was a very unusual form of activity. Workmen from the Public Works Department arrived in the village and immediately started digging a narrow trench, into which they placed many lengths of metal tubing to a strategic location where they erected a standpipe - a modern, and hygienic way of providing drinking water for the residents in that village, and adjoining villages.

Relaxing after the day's activity, Peter and Ellin were opposed by Alfred and Elizabeth in a game of Piquet; it was French. Elizabeth was the teacher. Wilfred was looking on.

"Among us, I think it is about time we drop all this formality," said Mr. Barrow. "It bores me. As from now, I am asking to be called Peter, and my wife Elizabeth."

"If that is the way you want it," said Mr. Skinner, smiling friendly. "I don't mind at all. You may call me Alfred, my wife Ellin and my nephew Wilfred. Other members of the family will also be introduced and called by their first names. Did you hear that, Hilda?" he called out to his sister-in-law who was sitting in another corner of the room and reading.

"I beg your pardon!" she said sweetly.

"Mr. Barrow has just requested that we call each other by our first names."

"Oh! that is grand," said she, bringing her slow rocking to a halt, "I was wondering when it would come. I hate superficial society stuff. I think it robs man of some of the freedom life is meant to offer."

"I think you have a point there," Peter said.

"That is just like Pete," said Elizabeth, placing her cards face down on the small bamboo table at which they were playing. "I sometimes envy him," she went on. "He has a way of putting people at ease that seems second to none."

"I can agree with you," said Ellin. "When he was on the island just a few weeks I felt as though I had known him all my life. While the house was being constructed, I suggested that he board here, but he refused. The excuse he offered was a reasonable one .... "you know how women are?" he said. "He appealed to my emotion and I was a cooked goose."

"I think he is some kind of philosopher," Elizabeth said boastfully. "I believe he has lived here before. The way .... "

"Do you mean in Barbados?" Alfred interrupted.

"No," replied Elizabeth. "On the earth."

"Do you really believe that man lives here more than once?" Alfred asked seriously.

"Vaguely," she replied, brushing it aside with a gesture of the hand, "but for now we'll discuss Pete."

"Go straight ahead and discuss me," said Peter, placing his cards on the table and folding his arms across his chest. "I'll be listening all through .... if you don't overdo it."

"I promise," she said, crossing her fingers .... "you make me forget where I was," Elizabeth said accusingly, frowning childishly at him. "Oh! .... yes .... whenever he presents himself he is liked, and I must confess that I'm sometimes jealous .... even of the men who seem to shower their attention upon him when he is met at a party."

"I hope you hear that?" said Wilfred, smiling sheepishly. "In the future, you will have to scrutinise your male acquaintances before you become very intimate with them."

"Well!" .... Peter pondered, "I don't think she suspects me of any homosexual tendency."

Wilfred blushed. "That is an ugly word," said he, drawing his lips into a thin firm line. "Especially in society."

"We are not in society," Peter said calmly. "I thought I'd made that clear a while ago. Where I am concerned," he went on, probing an index finger onto his stomach, "we're not even society people; but just plain, ordinary people .... like Mary and Joseph."

"Do you mean the maid?" Wilfred asked, "and .... "

"The yard-hand," Peter finished for him. "There is little difference between us and them," he went on slowly, "except that they are less fortunate financially; but potentially, we are alike."

"I should like to take you up on that," said Alfred, eyeing Peter doubtfully.

"I should like to advise you against that," Elizabeth said warningly. "That is his pet subject. Like I said a while ago, he seems to be some kind of philosopher. He has won a number of prizes from English magazines for short stories; and they were all written in a philosophical vein. His stories, although well told, were usually very simple. As for the characters, they were almost lifeless. I often wondered whether the lifelessness of the characters stemmed from the author's inability to do better, or if he had some special motive."

"I suppose you would like to know now?" Peter asked.

"Yes," Elizabeth replied.

"That is very unkind of you," Ellin said tonelessly, "why embarrass him here and now?"

"Embarrass?" Peter laughed. "I'm not easily embarrassed."

"Then out with it," Elizabeth urged.

During the silence which encompassed them, Alfred lit his pipe and filled the room with the aroma of his favorite tobacco, which had a pleasant scent.

"How to start?" Peter began thoughtfully. "Suppose I had to write a passage about two characters fighting; I guess I could make it as dramatic as any one else. 'A cuff to the mouth which brought forth a sudden stream of blood and sent the opponent sprawling to the ground.' That sort of thing is all right. It has its appeal to many readers; and I don't blame the authors who provide it. But that is not to my taste. A fight is just another fight where I am concerned; but the provocation exercised by one character and the tolerance displayed by the other is more important than the drama expressed by the author .... the characters' mentality. Quite often, I tell a story about a character in a situation and how he extricated himself, only to paint a picture of human nature. It is little wonder that my stories seem simple and the characters lifeless .... they are, on the surface."

"I see," said Elizabeth, nodding slowly. "I wonder if the readers of your works understand your approach?"

"Some of them would, I suppose," Peter replied. "I used to worry about that when I was a beginner; but as time passed I ceased to worry. I just wrote about characters confronted with life's vicissitudes as I saw it, and their methods of approach to an ultimate goal."

"That is marvellous," said Ellin, looking admiringly at Peter. "Why did you give up writing?"

"His father insisted that he studied agriculture," Wilfred interjected.

"What authority have you to say that?" Ellin asked.

"He told me so on the first day we met," Wilfred replied. Ellin looked inquiringly at Peter who confirmed Wilfred's statement by nodding.

"I think your father did the world an injustice," Ellin said.

"I suppose his father, like so many of us," Elizabeth said resignedly, "had failed to grasp the significance of his writing."

"Do you ever regret that you have not become an author?" Hilda asked. She had resumed her slow rocking; an index finger marked the pages of the book which rested on her lap.

"Sometimes," he replied tonelessly. He filled his lungs with fresh air. It lifted his chest. "Sometimes I'm terribly sorry."

"But why?" Alfred asked in surprise. "You're wealthy, happily married and successful .... they surely are the attributes of happiness."

"But they don't bring peace of mind." Peter said calmly. He stood up. He placed his chair close to the table and got behind it. "What time is it?" he asked, resting a hand on Wilfred's shoulder.

He glanced at the grandfather clock, which stood tall and formidable in its place against the cream-coloured wall. "Nine-thirty," he answered.

"You see," said Peter, running his fingers through Wilfred's gold coloured hair, "by the standard of society, I have overstayed my time by half an hour .... my first radical step."

"We don't usually go to bed early," said Alfred, as he beckoned to Peter to resume his seat, "we can sit it out a little longer. We aren't going to bed now, whether you leave or not."

"That's your affair," said Peter, smiling as he advanced towards the door. "I've already violated two laws for the night."

"Your conversation has been so stimulating," said Hilda, smiling fondly, "that we could do with you around more often."

"I will be," he promised, looking over his shoulder in her direction just as he reached the door, "as often as I am permitted."

"When a patient is in bad shape the physician usually prescribes medicine three times daily," said Ellin, touching his arm. "We could do with you no less."

"I am not a physician," Peter said.

"But you are medicine," said Hilda. "Not the kind which makes the mouth bitter, but that which gives stimulus to the mind."

"Is that a compliment?" Peter asked.

"No," Hilda replied.

"Then what is it?" Peter asked, looking into her large black eyes, which seemed to shine in the semi-darkness of the porch. "I should like to know."

"It is a fact," Hilda said flatly.

"You win," Peter said. He took hold of his wife's arm to support her down the steps, which were flood-lit by the flick of a switch at Ellin's command. "See you happy people tomorrow," he said, when they reached the bottom.

"Pleasant dreams!" Ellin said.

"Thank you," Peter returned, "but I don't dream half a dozen times a year....you may extend that wish to Liz; she dreams every night."

"Don't believe him," Elizabeth said, trying to cover his mouth with one hand.

They all laughed.

"Now! what is that? Happiness?" Alfred shouted.

"I guess so," Peter replied, waving his free arm.

From the lighted porch Alfred and his family watched the two figures as they slowly vanished into the black night; and only when brandished arms waved a final good-bye in the light through the opened door, did they re-enter the room.

Hilda was the last to enter the room. She extinguished the light in the porch. With her slim, pale fingers still resting on the shining cover of the light switch, she said: "I think Peter has some qualities like John."

"You don't mean my brother," said Alfred, "do you?"

"Yes," she replied.

"Mother," Wilfred said softly, "will you ever stop discussing Dad?"

"My son," said Hilda, slumping into a nearby chair, "your father was a fine man, and I will speak of him as long as there is life in my body."

"But it is doing you no good," said Wilfred, looking at her lean, pale face. "Dad has been dead for years and you are still lamenting. The impression you give, is that you are angry with God for taking him."

"Wilfred, I want to ask you something," said Hilda, "will you answer sincerely?"

"Yes, Mother," he replied.

"If I died tonight would you cry?"

"Yes, Mother."

"Would your grief be an expression of anger towards God?"

"Are we going to have that again tonight?" asked Ellin. "I can't stand it. I'm going to bed." She turned towards the stairway, and Wilfred followed.

"Are you falling in love with Peter?" asked Alfred, when they were alone.

"Not at all," replied Hilda. "He is like John in so many ways that in his company I am happy; then when he leaves it reminds me that John is gone."

Alfred nodded his big head understandingly.

"I wonder what goes on in his mind," she said.

"The same thing that goes on in mine," said Alfred, "how to become rich and independent."

"He is not that sort," said Hilda. "He is deeper than that. He is no materialist."

"He isn't, eh?" Alfred scoffed. "Then let him lose that beautiful wife he has and you'll see him crumble."

"I wouldn't like to see that," said Hilda, shaking her head sadly, "but I am doubtful that it would."

Minutes later they went upstairs to their respective rooms and to bed.

Samuel and Irine were among those selected to work for Peter, and Clifford was to be their driver. Two watchmen were to be selected and two more drivers. One was for the third gang and the other for the grass-pickers. Peter was to make the selection. He had left the responsibility of selecting the domestic staff to Elizabeth. She, instructed by Ellin, made her own decision. Together, it had afforded them much amusement.

"When you have to appoint a driver," Alfred told Peter on one occasion, "always choose the most loud-mouthed, tale-bearing from the group of workers. The fellow who likes to yap about his neighbours. Always remember, these workers are poor, ignorant and hungry; and when you appoint a driver, make him understand that you have chosen him above all the other workers because you are convinced that he will do justice to you. Make him feel that his job is important, that he is indispensable. Tell him you know he will not steal nor will he allow anyone to do so. When you have told him all these things," Alfred concluded, "you can rest assured that your estate is in safe hands."

Peter ignored all of this advice. It was dishonest and inhuman. It was contrary to his convictions, and would not subject his manhood to such an act. Three weeks elapsed before the selection concluded. During this period, Peter thoroughly scrutinised the workers. He rode into the field and conversed with them while they were on the job, visited and talked with them in the yard while they took breakfast.

Unaware of the motive behind his visits, the workers were responsive on every occasion; and from his own finding Peter made his choice. When those chosen were sufficiently trained in the execution of their tasks, Peter lapsed into a mode of living that was peculiar to himself.

Every Friday Peter and Alfred went to one of the city banks; and from their enormous deposits in the bank, withdrawals were made in order to pay the labourers on the following day. Journeying to the city was a pleasure. They went together by train or double-buggy; but when they went singularly, it was their respective horse-drawn buggies, controlled by competent coachmen.

Cooking was among the few things Elizabeth and Ellin had in common; and they taught each other a number of recipes. Familiar with the recipes of her childhood years in France, and those of her more mature years in England, Elizabeth had a wider variety of recipes to her advantage. Those Ellin offered were few, and peculiar to the Barbadian way of preparation; but they were accepted with much enthusiasm.

• • •

Entering the pantry where the servants stood waiting, Elizabeth said: "Cookie, come here a minute."

"Ye....yes please mistress," the cook stammered, "Uh .... uh coming now, mistress."

The cook hurried towards the pantry drying her slim, dark hands in her dingy, white apron. She was thin and short. Beneath the border of her white headtie, grey, plaited locks were showing.

"Yes, mistress," she said, bringing her hasty movements to a sudden halt.

"Cookie," Elizabeth said. Her voice was soft and there was a note of sympathy when she added: "Cookie, do I ever quarrel with you?"

"No, mistress .... you never quarrel with me," she answered without looking at her mistress.

"Then why do you act so afraid when I call you?" Elizabeth asked, looking down on the erect figure who stood before her.

"Mistress, all my years I been working in white people kitchen," she began, "from the time I did so high." She indicated. "And I .... "

"That isn't so long ago, Cookie," Elizabeth interrupted teasingly, "if you were that high."

The servants chuckled softly.

"Mistress, you like you making fun at me," said the cook, looking into her employer's eyes for the first time.

"I am an old woman with grandchildren."

"I certainly didn't think you were so old, Cookie," said Elizabeth, resting a gentle hand on her shoulder. "And at your age, I don't see why you are so fearful."

"Mistress, all my life I been workin' in white people kitchen, and I get so accustom to shoutin' and abuse from them, that everytime I hear 'Cookie,' I think it is another form of abuse."

"What do the neighbours in the village call you?" Elizabeth asked.

"They call me Cookie, mistress," she replied.

"Do you get frightened when they call for Cookie?" Elizabeth asked.

"No, mistress, that is different. Did you ever have a child, mistress?"

"No, Cookie."

The cook hung her head. She was silent for a moment.

"Ah!" she said with a sudden start. "But you have a cat and a dog. Did you ever have to lash the dog 'cause it mess up the house?"

"Yes."

"And after a little while you call the same dog to feed it; and although you have the dog's milk bowl in your hand he still run away. Did you ever notice that, mistress?"

"Yes, Cookie, I have."

"Do you know why the dog run away, mistress?"

"Yes, Cookie, he has not forgotten the lashes."

"Nor have I forgotten the many years of abuse, mistress. I can't forget."

"All right, Cookie."

After a brief moment of silence Elizabeth said: "As you all know, the master has gone to town and will not be back until evening."

"Yes, mistress," the cook said.

"Well .... I will prepare my own lunch, and the dinner as well."

"But mistress, can you .... "

"Oh! yes I can, Cookie," interrupted Elizabeth, tapping her lightly on the shoulder. "I can cook very well. As soon as the three of you can get through with what you have to do now, you can go home and return at four o'clock. I will take care of the rest."

"Oh! that is very nice of you, mistress," said the cook. "But what can I find at home to do now?"

"Play with your grandchildren," said the young, dark-skinned maid who was glad to be released for the few hours. "They would like that."

"At least," Elizabeth agreed, smiling fondly, "hurry with your work. Go, and be back at four."

There was little need to wonder why the cook was last to leave the house. She had nothing to do at home.

"Why you come home for, Grandma?" asked a little dark-skinned boy. "You los' yuh work?"

"No," replied the cook. She looked him over. He was wearing nothing but a khaki shirt which reached just beyond his large protruding navel. About his face, torso and the front of his shirt was yellow with the over-ripe fruit which he held with soiled hands while he ate. He only lifted his head to ask the question.

"Is that the bes' way you can eat a pawpaw?" the cook asked sternly.

The boy made no reply. There was annoyance in her gaze. "Why are you not in school?" she asked.

Except for the sucking sound as the boy forced his mouth amidst the soft, sappy skin of the fruit, there was no reply. She suppressed the urge to slap his clean-shaven head.

"My mudda say she en got no lunch to give me," he replied, throwing the skin away and wiping his face and torso with one end of his shirt, "so she tell me mus' to don' go school."

"Your parents are always working," said the cook, "and they never have money. Do they sell it?"

"I don' know, Grandma," replied the boy, tossing the marble he took from his shirt pocket into the air and catching it, "but she does got some money sometimes."

After a moment's thoughtfulness the cook said: "I want you to go to the shop and buy something for me."

"All right, Grandma."

Washing Day

She lifted her skirt, and from a pocket in her heavily laced petticoat she took a small sack of coins. Making an opening in the sack by releasing a tied string, she inserted two fingers and withdrew a coin. When she replaced the sack and re-arranged her clothes, she took from a pocket in her apron a piece of paper which she tore and folded the coin neatly and placed it in the boy's extended hand.

"Now don't lose this money," she began warningly. "The money you have is a sixpence. Buy a cake of sunlight soap, a box of Lion brand matches, half cent in Ball blue and a stick of candle grease. Can you remember that?"

Surprised, the boy looked at her, repeated the order as evidence of his recollection, and then ran off towards the shop.

"That boy is so hard-ears" said the cook, "it is a pity."

Having crossed her own yard, Ellin jumped the low, green fence of sweetlime trees which bordered the land on one side, crossed the narrow lane and jumped a similar fence of olive trees which bordered the land on the other side and walked briskly towards the back entrance of the house. At the door she called for the cook, but there was no reply. She opened the door. Still calling for the cook, she went quietly into the house. Her rubber-soled shoes made a soft noise on the wooden floor. When she called for every occupant who was likely to be there at that hour and got no reply, she hurried up the stairway. Along the corridor she shouted loudly: "Elizabeth!" There was a distant note of fear in her voice.

"Yes," Elizabeth answered calmly, as she stepped out of the door which closed noiselessly after her.

"I almost called my head off," said Ellin, "Didn't you hear me?"

"Yes," Elizabeth replied, drying her hair with a white bath towel. "I heard you."

Ellin was annoyed.

"Then why didn't you answer me?" she asked angrily.

"Because I wanted to frighten you," Elizabeth replied impishly.

"You will, if you don't do something about that," said Ellin, indicating the bathrobe which had flown open at the front.

"Sugar!" Elizabeth exclaimed, drawing the robe about her and tying the heavy cord into a firm knot around her slim waist which accentuated her hips.

"Do you call it by that name?" Ellin asked.

"No, do you?"

"Alfred does."

A look of surprise crept slowly into Elizabeth's eyes.

"What is the matter?" asked Ellin. "Have I said something wrong?"

"Not really," said Elizabeth. "But I didn't expect you to be so outspoken about it."

"Liz," she said, walking away, "I'm sorry if I've surprised you; but from the first day you looked into my eyes I knew I'd be compelled to answer your questions."

Elizabeth took a deep breath. She slowly moistened her lips with a thin red tongue; and through half-closed eyes she looked schemingly at Ellin's swaying hips.

"I'll be back," said Elizabeth, and she vanished behind a door.

When Elizabeth returned she was wearing a dress.

"I like that shade of pink," Ellin said.

"Thank you," said Elizabeth, sweeping the palms of her hands over her hips and along the front where the material was wrinkled. "I need an iron."

"It could do with a little pressing all right," said Ellin, "but it is good enough to wear around the house. What about the servants? Where are they?"

"I sent them home."

"Home?"

121

"Yes."

"You didn't dismiss them, did you?"

"No."

"But why did you send them away?" Ellin insisted.

Elizabeth laughed. She looked Ellin full in her eyes; then, pulled her nose and said: "Because I want to be private .... with you .... you don't mind, do you?"

"Why should I? I think all women have an insatiable desire for privacy."

"Good. In that case we'll have all the privacy we want until four o'clock when the servants will be back."

While they were preparing lunch Elizabeth explained her plans for the evening.

"Oh! that's grand," said Ellin, smiling happily, "and at the same time I'll have the opportunity to learn the preparation."

"That's right."

"When was this idea first born in your mind?"

"A week or so ago."

"And you kept it a secret all this time?"

"Yes. I wanted to surprise you."

The servants who had much to do at home and were glad to be released from their duties, were the first to return; but the cook who was reluctant to leave came hurriedly in five minutes after the clock struck four.

"How you come to be late?" the maid asked.

"Did the mistress ask for me?"

"No," replied the maid. "We jus' come in too."

"I went home and starched some clothes which I had planned to starch when I am off next Sunday."

"You think I would work in anybody kitchen for uh whole month an' get only one half-day home?" said the young, dark-skinned maid. "Not when I can stan' home an' say I sick. I live in a house that want cleaning too."

"Well child," said the cook in a motherly tone, "if you had a child or two to cry and tell you that they are hungry, you would be glad to work."

"Work so hard for just a few cents?" the maid asked angrily.

"When I was a young woman the pay was even less then it is today," said the cook, "but of course things were cheaper."

"Well uh goin' tell yuh somethin," said the maid, "I en workin' suh hard fuh nobody."

"The mistress busy in the kitchen," said the cook, breaking off the trend of the conversation, "so I'm wasting some time with you."

"But Cookie, how you come to speak suh good?" the maid asked enviously. "You had uh good schoolin'?"

"I scarcely went to school," the cook replied regrettably.

"An' how you come to speak so good?"

"That can be easily explained," said the cook. "If you live and work for white people as long as I have, and you are willing to learn as I have been, you too, will be able to speak properly."

"I would like to speak like you," said the maid, "but uh doubt uh would learn."

"Why?"

" 'Cause uh don' think uh would be able to let any white son-of-a-bitch push me 'round so long."

"Well, child," said the cook, shrugging her shoulders resignedly, "I've had a life time of it, and I'm too old to fight it now; although I don't think fighting would be the best thing."

"If we mus' get anything," the maid said angrily, "we got to fight."

"Fighting will do no good."

"Why?"

"Because if I strike you now, you will wait until tomorrow to strike me back, and I will wait until the following day to revenge you and so .... "

"I see what yuh mean," interrupted the maid. "Then what

123

you think is de bes' thin' to do?"

"To tell you the truth," the cook said thoughtfully, "I .... don't .... know; but I pray that God would inspire some author to .... "

"What is uh author?" interrupted the maid. She was eager to learn.

"An author is a person who writes books. I pray that God may inspire an author to offer to the world a solution which would serve as a cure for the hatred which is existing in this world."

Ellin wanted to be home to greet Alfred on his return. She said to Elizabeth goodbye, dashed out of the kitchen and raced across the yard; jumped one fence after the other, hurried across her yard and disappeared beyond the walls of her own kitchen. Summoned by the heavy rolling of the approaching double-buggy, Elizabeth hastened to the front door.

"Did you people have a hard day in the city?" she asked, as the buggy came to a standstill and Peter alighted.

"You bet," said Alfred, as he was driving off towards his home.

At the door, Elizabeth took Peter's white helmet and the brown leather case which contained the money.

"Ah!" Peter sighed. "After a hot day in the city, it's nice to come to a cool home and a loving wife." He brushed her lips lightly with his own.

"Thank you," she returned, placing the helmet on the hat-rack. "Where shall I put this?" she indicated the case.

"You may put that in the study," he replied, as he spread his dampened white jacket across the pegs of the hat-rack. "I'll be there in a minute."

He was standing under the porch catching a breath of fresh air when Elizabeth returned and stood at the door.

"Would you like to have something before dinner?" she asked lovingly.

"What have you got to offer?" Peter asked.

"Me."

"Not now."

"Then, how about a cup of hot milk?"

"That's better."

Peter was reclining in the study with his soft-slippered feet on the desk when there was a knock on the wooden door.

"Come in," he said. The door opened ever so slightly and Alfred poked his big head in.

"Come on in," Peter urged, "and have a seat."

When he entered, Peter noticed that his deportment was more conventional than was necessary for a casual visit, but he did not question it.

"Do you do anything else but read?" Alfred asked.

"Nothing that I enjoy better," he smiled.

"What are you reading now?"

Peter closed the book and held it up for him to see.

Alfred read aloud: "Dialogues of Plato."

Breaking the silence, Peter asked: "Would you like to read it?"

"No," Alfred replied abruptly. "I'm too old to learn that kind of stuff."

"No you're not," Peter said regretfully. "I'll tell you what I think. I think you are a little reluctant to relinquish and rectify some of your antiquated methods when dealing with people and situations. You have learnt by tradition; you are not alone, we all have; but tradition changes. Do you know what is responsible for traditional changes?"

"I have never given it a thought."

"Would you like to know?"

"I could."

Interrupted by the soft bang of the dinner gong, Peter rose, and taking special care to replace the book in the philosophical section of his huge bookcase, said: "Do you care to join me? Let's wash first," he added, entering the bathroom where they washed their faces and hands in the basin and dried them in a large towel, which was kept over the rack. Peter stopped in his tracks when he entered the dining room. Elizabeth, Ellin, Hilda and Wilfred were already seated at the table where there were two unoccupied chairs. Observing Peter's gesture of surprise, Alfred asked: "You don't mean you didn't expect us, do you?"

"I didn't really."

"Well it worked out just the way Ellin and I planned it," said Elizabeth. "A total surprise."

"I see," said Alfred, "the two of you arranged it."

"Well, I don't mind it much," said Peter, advancing towards his chair at the head of the table, "except for one thing. I don't ever sit at the table with a jacket unless we are having guests. In this case I am not having guests."

"And to prove that," said Alfred, chuckling softly, "I'll remove mine."

Hilda was first to break the silence while they ate.

"Whose recipe is this?" she asked.

"The French's," Elizabeth replied curtly, "It is called a gourmet dish."

"It is delicious," said Hilda. "I hope you've learnt to prepare it," she added, addressing Ellin.

"I hope so," Ellin replied.

"If I'd seen its preparation just once," said Wilfred, with a broad smile on his chubby face, "I would defy her to beat me at it after." Under the table, Hilda knocked her foot against his. He ignored its meaning.

"I like doing things," he went on, "things with my hands .... cooking, fancy work and things of that sort."

"Do you?" Elizabeth asked genuinely. "Then a country like

France would suit you."

"I guess so," said Wilfred. "See those antimacassars at home?" he went on proudly. "I worked them."

"You don't mean that?" Elizabeth said astonishingly.

"Of course I do," he replied haughtily.

"Wilfred," Hilda called softly.

"Yes, Mother," he answered, looking in her direction.

"How many times must I tell you not to say you worked those antimacassar?" Hilda asked.

"But, Mother, didn't I do them?" he asked for confirmation.

"Yes," she replied tonelessly, "but everyone needn't know of it."

"I believe he does it quite harmlessly," Elizabeth said.

"Besides, we wouldn't argue over such a delicious meal," Peter added.

"I've cooked enough for a second helping," said Elizabeth, "and the servants will still get their share."

"Let me have it," said Alfred, placing his silvers on either side of the plate. "Let it come."

"Serve the glutton," Ellin said humorously.

When dinner was over, they took to the sitting-room for a session of chatter while the stout, dark-skinned servant who had proved herself efficient around the table, removed the dishes. She wore a black dress with a stiff, white collar and a similar type of cuff at the wrists. Her white apron, which reached the hem of her dress, covered her proud bosom and fitted mid-way around her slim waist, was supported over the shoulders by two narrow straps which were crossed at the back and buttoned to its broad waistband. On her head was a white skull-cap and white canvas shoes on her large feet.

"Alfred, I think you are quite a nice neighbour," said Elizabeth, as she rocked slowly in her favourite bent-wood rocker.

"Am I?" Alfred asked. He was not sure whether he should feel elated or depressed. He was silent. He hoped that she would speak again. She said nothing. She purposely avoided his gaze.

"In what way," he went on cautiously, "may I ask?"

"It is months since I've been here," she said, "and you have never once suggested a ride that I may see your country-side."

"I .... I .... didn't know you could ride," he stammered defensively. He drew heavily on his pipe. He was thoughtful.

"The truth is," he said with more confidence, having regained some stability, "I had completely forgotten that you are a European and that quite a large percentage of women from the Continent do ride. I would chance to bet that the number of women who ride in Barbados could be counted on the fingers of both hands." He paused; then added: "Do you understand now, why it has slipped me?"

"Yes," she replied. "but now that you know, aren't you going to invite me?"

"I guess I will have to," he replied, eyeing Peter questioningly, "with his permission."

"The pleasure is all yours," said Peter, extending a hand towards Elizabeth which indicated consent, "any day you find it convenient."

"I think you are very generous, Peter," said Hilda. "I thought you would want to go along."

"Hilda, I wouldn't say that I couldn't go along and enjoy myself," said Peter, "but I would enjoy myself more if I stayed at home and took to a book. Why should I deprive Liz of outdoor life if she finds it pleasurable?"

Minutes later a servant appeared in the doorway. She asked to be excused and announced that she and the other servants were ready to leave.

"Is the back closed?" Elizabeth asked.

"Yes, mistress," the servant replied.

"And everything in order?"

"Yes, mistress, everything in order."

"All right, you may go through the side door. Get home safely."

"Thank you, mistress. Good night! Good night everybody!"

"Good night!"

"Do you always allow your servants to leave so early?" asked Alfred, when the servants were gone.

"This is not early," Elizabeth answered, somewhat surprised. "If we did not have friends they would be gone long ago."

"Why do you permit them to go so early?" Alfred asked.

"Why?" Elizabeth asked. "Because they have nothing to do. You don't mean you keep yours hanging around when they have nothing to do, do you?"

"Liz, you should first find out who dismisses the servants," Peter cautioned.

"I do," Alfred answered.

"Well that is where we differ," said Peter. "I am owner of this estate .... Liz is mistress of the house and I am master of the field; but that does not deprive us from the right to discuss, and make suggestions for any difficulty that may arise."

"Alfred is not like that," said Ellin. "He is a good provider, but he is sole master; and everything he does is right."

"He is much unlike his brother," said Hilda, "in the latter."

"It is unfortunate that you are at my home and not the other way around," said Peter, "or I would go straight ahead and discuss this matter."

"I should like to hear you on it," Alfred said.

"First a question," Peter began. "Why do you keep your servants around when there is nothing for them to do?"

"Because they have been accustomed to nothing better," Alfred replied, "and I don't want to create a precedent."

"Well, I am sorry if Liz is responsible for one," said Peter, "but she will not be deterred by me. In the first place," he went on in a more serious tone, "I don't see why anyone should be ashamed to create a precedent which is constructive and for the benefit of mankind."

"Peter, you have the wrong end of this argument," Alfred said warningly, "these people have lived under these conditions for years and they expect nothing better."

"You are not by any chance implying, what was good for your father is good enough for you?" Peter asked.

"Not really," Alfred replied cautiously. "But who am I that I should change it?" Silence fell upon the group.

"Do you remember I asked you a while ago if you knew what is responsible for traditional changes?" Peter asked.

"Yes," Alfred replied.

"You said you didn't know .... or words to that effect."

"That's right."

"I'll tell you," said Peter, sure of himself. "Man's concept is responsible for traditional changes. When an idea is effected, the result is a change .... like Liz. It is her idea to release the servants early, hence the change. Do you know why? Because they are right; and only that which is right and good is of God; and God is universal."

"Alfred, I forewarned you about my husband in connection with things philosophical," Elizabeth said pensively. "I hope you have not considered him impolite."

"Not in the least," Alfred said boastfully, as though he had won the discussion. "I don't mind at all. I do admit that I've learnt a great deal, but I would like to take up the subject some other time." He rose in preparation to leave.

"Peter, I think you are dynamic," said Hilda, happy to be in his company.

"I wonder what makes Alfred tick," said Elizabeth, as they were preparing for bed in their cosy, pink-coloured room.

"I can tell you," Peter said casually, "if you want to know."

"Go ahead," she urged, "let's hear it."

"Are you interested or curious?" He asked.

"An equal mixture of both."

Peter was thoughtful. He had adorned himself only in the trousers of his pajamas. His torso remained uncovered. Taking a seat on the edge of the bed, he said firmly: "Anything between being the father of a child and destroying a man will make Alfred Skinner tick; and to be a little redundant," he went on, eyeing her shapely, nude figure as she fought to get her head through the small opening of her nightgown, "an affair with any woman as lovely as you are."

"You are terrible," she snapped.

"Not me," he returned calmly, "Alfred is."

"What gives you the right to say that?"

"I can see it in him."

"We are warned about you half-baked psychiatrists and the diagnoses you all make."

"I know," he said, swinging his feet off the carpeted floor and lying on his back with the palms of both hands under his head, "and I also know, that any individual who is as egotistical as Alfred Skinner will stop at nothing. If being the father of a child makes him feel that he has achieved much, and much could be achieved by the destruction of a man, Alfred would do either."

"Hello, Irine! we en work so close to one another for de longest time," said Dorothy. "Not since you got a new master."

"That is true," Irine said. They were working in the adjoining fields of different owners.

"How you like your new master?" Dorothy asked.

" 'E is uh perfect gentleman," replied Irine. "Since I did workin' day I never hear 'e call anybody a fool. Sometime' 'e does come in de field an' talk to we while we workin,' and sometime' while we in de yard eatin' breakfas'."

"You think 'e better than we ole time master?" Dorothy asked.

"I en think; I know 'e better than he," Irine sneered.

"Clifford is still we driver," she went on, "an' you know how bad 'e use to curse? Well 'e don' curse so bad now; uh don't know if de master talk to 'e 'bout it, but 'e is a change Clifford. The truth is, everybody does work peaceable. We don' get so much lickmout' talk like before. He say this an' she say that an' de master say these. You know people is people, an' you would still get uh li'l talk, but nothin' like before. We does live like one family now."

"Chile, over here is de same way," Dorothy said sadly. "The ole bitch I workin' at like 'e would change from bad to worse, but not better."

"Why you don' change from cursing?" Irine asked.

"You think anybody could work 'round that sow without cursing?" Dorothy threw back.

"I use to," Irine reflected, "You remember?"

"But look how lucky you is to get de shift over with that nice gentleman?"

"It isn't luck, Dorothy," she said calmly. "If you was to stop goin' at that old woman who does tell fortune, things would be better with you. Learn to trus' God, an' He will make a way."

Peter's technique in administration was superb. He had a vast variety of trees planted which were to provide shade, fruit, fencing and fragrance for the home. These trees were all cared for; and they thrived with amazing swiftness. He made a special study of the soil, and soon his general crops of sugar cane, sweet potatoes, yams, eddoes, black-eyed peas and Indian corn, which varied in accordance with their seasons, were yielding most favourably. The workers whom Peter chose for executive positions were greatly responsible for such an accomplishment; but that was not all. There was a genuine co-operative spirit existing between employer and employee. Except for Clifford who had his early training under a different master, the others proved to be quite obedient.

• • •

"Clifford, you are now working for me," Peter told him on one occasion. "Not for Mr. Alfred Skinner who is your former master. When you were working for him you were expected to do things the way he wanted them done; now, you will do things the way I want them. Another thing," he went on after a pause, "you are in the habit of bringing the villagers' private affairs to me; I want nothing to do with things of that sort. I want you to see that my work is done in the manner I have advised you. I do not abuse you, and I will not have you abusing the workers. You are from among them, if you remember. I have warned you twice before, and this warning is final. If my orders are too rigid for you to execute, you have a choice. Your forner master is still alive."

The day appointed for the ride turned out to be one of those windy, but brilliant sunny days, when small patches of snow-white clouds raced swiftly across the blue sky, with birds chirping sweetly as they journeyed from tree to tree in the brilliance of the afternoon sunlight.

"You are much unlike a woman today," said Alfred, as he came through the door of his own home and unexpectedly met Elizabeth already seated in her saddle.

"Because I am wearing this get-up?" she asked, tugging gently at her garments as she met his gaze.

"Not really," he replied, advancing towards his own harnessed animal, which Joseph, one of his yard hands held firmly. "But your desire to go riding is like a child with a new toy."

"Be it so or not," she said, smiling friendly, "don't treat me like one on this ride."

"I have a very wild animal here," said he, "who must burn up some of her pent-up energy before I can woo her."

"She's like me," said Elizabeth, when Joseph was out of earshot.

"You better wait here," said Alfred, slipping his foot into the stirrup, "until I cool her off."

133

Crane Beach

"I could do with a little of that myself," she said, as Alfred and his black mare shot down the gap and vanished in a thin trail of white dust.

Alfred drew his animal to a halt and turned her around; but he was greatly surprised to find that Elizabeth was only a short distance away.

"I didn't know you could ride so well," said Alfred, when they were abreast.

"Only horses," she laughed. After a pause she added: "I started riding when I was very young."

"Why didn't you say, learnt to ride?" he asked.

"Would it have meant the same?" she countered.

"W.e.l.l, no," he replied. "I wouldn't ride anything less wild than this," he added, patting the horse's sturdy neck.

"How about me?" she asked.

Alfred drew his animal to a stand-still and stared intently at her.

"What's wrong?" She asked astonishingly.

"Such ambiguity I've never heard in all my life," he told her. "You've kept it up ever since we were ready to start riding. I have never heard you speak in such a manner before and I have a suspicion that you are trying to prove my fibre. If that is what you are after, I can save you some of your difficulty. I am a man of few scruples," he went on after a moment's silence. "And I suffer from little or no remorse." He spoke as if to bolster a waning virtue.

"It's the same here," she threw back shamelessly, spurring her horse into a quick trot. They rode some distance in silence; then, as the horses walked quietly side by side, Elizabeth dropped the reins about her own horse's neck. "I should like to rest a while," she said. She slowly drew the fingers of one hand through those of the other hand. "I am sore."

"There was a time when the doctor stopped me from riding for a few months," Alfred told her. "When I resumed riding my fingers were sore like hell."

"It was unfortunate that you sat on your fingers," she teased. "In my case it is different."

Alfred found a cluster of trees and led her there. When he had tied the animals at a safe distance, he returned to where she stood awaiting him.

"Is this your haunt?" Elizabeth asked.

"You have been toying with me all day," he said, tugging her into his strong arms and kissing her full on the mouth. Her arms shot around his stout neck to return his kiss with equal force.

"It is nice and peaceful here," said Elizabeth, as she sank to the cool earth. For a moment, he stood looking down on her sleek, black hair before he sat next to her. "I think...." The rest of her words were blotted out when his lips crushed down on hers in a long, fervent kiss.

"You brute," she snapped, when she shook free, "do you want to suffocate me?"

"Until now, I didn't think you were suffocating," he smiled. "I thought your reaction was a pleasurable one."

"Who said it wasn't, silly?" she returned, lying flat and resting her head on his muscular legs. "I could spend the rest of the day here."

"You would, eh?" He asked, running his fingers through her hair.

"Yes .... I long wanted to know what your kisses were like."

"Now that you know, what would you say?"

"They are stimulating .... and they make things walk although they have no feet."

As they rode quietly homewards bathed in the crimson rays of the sinking sun, Elizabeth asked: "Do you know any place along the beach as cosy as where we have just left?"

"Yes," Alfred replied.

"You are terrible."

"Why did you say that?"

"Because you didn't have to think of a place," she told him, "you certainly know the haunts, eh?"

He shrugged his shoulders in reply.

When Alfred and Elizabeth went galloping into the front yard, they were greeted by Peter and Ellin.

"I hope you enjoyed your ride," said Peter. "I imagine you were yearning for it."

"You bet I was," Elizabeth returned childishly. "I hope I'd be permitted to go riding more often."

"It will be quite alright with me," Peter said genuinely, "if Alfred can find it convenient."

"But suppose Ellin has objections," Elizabeth said.

"Why should I? You have just as much to lose," said Ellin, resting a friendly hand on Peter's shoulder. "That is numerically, but intellectually, I would pity your taste."

"That is a mighty terrible thing to say against yourself," Alfred said.

"I guess it is," said Ellin. "But in the land of the blind the one-eyed man is king."

"I should like to go to the beach the next time we go riding," said Elizabeth, diverting the trend of the conversation into a lighter vein. "I simply adore the sea .... do you remember your summer trips to France, Pete?"

They were standing under the porch. The animals had been led away by Joseph whom Alfred called as soon as he and Elizabeth alighted.

"One does not easily forget the little intimacy which led to matrimony," he told her; "whether the result be pleasurable, or miserable."

"What a beautiful expression," said Elizabeth, looking at Ellin and Alfred. "I think it is good enough for an epitaph."

"It is the most beautiful expression I've ever heard," said

Ellin. "It expresses so much in just a few words."

"You wouldn't be able to hear any more of him now," said Elizabeth, "I need a shower."

"You and my sister-in-law Hilda are the strangest people I've ever met," said Alfred one evening as they were all sitting under the porch.

"Why do you think so?" Hilda asked, tense with curiosity.

"The two of you are always willing to advise others about that which is good and religious," Alfred challenged, "and only once in a while will you go to church."

"You know, Uncle," said Wilfred, in his high-pitched voice, "I have often wondered the same thing. Not so much about Mother's reluctance, but Peter's. The truth is," he went on quickly. "I had always wanted to question Peter about it, but on second thought I decided that it was personal."

"Peter has never been much of a church-goer," said Elizabeth, "as far back as I can remember."

"That isn't true about Mother," said Wilfred. "Before my father died and shortly after, Mother went to church regularly."

"Near to church and far from God," said Hilda. "Did you ever hear that before?"

"Yes," Wilfred replied.

"Nobody can vouch for that better than I can," said Hilda, "and this is a confession. During those years when I went to church regularly, I was a sincere worshipper of God. I used to pray two or three times every day .... not lip service. I said prayers from the depth of my being; but today, now that I seldom go to church, I am a better individual."

"That could never be," Alfred stormed reproachfully.

"Oh yes!" said Peter. "It is quite possible."

"How could it be?" Alfred asked.

"Let Hilda explain it," said Peter with some confidence. "It is she who had the experience. If it isn't convincing, I'll eat my hat."

"You haven't got one, Peter," Elizabeth said humorously. "Or rather, not a creditable one."

"Thank you for reminding me," he chuckled.

"When I went to church regularly," Hilda began boldly, "I used to pray with sincerity. But I used to pray for Hilda Skinner, her son and husband. I used to see Hilda as a good woman striving for the Kingdom of Heaven. I cared little or nothing for those who went to church or those who didn't go. I was interested in myself. Today, now that I stay at home, I can see people all around me; and I love them dearly. Secretly I share their joys and sorrows."

When she said nothing more, Peter asked: "How do you like her explanation?"

"It sounds reasonable," Alfred answered. "But that is not good enough. By their fruit ye shall know them."

"Man is neither capable of measuring man's fruit," Peter said calmly, "nor is man's fruit revealed to man."

"Why do you say that?" Alfred asked.

"I don't know what you mean," Peter said.

"Man is not capable of measuring man's fruit," Alfred repeated.

"Do you think he is?" Peter asked.

"Yes," Alfred answered.

"Suppose I ask you what is Ellin going to prepare for breakfast in the morning, do you think you would be able to tell me?" Peter asked.

"Yes," Alfred replied.

"How is that?" Peter asked.

"I tell her what to prepare."

"I see," said Peter. "But would you be able to tell me what Elizabeth will be preparing?"

"No, man," Alfred laughed.

"Why?"

"Because I don't know what is going on in her mind."

"Then how are you going to measure man's fruit?"

"By little deeds of kindness," Alfred threw back.

Peter laughed. "That is where you, and many others go wrong. Man's fruit is neither measured by going to church, nor by little deeds of kindness."

"Why?"

"Because neither is an indication of a good individual. A great many people take interest, and derive much pleasure from doing good. It makes them happy; happy because they are in the fortunate position to offer assistance, and happy because there is the unfortunate who must seek aid from them. Such persons are egotists and their kindly deeds are only superficial; but they give relief to these egotistical individuals who are seeking a reward."

"If I am to accept all you've said as truth," Alfred said passively, "what is good?"

"Goodness is a quality," said Peter, "not kindly deeds. A kindly deed is not necessarily a good deed. It is the motive behind the deed that is important."

"But how are we to know the motive?"

"Like I told you a while ago," said Peter, "the motive, or fruit, is not revealed to man. Man has no way of knowing how good man is. The motive is spiritual."

A long silence followed. Alfred was thoughtful. "Suppose we call one kindly deed material and the other kindly deed spiritual," Alfred began slowly, "could that be accepted?"

"I guess so," Peter replied.

"Then it is my opinion," Alfred said boldly, "that if one individual does a kindly deed for material reward and the other does a kindly deed for a spiritual reward, reward is the motive in either case."

"I disagree with you."

"Explain your reason."

"Man, through sin, has fallen from the status which God

made him;" said Peter. "And, when man comes to realise what God has done for him through Jesus and he accepts the meaning of the cross in its entirety, he realises that he has a duty of kindly deeds to perform. These kindly deeds are spiritual, and for them, there is no reward. Man, having fallen from a status, must first accept the cross, and the kindly deeds which follow as a result, are like the steps of a ladder which takes him whence he had fallen."

"I have already warned you against taking up such subjects with Peter," said Elizabeth, breaking the silence and preparing to leave. "Next time try agriculture."

"Agriculture?" Alfred stormed. "I would be defeated in that as well. Have you not noticed how his crops flourish?"

"Yes," Elizabeth replied, "but he may not be able to offer convincing reasons why they do."

Elizabeth wore a black swim-suit beneath her dress; and while Alfred was busy securing the animals to a tree, she kicked off her shoes, dropped her dress in a little heap next to them and plunged into the sea.

"Elizabeth!" Alfred called from among the trees some distance away. He called again and again, but got no reply. He ran to the place he had left her. She was gone. Her clothes bore evidence that she had been there. He looked to the sea. Some distance at sea amidst the white, foaming waves he spotted the little black thing that was Elizabeth's head. Alarmed, he cone-shaped his hands to his mouth and shouted her name several times; but his voice was carried away by the strong wind and roaring waves. He hastily removed his clothes. He left them at the water's edge and dived into an oncoming wave. He swam with amazing speed. He did not know if he was carried by the tide or driven by fear; but one thing he knew which created more fear, was the fact that the sea off the Crane Hotel was notorious for the lives it claimed regularly. Only when they rose simultaneously on the mountainous waves was he able to catch a glimpse of Elizabeth's head. There was a long interval when he did not see her; but when he did, he was quite close. He hurried in her direction; but she suddenly disappeared.

"Lord!" he exclaimed. "What is this?" He filled his lungs with air and submerged. Far below, the sea bed was black with moss and the water was a deep blue. He scanned the sea for Elizabeth's body, but it could not be found. He was mad with fright. He emerged swiftly. He filled his lungs with air and submerged again. He thought of the many people who had lost their lives in this area; the bodies that were never found, those bodies that had washed ashore after two or three days with limbs severed or face disfigured; those escorts like himself who had to answer questions and give convincing reasons that the death was accidental.

"Good God in Heaven," he said, filling his lungs before submerging once more, "help me to find her." He searched until he felt his chest would burst for want of air before he shot to the surface just in time to see Elizabeth racing towards shore.

"I .... I .... hate your sense of humour!" Alfred thundered breathlessly when he returned to shore. Elizabeth was lying on the white sand. Her head was resting on the palms of her hands and her feet were crossed at the ankles. Lying thus, accentuated her firm bosom.

"Next time you feel like playing tricks," he went on angrily, "choose a more sensible place."

"Catch your breath," she laughed, patting a place on the sand next to her. "Have a seat; you need it badly."

"I am not fooling about this," he shouted. "Suppose I had done what came to my mind."

"What was that dear?" she asked, still laughing.

"I was tempted to fill my lungs with water."

She snapped into a sitting position. A hand covered her mouth. Her face suddenly grew pale. She was frightened. All of the humour

142

was gone. There was seriousness in her voice when she asked: "Is that true?"

"Of course it is true," he answered mildly, and breathing more evenly. "You nearly scared me to death." He took a seat.

"But why would you have taken your life if I did not survive?" she asked seriously.

"It would have been better than facing the law," he told her flatly. "We left for the beach together, you know. I don't suppose you thought of the reaction which such an act could have produced."

"I didn't really, although I'd done it to Pete on one occasion with a similar effect," she said. "I didn't stop to think of the consequences in your case. To be honest with you, I like excitement. If I were a man...."

"Go on."

"I'd load all the pretty women I come in contact with."

"Where did you get that word from?"

"What word?"

"Load."

"I picked it up here on your beautiful little island."

"You're learning fast."

"The sun is hot here," said she. "Let's find some place where it's cool and snug."

Alfred found a place beneath the twisted branches of a cluster of grape trees. It was cool and snug.

"It is more conducive here," said Elizabeth, nestling up to him and fawning his hairy torso.

"Conducive to what?" Alfred asked.

"Pent up emotions," she answered, reaching up to be kissed. He kissed her. When she was released she sank to the hard, sandy soil and beckoned Alfred to lie next to her. He did so, and they leaped into each other's arms. He kissed the tender lobes of her ears, her forehead, her eye-lids, and finally, her soft luscious lips which seemed to set her on fire as his tongue darted for an instant between her parted lips. And while his hand explored her body, her breathing quickened rapidly and her heart raced madly.

"Ta....ta....take me, Alfred," she panted, tossing restlessly on the leaf-covered ground.

"Take me .... here and now."

Devoid of restraint, Alfred was upon her like his brother from the caveman era. This, she did not mind. In fact, she enjoyed it. And during the moments of ecstasy, she sank the nails of her fingers several times into the fleshy part of his broad shoulders. She sighed, and ground her teeth and called him sweet names in low, breathless, uneven tones. She wiggled convulsively on the rumpled, dry leaves which cried out rebelliously under their agonising torture. Time passed; and while thus, they were like the mighty waves which mounted to gain more momentum as they rolled on an on until they met a disappointing climax when they lost intensity, and served no other purpose than to wash the awaiting white lips of the sand and then raced gently, whence they came.

"It is all my fault," Elizabeth explained to the family circle who were anxiously awaiting their return. "First, I played a dirty drowning trick on Alfred .... similar to the one I played on you, Peter. It made Alfred a nervous wreck. After that, I had a long time trying to rekindle his desire to bathe. We found the water so pleasant and refreshing, that we lost complete track of time. And last but not least, the weather tricked us."

It was one of those evenings when the light from the early risen moon blended so harmoniously with the waning afterglow of the sun, that one was completely unaware of the fact that the former had assumed duty from the latter.

"We did not notice that the day was spent," Elizabeth went on, "until we discovered that we were being mocked."

"Mocked?" asked Hilda. "What do you mean?"

"We had shadows which were mocking us." She answered. "Then, we realized that it was night."

"That is a beautiful expression," Peter said. "Ellin was mighty worried," he added quickly. "Mostly because she thinks that bathing there is too dangerous. I really would have galloped out there, but to my mind it would have had a suspicious appearance."

Hoping to dismiss from Peter's mind any thought of visiting their rendezvous, Alfred said, "She can swim like a fish, and so can I."

"You know something," said Peter, when they were preparing for bed, "to my mind, Ellin was unduly worried this afternoon."

"Was she?" Elizabeth asked, making little slits of her eyes. There was irony in her tone. Peter noticed. He said: "Her husband was in danger of losing his life, you know."

"And so was your wife," she snapped.

Peter nodded. "You don't need to get angry," he said pleasantly, "if she is suspicious about her thrill-seeking husband."

"I would not have to," she returned angrily, "if I were not involved." She threw her dress madly across the room. It fell to the floor. "That woman thinks I am a tramp," she stormed.

"Liz!" Peter cried softly, "you are acting like a child."

"Child!" she shouted. "That woman is wordlessly accusing me of an affair with her husband and you call my reaction to a lie, childish. How would you have acted if Alfred said something which indicated an affair?"

"I, knowing you to be honest," he said warmly, "would dismiss it as a badly constructed sentence."

"Sometimes I think this earth is no place for you."

"Why?"

"Because you only look for the purer things."

"That is what we should do," he told her instructively.

"The impure things are all around us; but they appear more obvious when you look for them. And since we will get nothing beneficial from evil things, we should not look for them, but strive to see those things that are good, pure and holy."

"Oh no you don't, Peter Barrow!" said Elizabeth, yanking his pajama jacket out of his hand. "You are to put out the light tonight, and you're not getting into bed before me."

"But you are not dressed for bed yet," he protested, struggling to retrieve the jacket which she held behind her.

"That isn't fair," she laughed, "I put out the light last night."

"Who got into bed first?" he asked, laughing at her childishness.

"You did."

"Well," he said, releasing the jacket and snatching her nightgown off the bed, "what is the game? Who gets into bed last should put out the light, isn't it?"

"Yes, but recently you have been beating me to it too often."

"That is no fault of mine."

Peter was already wearing his pajama pants. When she was completely nude and required the nightdress, she held out the jacket to him and said: "Here is your jacket. As soon as I get into my nightdress the race is on; but you must fasten every button before you get into bed or you will be disqualified."

"Throw it to me," Peter said.

The two garments swiftly passed each other as they journeyed to their respective owners. Elizabeth was sure that she had created enough difficulty for Peter in asking him to fasten all of the buttons. That would give her ample time to throw the nightdress over her head and rush into bed. Peter caught his jacket, thrust his hand into the sleeves, fastened the buttons and rushed for the bed.

"Oh no, Pete!" Elizabeth cried, checking his approach, "you have cheated. This is dishonest."

146

Peter had secretly made a close knot of the upper section of the nightgown. It retarded her progress. They laughed heartily while Peter unfastened the knot and slipped the garment over her head.

"I've tricked you," he said, as they got into bed. He extinguished the light. The switch was at the head of the bed.

Minutes later, Peter drew close to her and kissed her. "Liz," he said, his hand covering one of her firm breasts.

"I'm sleepy, and tired from exertion in the sea, Pete," she said, drawing away from him. "No love-making tonight."
He kissed her again. "I guess you would be tired," he said understandingly. "You haven't had a seabath in a long time. Good night," he whispered in her ear after a short pause. "May God take care of you during your sleep."

"Good night," she returned.
Peter moved to the farther corner of the bed and went to sleep.

Elizabeth was not sleepy as she said. She wanted to be alone with the memory of those blissful moments she spent in the shade of the grape trees. She wished she was there now; that the hand which had just touched her was Alfred Skinner's. The hand which shocked her like electricity when it explored her sensitive body or caressed her quivering breast. The hand that caused her to burn with desire and plead shamelessly for the act of coitus, whose fulfillment was beyond any she had known. She remembered Alfred's body. It was hard against her own. She heard his wordless cries, his rapid breathing as they had striven together for the white goal. The thought maddened her.

"What is it?" Peter asked, snapping on the light and looking into her face which was sprinkled with little beads of perspiration, "I heard you sighing and I felt the bed shaking, is something wrong?"

"No, I guess I had a bad dream," she lied, putting out the light. "Go back to sleep."

When Elizabeth woke with a start, the golden rays of the sun were already warming the breeze, which, drifting through the half-opened windows of the bedroom, was pregnant with the fragrance of green vegetation. She sat up in bed. Fearful, she thought it was Friday. She would have hated it to be. She smiled at the thought that it was not. Friday was yet another day off. She was glad; glad for the interval during which she would be able to construct her plan .... a plan that required skillful construction if it was to be successful and lead to its ultimate goal. She slid to the edge of the bed and slipped her toes into her slippers. She crossed the room and forced the sash windows to their uppermost; and as the gentle breeze passed, it dallied amorously with her shining, black hair.

During the day Elizabeth travelled many times across the two yards to discuss a fashion for a dress, a bit of gossip which she overheard from the two young servants, and to take a bottle of pepper sauce which she had the cook prepare. These visits were not as casual as Ellin thought. Little did she know that she was constantly under the eagle-eyed scrutiny of Elizabeth who watched her every gesture and facial expression. She noticed too, the tone of Ellin's voice and the briefest of reluctance to participate in any conversation in which Alfred was involved. His name seemed to be taboo. Hard as she tried, Ellin was without power to fully conceal the emotional storm that was slowly building up within her breast; but Elizabeth was not prepared to allow anything to sever their friendship. Tomorrow was Friday .... the day she had set to put her plan into operation. 'If you don't do any worse than you've done today,' Elizabeth said to herself 'when the sun goes to rest, you would not have failed.'

• • •

Elizabeth was prepared to be extremely cautious when the group met that evening for their usual after-dinner chat. They had no set method for their visits. One week they were almost equally divided, and the next week they were heavily outweighed on one side or the other. Some evenings they met on the street where they stood chatting for some time before they decided on who should visit whom. This evening, Peter and Elizabeth were the visitors. On their arrival, they were heartily welcomed by all. Elizabeth was vaguely surprised when she found herself being led by Ellin's hand to a corner of the sitting room.

"We are going to surprise the boys with a dinner tomorrow," she whispered close to Elizabeth's ear. "Here at me."

"Good," said Elizabeth, glad for the offer. "We'll discuss it in the morning as soon as they have left."

Resuming their places among the others, Ellin said: "I heard today that Vesta can't use her right arm."

"Who is Vesta?" Peter asked.

"You don't know her?" Ellin replied. "Alfred does."

"Vesta is an old friend of ours."

"What is the matter with her arm?" Alfred asked.

"The woman next door injured her," Ellin replied.

"Did they have a fight?" Elizabeth asked.

"Not a physical fight," Ellin replied, "an oral one."

"Don't be absurd," Elizabeth laughed. "How can anyone get injured in an oral battle?"

"Why, don't you know that people can hurt you," said Ellin, "without striking you?"

"Yes," replied Elizabeth, "if they ill speak you."

"I don't mean that way," Ellin said.

"Then how do you mean?" Elizabeth asked.

"There are special types of powers and liquids which can cause good or ill to befall you," Ellin replied.

Peter and Elizabeth laughed heartily.

• • •

Addressing Peter in a calm, but stern voice, Alfred asked: "You don't believe it can happen?"

"Who in their right mind could believe such rot?" Peter answered.

"Near to church and far from God," said Ellin. "The two of you wouldn't allow the pews in the church to cool, and yet you have no confidence in God."

"Now what does God have to do with this?" Ellin asked.

"If you had stopped to think," said Hilda, "you would never have asked that question."

"Why?" Ellin asked. There was a note of surprise in her tone.

"Because you are so right," Hilda answered calmly. "God has nothing to do with anything wicked; and only when you have no confidence in His protection and care will you believe that evil can prevail."

"I can neither pick head nor tail from what you are saying," Ellin said coldly.

"You don't mind if I try?" asked Peter. "Do you?"

"If you think you can do a better job," Ellin replied.

"Suppose you were in this room alone," Peter began slowly, "and a ten-year-old rushed suddenly through the open door and threatened to beat you up with his fist, what would be your first reaction?"

"I would be afraid," she replied, "and probably yell for Alfred."

"I think that would be the most natural reaction," said Peter, "because of the possible danger. But would you be as fearful with Alfred at your side as if he had not been there?"

"Of course not," she replied.

"Why?"

"That is silly to ask."

"I don't mind being silly once in a while," Peter smiled, "but I would like my question answered."

"How could I be afraid of a little ten-year-old boy when a big giant of a man is standing next to me?" Ellin retorted. "Do you see how silly you make yourself when you ask that question?"

"I wouldn't make that assertion too strongly," he told her, "if I were you."

"Why not?" Ellin asked, looking serious.

"Because it expresses the fact that you have more confidence in the strength of your broad-shouldered husband," Peter explained, "than in the source of his strength."

"You have a plaster for every sore," Ellin said.

"It may be necessary," said Peter, going through the door. "It all depends upon the infection."

In bed, Elizabeth lay awake for the greater part of the night. She was occupied too deeply with her plan to worry about sleep. She frequently rehearsed the first act of her plot, in which a major section of her happiness would soon be housed. It was only after she realised that her plot was almost faultless that the desire for sleep came to her.

Elizabeth was up very early the following morning. The first chirpings from the birds in the trees across from her bedroom windows had awakened her. From her bed, she looked through the misty, half-lowered sash-windows. Outside, the first rays of sunlight were appearing. She slipped quietly out of bed and forced the windows upward to permit more light and air to enter the room. She filled her lungs with air, which was pregnant with the freshness of the new day. Poking her head through a window, she looked to the sky. It was patched with numerous pieces of cloud. They varied in colour from a dark, frightful grey, to a beautiful radiant pink. As she averted her gaze and looked to the landscape, she was mesmerised by its beauty. For comfort, she sat on the broad windowsill and watched the clouds as they took on new shapes and different colours drifting across the sun as the morning grew gradually older.

Since Peter and Alfred were journeying to the city by train, they had to be taken to the station. They were conveyed by buggy. Elizabeth accompanied them. She had done so on many occasions. She liked to make a mock of the small locomotive and its burden, which varied from man to beast. Quite often some of the locomotive's wagons were laden to capacity with sugar cane which was unloaded in those factory yards through which it passed en route to, and from, the city.

"Are you ever going to stop laughing at our trains?" Alfred asked on one occasion.

"Yes," Elizabeth replied.

"When will that be?" he asked.

"When I've seen them long enough to become bored with them," she replied laughing.

"I thought that was why you laughed."

"No, I laugh because they look so funny," she said, "they seem to tickle me."

"You've been living here long enough to be called a Bajan," he teased, "and you continue to make jokes at our train. Don't you think it is about time you become acclimatised?"

"I am," she answered, "but I exercise my tolerance with other things," she said laughing heartily.

"That is one of the many things I admire about Liz," Peter said, "one minute she is a startling example of sophistication and a second later she can express all the reformation that could be desired. I sometimes wonder what goes on in her mind."

When Elizabeth returned from the station she found the little dark-skinned boy, whose duty it was to care for the flower garden, digging in the moist, black soil. As she approached, she noticed that the seat of his knee-lengthed trousers was torn.

"Have you anything with which I can cut some roses?"

152

Elizabeth asked. Her voice startled him. He stood erect.

"O....o....only a knife, mistress," he stammered frightfully. He gave her the knife. He slumped down on his haunches and resumed digging.

"Oh! dear me!" Elizabeth exclaimed. She dropped the knife and it fell harmlessly to the ground. "The thorns stuck me."

"Le' me cut dem for you, mistress," said the boy, rushing to her assistance. "You show me de ones you want cut."
She pointed here and there at those most suitable to make a colourful bouquet.

"These will be enough," she said, as she took them one by one to arrange them. "We'll leave some for the next time."

"Yes, mistress."

"Thank you, son," she said, as she turned away and vanished behind a door which closed after her.

"I'll be next door for the greater part of the day," Elizabeth told the servants. "The master and I will be dining there tonight; but Cookie will prepare something for all of you. See that you do your work," she added, going through the door, "and don't be eye-servants."

"All right, mistress."

"De mistress upstairs," said the maid who took the flowers.

"Thank you," Elizabeth returned. "Put those roses in a vase with some fresh water," she added, moving towards the stairway. "I'm going up."

"It is hot like bloody hell already," said Elizabeth, when she stood before Ellin, "and the day has just begun."

"That is true," Ellin agreed, "but where did you get this bloody hell talk from."

"I picked it up in England."

"Oh!"

"I accompanied the others to the station," said Elizabeth. "Did you know?"

"No, I didn't," Ellin replied, "or I would have gone myself.

Sometimes I get tired of the house, and a couple of minutes outside refreshes."

"That is why I went," said Elizabeth, "but I'm so hot now that I could do with another bath."

"Are you implying that you had one already?"

"Yes, but I think this high-necked frock is adding to my discomfort," said Elizabeth, releasing two of the buttons at the throat.

"You can make yourself more comfortable than that," Ellin urged. "The servants won't be up here again for the rest of the day. I am going to take a shower soon, and you can do the same if you like."

"Okay."

"But before I shower, I'll finish reading these few pages."

Elizabeth chose a book at random and stretched out on the couch. Minutes later Ellin closed the book with a loud bang. "There," she said, placing the book on a nearby table.

"That is finished." She walked over to Elizabeth and added: "One minute you're all words and the next you are as quiet as a lamb."

"You don't expect me to be noisy while I'm reading," said Elizabeth, smiling sweetly, "do you?"

"It is a pity you couldn't."

"Why?"

"Because I like the huskiness in your voice," Ellin answered. "It is charming."

"Thank you," said Elizabeth, meeting her gaze, "if it is a compliment."

"It is a fact." Elizabeth extended her gratitude and returned her eyes to the book. But she was not reading. She was too busy re-assembling her plot to notice the words on the pages before her.

"I'm sorry to disturb you," said Ellin, "but .... "

"You are not disturbing me in the least," Elizabeth

interrupted. "I'm going to take a shower and get back to this book; it seems interesting."

"I interrupted you to suggest that," said Ellin, "but I've never read the book." Elizabeth dropped the book onto the colourful mattress cover of the couch and followed Ellin into her bedroom.

"You may use Alfred's robe and bathe first," said Ellin, tossing it onto the bed. "I'll wear my own housecoat. In the meanwhile I will go down stairs and fetch two drinks," she added quickly, going towards the door, "to use after we've showered."

When Ellin returned from the bath Elizabeth was standing before the life-size mirror. She was combing her hair. It was soft and black, and it reached the nape of her neck. She heard the door open, Ellin's sudden gasp of surprise, her soft approach, and when it halted nearby. Looking into the mirror, Elizabeth observed that Ellin was not looking at her physical being, but at her more frontal view in the mirror. Realising this, Elizabeth turned slowly and faced her. Ellin was silent and motionless, but her eyes were quite active. She scrutinised Elizabeth's calves, her long shapely legs, her narrow but fleshy firm hips, the cavity that was her navel and the slimness of her waist which accentuated her pointed, pink-nippled breasts. When their eyes finally met, Elizabeth stared intently.

"Y....y....you are stunning," Ellin stammered, "and so gracefully shaped that you could easily impersonate a Greek goddess. I didn't know that you were so evenly tanned."

Elizabeth was silent. It was embarrassing. She knew it was. She wanted it that way. Soon Ellin would have said all she had to, and too late discover that to agree was her only alternative.

"Almost every day I take a sunbath," Elizabeth said finally, "in the raw."

"In the raw?"

"Yes."

• • •

Ellin was mesmerised by Elizabeth's beauty, her symmetry and her seductive black eyes which held her motionless. Elizabeth stepped slowly forward. She folded Ellin in her arms and kissed her; lightly at first, then long and compellingly. The comb fell to the floor, and in the silence of the room it resounded like a cannon. Ellin was startled by the sound. She looked frightfully around.

"There's nothing to be afraid of, darling," said Elizabeth, as she locked the door. "It is only a comb. It seems a lifetime since I've waited for this moment," she went on, as she slipped off Ellin's housecoat which fell to the floor with a hushed sound. "You are beautiful."

She led Ellin to the bed and climbed in next to her. Ellin had neither the physical strength nor the mental stability to resist Elizabeth, who employed every conceivable means to arouse the latent desire for lesbianism. And in the privacy of her own room Ellin found a love that she had never known.

'That is act one from my plot,' said Elizabeth to herself, elated with her accomplishment. 'But don't compliment yourself too quickly, you have yet another bridge to cross. As for you,' she smiled triumphantly, as she looked down on Ellin who was prostrate and panting, 'you'll never again accuse me of having an affair with your husband; not after the experience you've just had.' She took the housecoat from the floor and placed it over her shoulders. She drew the white sheet over Ellin's body and then went into the bath.

Ellin was sleeping as soundly as a kitten when Elizabeth returned from the bath. She reached out and kissed the sleeper's parted lips, who stirred ever so slightly. Her eyelids quivered; gently at first, then slowly they opened. The eyes that were once green and beautiful, were now dim, and almost colourless. Her lips trembled as though she wanted to speak but no sound came. Her hand moved slowly to avoid Elizabeth's kisses.

"D....don't Liz, please!" she begged. "Not again."

"Some other time?"

"Maybe."

"Don't say maybe," Elizabeth implored, taking a seat on the edge of the bed. "Say yes."

"Yes."

"Promise."

"I promise."

Minutes later Ellin rose and took a bath. When she and Elizabeth had taken their drinks of brandy, they went about their task of preparing dinner and spoke nothing of what had happened. That night, dinner was served in the gayest of moods.

Moving towards the border of the field in which Irine was working and the boundary of her own field, Dorothy made sure that there was no one within earshot before she said: "Uh see me massuh carry out you massuh wife de other day. 'E soon live wid she now .... if 'e en living wid she already. 'Cause all he like 'e want to do is live wid every woman 'e see. I don' know why some woman don' give 'e uh dose uh sickness."

When Irine remained silent Dorothy added: "Dat red gal Olga lef' she aunt house and gone livin' in de nex' village wid Vera. She is uh bad eddoe, dat woman Vera. She influence dat young girl an' make she lef' she aunt place. Uh wonder wha' dese people goin' tell God."

"What you goin' tell Him?" Irine asked ponderingly. "You ever stop an' ask yuhself?"

"Now wha' you want me to do if uh hear somethin'.... uh can' prevent muhself from hearin'."

"You does hear so much," Irine told her, "dat sometimes I does believe dat you ask questions."

"Yuh like yuh drunk," Dorothy threw back. "Uh hear dat Samuel lef' Gladys, too .... 'e ketch she wid uh man, but uh din tell yuh dat."

"I can tell yuh dis," said Irine, "Samuel is my husband, an' I pray an' ask God to sen' 'e home to me an' 'e son, an' God hear my pray. I don' know if Samuel lef' Gladys or not; but uh know 'e start sleepin' home again an' I doin' my duty as uh wife."

"Wha' I en say yuh shouldn't," said Dorothy, "I only tell yuh wha' uh hear."

"Yuh know something, Dorothy?"

"No."

"You en such uh bad person, yuh do things with good intentions, but yuh do them de wrong way."

"How?"

"Every since dat day when you carry me to dat obeah woman I know you did want to see me an' Samuel back together; but yuh do it de wrong way."

"How?"

"You should of ask me to pray to God. Only He can make things brighter. Look to God, an' yuh will see de light."

The rain had fallen for the greater part of the day and continued into the night. There would be no visitors. Hilda was glad.

"Alfred, it has been a long time since I wanted to discuss something with you," she said.

Taking his pipe from his mouth he asked: "What is it?"

"It is about this young man, Wilfred," she sighed. "This boy is fast becoming a drunkard," she went on, "and a gambler too."

"Gambler!" Alfred exclaimed, looking at Wilfred.

"Yes, he gambles," said Hilda. "He can't deny it. I have found evidence in his pockets .... cards on one occasion and dice on another."

ih like yuh drunk," Dorothy threw back. "Uh hear dat
el lef' Gladys, too .... 'e ketch she wid uh man, but uh din
h dat."

:an tell yuh dis," said Irine, "Samuel is my husband, an'
an' ask God to sen' 'e home to me an' 'e son, an' God
ny pray. I don' know if Samuel lef' Gladys or not; but
ow 'e start sleepin' home again an' I doin' my duty as uh

'ha' I en say yuh shouldn't," said Dorothy, "I only tell yuh
h hear."

ih know something, Dorothy?"

).''

u en such uh bad person, yuh do things with good
ions, but yuh do them de wrong way."

ow?"

ery since dat day when you carry me to dat obeah woman
v you did want to see me an' Samuel back together; but
) it de wrong way."

ow?"

u should of ask me to pray to God. Only He can make
brighter. Look to God, an' yuh will see de light."

e rain had fallen for the greater part of the day and
ued into the night. There would be no visitors. Hilda
ad.

fred, it has been a long time since I wanted to discuss
hing with you," she said.

; his pipe from his mouth he asked: "What is it?"

is about this young man, Wilfred," she sighed. "This
fast becoming a drunkard," she went on, "and a gambler

imbler!" Alfred exclaimed, looking at Wilfred.

s, he gambles," said Hilda. "He can't deny it. I have found
ce in his pockets .... cards on one occasion and dice on
r."

158

came. Her hand moved slowly to avoid Elizabeth's kisses.

"D....don't Liz, please!" she begged. "Not again."

"Some other time?"

"Maybe."

"Don't say maybe," Elizabeth implored, taking a seat o
edge of the bed. "Say yes."

"Yes."

"Promise."

"I promise."

Minutes later Ellin rose and took a bath. When sh
Elizabeth had taken their drinks of brandy, they went
their task of preparing dinner and spoke nothing of
had happened. That night, dinner was served in the gay
moods.

Moving towards the border of the field in which Irin
working and the boundary of her own field, Dorothy
sure that there was no one within earshot before she said
see me massuh carry out you massuh wife de other day. 'E
live wid she now .... if 'e en living wid she already. 'Cause
like 'e want to do is live wid every woman 'e see. I don'
why some woman don' give 'e uh dose uh sickness."

When Irine remained silent Dorothy added: "Dat r
Olga lef' she aunt house and gone livin' in de nex' villag
Vera. She is uh bad eddoe, dat woman Vera. She influen
young girl an' make she lef' she aunt place. Uh wonder wh
people goin' tell God."

"What you goin' tell Him?" Irine asked ponderingly.
ever stop an' ask yuhself?"

"Now wha' you want me to do if uh hear somethin'
can' prevent muhself from hearin'."

"You does hear so much," Irine told her, "dat someti
does believe dat you ask questions."

strong arm and forced him to resume his place next to her. "After our first affair on this spot," she went on quietly, "I knew that I had to have you; that nothing was going to stop me; that Peter would never suspect me, but I was afraid of Ellin. Afraid that she might have done, or said something to break the friendship; so I made a pass at Ellin. I told her that I love her; that no other woman attracted me, that I wanted to have an affair to prove my love for her; that I went out with you, only to kill any suspicion in you. I fought to kiss her on one occasion."

"What happened?" Alfred asked curiously.

"She slapped my face. I was glad, but I cried. I cried bitterly. I thought my crying would have aroused enough sympathy in her to make her submit. It didn't and I was glad when it failed."

"I don't understand it," Alfred said thoughtfully. "You wanted an affair with Ellin. You fought to kiss her, she slapped your face and you were glad. You cried bitterly with the hope that it would weaken her resistance; yet, you were glad when it didn't. It doesn't make sense."

"Don't be silly, Alfred," she snorted, sitting up. "I'm no lesbian. I didn't really want an affair with her, but I wanted her to believe that I was in earnest; and when she objected to my request, it gave me more scope to persist, and in doing so, convince her of a trait that I do not possess. You see," she went on coyly, "I told her that my going out with you meant nothing to me .... I didn't want you; but if I continued to be in your company regularly, you would never find time to suspect us."

"I s-e-e," said Alfred, who was undoubtedly convinced; "that is why Ellin has never objected to my going out with you. It was much unlike her to act in such a casual manner. I think it was very clever of you." He took her in his strong arms. 'You are extremely cunning' he thought, 'much too cunning to be trusted.'

"I hope you understand why I did it," she said, looking

161

suspiciously into his eyes for any trace of distrust.

"Yes." He kissed her.

'Look how gullible men can be,' she thought.

"I had never been kissed by a woman before," said Ellin, "until you did a few weeks ago."

"Really? That is more honourable than I can say," said Elizabeth, pouting her thin lips, "if one thinks it honourable. I am French; and anything in sex is right. I have been kissed by many women, but this is the first time that I've been the aggressor."

Ellin's mouth fell open. She was astonished by Elizabeth's frankness.

"Yes .... this is the first time I have been the aggressor," Elizabeth repeated.

"But why did you choose me?" Ellin asked.

"Because I had never been attracted so forcefully before," she lied, gazing into Ellin's eyes. "Not even half so much. I hope you understand."

"I understand, but .... "

"Kiss me," Elizabeth interrupted.

"Let's forget about it."

"Forget?" she cried. She was afraid. Ellin was not convinced. "How can I forget it when you've promised so faithfully?"

"Do I have to keep my promise?"

"You must," Elizabeth replied, leading her into the bedroom, "if you want to be trustworthy."

'It is a long time since I've last read something light,' said Peter to himself, as he stood before Elizabeth's section of books. 'I'll try one of these.' Much unlike Peter, Elizabeth had a flair for literature which dealt with love and sex. Peter raised a hand towards the books. He took one at random. Its cover read: "A Cheating Wife." 'Why do authors write such stuff,' he questioned himself sadly, 'is it that they write for commerce, or is this their concept?' He could not decide which it was, so he dismissed the problem with a shrug of his shoulders. As he casually opened the book a few sheets of paper slid from between the pages and fell to the floor. He picked them up. Observing that it was a letter he said to himself: 'I wonder what mood possessed me when I wrote this, I'll read and see.'

Peter walked leisurely across the room to his reclining canvas-bottomed chair. He took a seat, stretched out and crossed his feet at the ankles. He placed the closed book gently on the floor beside him, and patiently opened the folded pages of typewritten paper.

'*My Dearest Liz,*'

he read, smiling fondly. 'It is with the deepest regret that I have to write you these few lines' …. "I don't ever write in this vein," said Peter to himself, frowning slightly. He looked to the right hand corner of the paper. The address was the same as his former home in Kent, but the letter had no date, and the house number was different. "Is this some kind of a joke?" he went on, "I don't know, but I'll read it through."

'*My Dearest Liz,*'

he began again, 'it is with deepest regret that I have to write you these few lines. I received your letter by the morning delivery and I have foregone my lunch in order to reply. I know that you are angry because I did not come to see you off; but I was terribly hurt. I guess it was unreasonable of me to expect you to miss the boat a second time. Once was enough, and I suppose your outburst of anger was justifiable. But how reasonable can a man be when he is in love; especially with another man's wife …. a woman whom he may never truly possess. The mere thought that Peter is enjoying

163

your artful love-making is driving me mad. As long as I live, I will remember those nights we spent locked in each other arms. Liz, why did you leave me just when I wanted you most? The winter is here, and we could have spent all the hours of night locked in the cosy fragrance of your home. I can still feel the smooth softness of your nude body against my own. Liz, please try to come back for a few weeks vacation. My time is running out, and I have only a few minutes left to collect a snack and get back to work. Write soon and let me know all about your sweet self and the way Peter treats you.

I am, yours as ever

Dexter.

N.B. Take care of yourself for my sake.'

As Peter read, small beads of perspiration appeared on his forehead, his nose and upper lip, slowly at first, then swiftly, until he was sleek with perspiration. He made a swift sweeping stroke across his forehead with the index finger of his free arm, and a stream of water fell to the floor. Quite unconsciously, he slowly and nervously shifted his position several times during the course of his reading. His saliva grew thick, and difficult to swallow. It shook his head every time he tried to swallow. His breathing became quick and irregular.

"This is the strangest joke .... " said Elizabeth as she entered the study. Amidst her laughter she spoke; she stopped suddenly when she saw Peter. He was sitting on the edge of the chair. His feet were drawn up. Both elbows were resting on his knees and his face was buried in the palms of his hands.

"Peter!" she cried. "What is it?"

Slowly he raised his head. His face was red. Tears were in his eyes, and they were wild with rage. As she gradually removed her hand, her eyes caught the book on the floor. She knew it by the title. It was hers. 'Why was he reading it? Why should it disturb him?' she asked herself. She could find no answer. Suddenly she observed the sheets of paper in his hand. 'Could it be those papers?' she thought. She was doubtful. "What is it, Peter?" She asked again.

"This," he growled, shaking the sheets of paper before her. "Explain this."

It was without doubt that the contents of the papers were responsible for his condition; but Elizabeth had not the vaguest idea of the nature of the letter. During the silence, her mouth opened several times as if she wanted to speak, but no sound came.

"Explain this!" Peter thundered, rising to his feet, "you cheating son-of-a .... "
His fist exploded against the side of her head and she toppled into a little heap on the floor.

'Peter!' a still small voice within him said, 'what are you doing?' He walked hurriedly out of the room.

Outside, the sky was bright with the afterglow of the sun which had just gone beyond the horizon. Peter walked aimlessly about his yard. All of the workers were already gone; even the night watchman. He would return sneakingly at an hour when he thought it best. Peter walked slowly. With hands clasped behind his back, he was thoughtful as he looked to the ground. He remembered the incident on board the 'S.S. LATHENA' .... the ship which brought Elizabeth to the shores of this island .... the strange way she reacted when he took her in his arms and kissed her. He felt cold and hot at one and the same time. The stall in which the animals were kept loomed suddenly before him. He looked in. The cattle were gently chewing on their fodder .... the green tops from the sugar cane. The horses, asses and mules were munching on their share of the green vines from the sweet potato and the suckling pigs were feeding on the milk from their mother's breast. Not far away from the stall, two large dogs were lying quietly at the door of their kennel.

'All is peaceful with the animals,' said Peter to himself, 'and only man is vile.'

The gong told Peter that dinner was ready, but he did not leave the yard immediately. He was hoping to find Elizabeth awaiting him at the table. He was surprised when he did not find her there. He went upstairs and found her already dressed in her nightie and lying in bed. "The mistress will not be down for dinner," Peter told the attendant who was preparing to serve him. "She has suddenly developed a headache .... I'm not much in a mood for eating," he went on after a pause, "I'll serve myself and let you know when I'm finished."

"Very well, Sir," she said, and left the room.

Peter ate little of the food placed on the table. He had lost all desire for food and drink. He had little desire for anything. "You can remove the dishes and clean up," said Peter, after he had successfully forced a morsel down his throat which seemed congested.

When Peter dismissed the servants he went for a quiet stroll. He was in no mood for talking. He wanted to be alone; but he stopped at Alfred's for a while. Ellin was greatly disturbed when she heard of Elizabeth's illness.

"It is not as bad as you are trying to make it," Peter told her. "Liz developed a headache and she has gone to bed. That is all there is to it. She will sleep it off and be as good as new in the morning."

"But she may be angry if I don't visit her," said Ellin, "especially when she learns that I knew of her illness."

"She may be annoyed if you disturb her slumber," said Peter. "It may worsen the headache."

"I agree with you, Peter," said Alfred. "It can't be so bad."

"It isn't," Peter said.

Peter left shortly afterwards. He walked slowly along the way. Absorbed in thought, he passed his home by a few yards. As he returned and stood at the door, he recalled the incident most forcefully. "Should I take you over the threshold?" He had asked Elizabeth on that very early and beautiful moonlit morning when he brought her to their new home.

"I don't see why you shouldn't," she had replied. He took her over the threshold; and while he still held her lifted, his lips found hers. They were happy to be together, or so he thought. He opened the door. Before entering, he looked at the entrance which once led to all the happiness that could be expected in a home. He shuddered at the thought of what was left of it.

The book was still lying on the floor where he had gently placed it. The sheets of paper were scattered about the room. From a distance, he looked at them for a long time before he walked slowly about the room and picked them up. He reassembled the sheets and placed them neatly between the pages of the book. He looked at its title and smiled weakly. 'I'll probably read it some other time,' he said to himself, 'if I find it convenient.'

When he replaced the book on the shelf he switched off the light and sat in the dark. His mind ran in circles. He thought of those summer trips to France .... those pleasurable days of courtship and his long and happy married life. He wondered if he had been a fool all this time, but he concluded that he was not a fool. It had been his policy to accept all men as honest until he found them dishonest. Until now, he had no reason to doubt Elizabeth's sense of honesty. He held firmly to his conviction. Confidence and doubt are two separate and distinct forces; and they cannot be fully operated at one and the same time. When two people make a covenant, they are expected to keep it, and if it is broken by one, the other should never feel remorseful because of his partner's shortcoming.

It was long after midnight when Peter sneaked noiselessly into bed; but he was up and about the yard very early the following morning. At breakfast, he and Elizabeth spoke only for the benefit of the servants who were to be kept uninformed of the strained relationship.

"It looks like we're going to have a sunny day," said Peter, taking his seat at the head of the table.

"It does look so," Elizabeth agreed. "Monday was similar, but we had a hell of a lot of rain during the afternoon."

"That is true," Peter said, after he sipped his tea. "The weather is sometimes like life."

"Oops!" Elizabeth exclaimed, as she spilt some of her tea on the table cloth. Their eyes met for a brief instance. Peter was silent. His sentence shocked her. Her hands were shaking nervously.

"Excuse me," she added. She got up from the table and hastened out of the room.

"Good morning."

Peter looked up from his breakfast to see Ellin standing in the doorway of the breakfast room.

"Good morning," he returned, smiling, friendly. "You are late for breakfast."

"I came to see the patient."

"The patient is up and around," he told her. "She has just excused herself from the table."

"Then she was actually taking breakfast?" Ellin asked, as she advanced. She was greatly relieved.

"Did you think she was poorly?"

"Not really," she replied. "I'll see if I can find her."

• • •

Elizabeth was lying across the foot of the bed when Ellin entered the room. She got no reply to her soft knock on the door, so she took the liberty to open it. She closed it gently after her and crossed the floor on the ball of her feet. She looked down on Elizabeth. She was lying on her stomach. Her arm hid her face. Her feet, which protruded the edge of the bed, still bore her soft house slippers.

"Are you asleep?" Ellin whispered.

"No," Elizabeth replied. She looked up. Her eyes were red. Ellin knew she was crying. She sat on the edge of the bed and took Elizabeth's head in her lap.

"What is it?" Ellin asked sympathetically. "Is there anything I can do for you?"

Elizabeth shook her head.

"Have you any pain?" Ellin asked.

"If there is, I don't seem to know where it is," she answered.

"You don't suppose that you are pregnant, do you?"

"Pregnant!" Elizabeth exclaimed frightfully. She snapped into a sitting position. Her lips grew pale and her eyes took on a wild stare. Her hand slowly covered her half-opened mouth. "Pregnant!" she repeated, in a muffled tone. She got up and walked feebly across the room and stood at the window. She reached up and took hold of the window jambs. She rested her forehead against the windowpane. It was cold and soothing and she closed her eyes.

In the dark, Elizabeth saw a small, white-painted cradle. In it, lying on the snow-white bedclothing was a sturdy little baby boy. He was laughing and catching at his chubby feet which he kicked out playfully in the air. His eyes were brown; and his big head was covered with sleek, brown hair. At the foot of the cradle, she saw the lower limbs of a man. Her gaze rose slowly to the abdomen, the chest, the neck and finally the face. It was the face of Alfred Skinner. He bore an unmistakable resemblance to the boy in the cradle. Frightened, Elizabeth opened her eyes. "No! no! no!" she shouted. "I'm not pregnant." She ran blindly across the room. She fell on her knees at the foot of the bed and buried her face in Ellin's lap. "I'm not pregnant," she sobbed mournfully. "It can't be." And while she cried Ellin gently stroked her soft, jet-black hair.

A long time passed during which Elizabeth cried uncontrollably. It shook her convulsively. Ellin was silent. She could find no suitable words for consolation. She continued to stroke Elizabeth's head and shoulders.

When Elizabeth was able to control her crying, she then realised how unbalanced she had been. She recalled the true cause of her grief, but she did not reveal it. It had nothing to do with pregnancy. She could not understand how a simple question could have so easily led her into an uncontrollable state of emotional chaos. She had been a blundering idiot. "Don't tell Peter about this, please," she begged.

"I wouldn't," Ellin promised.

"I wouldn't like him to know," she went on, "men are so vain."

"But you can't hide pregnancy," Ellin said warningly. "At least, not very long."

"Don't start that again," she returned. "I can't stand it."

Ellin was greatly surprised by Elizabeth's unwillingness to become a mother. She was advancing in years, true enough, but many women had babies during their more mature years. These women were usually very proud. She saw no good reason why Elizabeth should not be grateful for a son or daughter. A child would make Peter extremely proud of himself and his family. He would have his own offspring to tutor in the science of philosophy. He always devoted such a lot of his leisure time to the company of my own son, that there was little more he could do for his own son; a son by the woman of his choice.

When Ellin could find no justifiable reason for Elizabeth's indifference to motherhood, she abandoned the self-inquiry.

As time went by, the relationship between Elizabeth and Peter became more and more strained. For Elizabeth, it was unbearable. They spoke to each other only in the presence of the servants, when they went visiting or when they entertained.

To avoid the cold, dull, piercing boredom of the house Elizabeth took a book and a reclining chair into the yard. The sun was receding. She looked for a shady spot. Finding a suitable one alongside the fence which had grown tall, and almost covered with bean vines, she placed the chair there and took a seat. It was drab, but it was peaceful. From the kitchen, the aroma of tasty food was drifting westward in the gentle breeze.

She had only read a few pages when she heard voices. She looked around. She saw no one; but she soon realised that the persons responsible for the sounds were securely hidden behind the thickly grown, vine-covered fence. The voices slowly grew louder until they were opposite to where she was sitting. She could hear them distinctly now, although they spoke in low whispers. They were the voices of two people. One was undoubtedly the gruff voice of a man; and the other, the soft high-pitched voice of a woman. Elizabeth was stirred with curiosity. She ignored her own predicament and inclined herself closer to the fence and listened attentively.

"You took so long to get here," said the woman in her high-pitched tone, "that I thought you'd never reach."

"Uh had to bathe an' change my clothes first," came the gruff voice of the man. "You did want me to come in muh dirty clothes?"

"No."

"Then why you can' wait a few minutes?"

"I don't mind waiting, but the time always seem longer than it really is. Come and kiss me."

There was a long silence. It was broken by a smack.

"Let us make love," came the high-pitched voice.

"Not this evening."

"Why?"

" 'Cause I don' feel like doin' it."

"I can't understand you when it comes to love-making. One week you would do it every evening and the next week you don't want to do it at all."

"Don't open de front of muh trousers."

"Don't be silly, you don't like it?"

"Yes; but I don't want to do it this evenin'."

"All right. Don't let us quarrel.

During the long silence that followed, Elizabeth heard only the low, blissful sighing and the sound of lovers parting lips. She wished that she had a similar opportunity.

"I goin' home," said the gruff voice.

"Are you coming tomorrow evening?"

"I will give you the signal."

As they spoke the sound drifted westward. Following the fence which curved inwards at the end, Elizabeth slumped into hiding and waited to see who were the lovers. As suddenly as a flash of lightning, her whole nervous system revolted and she wanted to vomit. She hated the curious side of her nature which led her to where she now stood. She wanted to run away, but she was too weak. To give relief to her tension, she wanted to scream, but it would have betrayed her presence. She hated herself, her eyes, and the fading light which should not have allowed her to recognise Wilfred and his uncle's yard-hand, Joseph.

• • •

"There is something about Elizabeth that strikes me as very strange," Alfred said one day. "Have you noticed?"

"I think so," replied Ellin. "She has lost weight, got pale and comparatively shy."

"That is true," said Alfred. "I wonder why?"

"I think she is pregnant."

"Preg....pregnant?"

Ellin looked astonishingly at him. He avoided her gaze.

"What is so funny about that?" Ellin asked sternly.

"Funny? There is nothing funny," Alfred replied, "but it just struck me as strange after all these years."

"Time has nothing to do with it," said Ellin. "A child should be the ambition of every married couple; and the longer they are deprived, if we may so call it, the greater the enthusiasm should be when one is forthcoming."

"I guess women are more sentimental about such things," he said dispiritedly.

"Marriage is not one-sided," she told him. "It takes two to make it a success, and the enthusiasm should be the same."

"I guess you are right."

Alfred was greatly perturbed. He wondered if Elizabeth was really pregnant. He hated the very thought of it. Pregnancy would reveal the true intimacy of their frequent visits to the beach. Such a revelation could be extremely dangerous. Until then, he did not realise that the interval between their last clandestine meeting had been so long; that she had been avoiding him. He could not bring himself to believe that it was deliberate.

"See that you don't breed me," she told him on one occasion. "Pregnancy would betray us. Peter is not impotent, but he is incapable of fatherhood. He was told so by his physician in England. He still has the ability to perform the sex act," she laughed.

"Successfully?" Alfred asked.

"Now Alfred!" she stormed, "don't add insult to injury."

It was dusk. The sky was dotted with small, black bats which were darting madly about the rapidly approaching night. Peter and Alfred were sitting on a long wooden crib, which was situated under a lofty mahogany tree amidst the beautiful flower garden.

"What is there in your home that interests that boy of mine?" Alfred asked.

"It's my library, I guess," Peter replied.

"He spends more time by you than in his own home."

"I suppose that is true, but before we discuss that, I should like to make a point."

"Go ahead."

"There is something about the way you refer to your son that I do not like. You usually say: "'That boy of mine....my boy'. "Why not say, my son, or my son Stephen."

"What difference would it make?"

"A great deal of difference; and I hope that what I'm going to say now is reminiscent and not informative. The expression 'boy' is belittling, and it could be very dangerous if it is repeatedly expressed in his presence."

"In what way, may I ask?"

"It could destroy a quality which is so very necessary to the character of a man."

"What special quality is that?" Alfred asked with a smile.

"His initiative. A man devoid of such a fine quality can never be successful."

"I don't see how my calling him boy could destroy his initiative."

"You don't even talk to the youngster."

"Did he tell you that?"

"He did not have to tell me. I discovered it on my own."

"How did you?"

"By the little things he so often comes to ask my opinion. If you were there for him, he would never have to come to me. A child should be taught to respect its parents, not to fear them." After a pause he said: "If I were to ask you something would you be annoyed?"

"The funny thing about you is this," said Alfred, "you sometimes start a subject which annoys me; but I am so enlightened by the time you have concluded, that I forget how annoyed I really was. So .... go ahead."

"Did you ever sit and have a good chat with Stephen?"

"About what?"

"The kind of course he would like to pursue after school."

"No."

"Why not?"

"Because there could be only one course."

"What is that?"

"Agriculture."

"But suppose he wanted to study a profession .... medicine, law, theology or engineering?"

"There are less headaches and more money in agriculture than in any of the professions you've called."

"That may be true, but will earning money make him happy?"

"I don't see why it shouldn't."

"Isn't my case a good enough example of that sort of thing?"

"Your case?" Alfred asked concernedly. "What do you mean?"

"You forget too quickly, Alfred. As a youngster I wanted to take up writing."

"Did he tell you that he wants to be an author?"

"No .... we've never had a discussion of this sort."

"Then why have you brought it to me?"

"Because I think he deserves the right to his choice; and if he is given such an opportunity, he will realise ever so slightly that less dictatorship exists than he really thought, and therefore venture into the world with less resentment in his mind."

"But why would it be likely for him to carry resentment into the world if he is deprived of this right?"

"Because there is a natural tendency to resent tyranny."

It was well after midnight, and Peter was still awake. He was lying flat on his back. His eyes were wide open. In a room that was lit only by the light from the twinkling stars as they shone through the half-opened sash windows. Peter stared at the white tester which seemed to be a dark blue in the dimness of the room. His feet were crossed at the ankles and his blond head was resting on the palm of his hands. He was thoughtful - thoughtful of the restlessness of his wife; the woman who was lying a little more than an arm's length away. He was perturbed by her restlessness, but he said nothing - nothing as he had said in weeks now. He was not in the least surprised when he heard his name called. It was just above a whisper, not meant to disturb a possible sleeper.

"Yes," Peter answered with matching softness.

"I feel awful," she said, sitting up in bed.

Peter reached for the switch. He snapped on the light. He scrambled hurriedly across the heavily embroidered bedspread and sat at her side.

"I feel awful," she repeated, throwing her arms around his neck and resting her head against his chest. It was warm and comforting. She could hear the mild rhythmical beat of his heart. It was soothing to her ears. It was a long time since she last heard those familiar sounds. In an effort to shut out the very recent past she closed her eyes; but she only succeeded in blotting out the light. She saw a defeated Peter sitting on the edge of his reclining chair with his face buried in his hands. She heard the quickening of her own heartbeat, her hurried steps as she raced across the room, the soft thud of her knees on the wooden floor as she fell before him. "Peter!" she exclaimed; and a hand reached out and touched his shoulder. "What is it?" she asked repeatedly. His eyes were frightening and his voice was like the roar of a ferocious beast when he said: 'This.... explain this .... you cheating son-of-a....' as suddenly as his fist exploded against the side of her head, she recoiled from his embrace.

"No! no!" she shouted.

Peter swiftly recaptured her. "What's the matter, Liz?" he cried, patting her back tenderly. "Tell me."

"I....I'm afraid."

"You don't need to be," he said reassuringly. "I'm here with you."

"Peter," she whispered against his chest, "sometimes my heart beats so rapidly that I feel it would burst; then another time it is so week that I feel as though I'm going to die."

"Do you want me to call a doctor?"

"No."

"Why not?"

"In the morning I...."

"You may feel worse during the night," he interrupted.

"I hardly will," she said.

"Why don't you take a shot of brandy?" he asked. "It may settle your nerves."

"Thank you."

"No! no! don't leave me," she begged.

"I'll be back in a minute," he told her.

"No, I'm afraid."

"All right."

He held open her housecoat. She went into it and tied the band around her slim waist. He dressed himself in his own robe and supported her down the steps. Peter poured her a large brandy and helped himself to a small one. "That should make you feel better," he told her after they had the drink.

"I do hope so," she said, "because I can't sleep."

"Why don't you take another?"

"No, that one should be enough."

Peter supported her up the stairway and led her to bed.

"Let me rest on your arm, Pete," she whispered, when the room was again lit only by the stars from without. "I feel chilly."

"You are cold," he said, as she drew close to him. "Let me cover you with a blanket." She was silent. She did not release his arm. She needed no blanket. She wanted him; the warmth of his body and his love. And while time passed he could feel his arm slowly moistened by tears, and her frail body shook ever so slightly until she fell asleep. And while she slept comfortably in his embrace, a million and one things raced uncontrollably through his mind.

"I'd rather go to the doctor," said Elizabeth, when they had taken breakfast.

"Why?" asked Peter. "It would be more convenient for you if the doctor came here."

"I know that," said Elizabeth, "but I'm not decrepit. To my mind, a doctor in a house tells a real sick story .... a story that I am not prepared to tell."

"Should I phone and make an appointment?"

"You could."

"But suppose you can't get an appointment today?"

"Tomorrow will do just as well."

"I hope not; you may get sick on me tonight."

Peter went to the telephone. He briskly turned the little black handle which jutted out the side of the instrument against the wall, and immediately came the soft tingle of a bell. He placed to his ear the short black earpiece with its long cord which disappeared in the other side of the instrument.

He listened attentively. "Good morning, exchange," he said, in the black, horn-shaped mouthpiece which protruded from the front of the instrument, "Give me 4859, please....Good morning, Doctor Watson....this is Peter Barrow...I would like to make an appointment....Ha, ha, ha,....No, not me....it's the wife....I'd never bring her to you if I knew....not any smarter than you are. Do....the whole needs no physician, says the Good Book....how soon?....that'll be grand....I should be able to make it....thank you ever so much, Doc."

Elizabeth was standing just a short distance away when Peter replaced the earpiece on its tiny hook, and turned the little handle to produce the tinkle of the bell, which notified the Telephone Exchange that he was finished with his connection. "We have one hour and a half to get to the doctor's office," he told her. "Do you think you can make it?"

"Of course I can make it," she answered confidently, "with time to spare."

"Then I'll get the coachman to...."

"No you're not," she interrupted. "You are taking me." He looked over his shoulder at her, smiled, and went to the back door and gave the order to have the animal harnessed and attached to the small buggy.

Doctor Watson was standing in the doorway of his waiting room when the buggy came to a halt. His white, drillsuit was spotlessly clean. Except for a smudge across the tip of his right shoe where it seemed to have been crushed, they were as white as milk. A coarse, goldlinked chain stretched across his fat stomach to secure the large gold-cased watch, which was kept in the pocket of his white waistcoat. His hair was blonde and thinnish at the top of his big head. His grey eyes were warm and friendly when he said: "Come into my parlour, said the fly to the spider."

"I know you have purposely misquoted it," said Peter, as he

rested a gentle hand on Elizabeth's shoulder and accompanied her into the office, "because it makes you feel less guilty." Elizabeth eyed Peter narrowly.

"That is a very dirty thing to say," she challenged, "under the immediate circumstances."

"I don't believe what he said is any cleaner than what I've said," Peter told her, "under the immediate circumstances." They all laughed heartily.

"Under the immediate circumstances," said Dr. Watson, shaking the bottle of mixture he compounded after he had given Elizabeth a thorough examination. "This should assist greatly to the restoration of your physical health."

"I sincerely hope so, Doctor," she replied.

"Carefully follow the instructions on the label," he said, "and eat and drink as much as possible."

"Very well, Doc," she said.

"Why did you say the medicine should cure her physical health?" Peter asked. "Do you know of other cures?"

"Peter, why are you so argumentative?" Elizabeth asked.

"I haven't had an argument in a long time now," Dr. Watson interjected, "I could do with one."

They were all sitting in the office; and since there were no patients in the waiting-room, the doctor had no need to hurry.

"Yes, Peter," he answered, "the mental and the spiritual."

"It is strange," said Peter, "but few people seem to think of a racial cure."

"I'm sorry to say," said Dr. Watson, "there isn't such a thing."

"You are not serious, are you?"

"Of course I am."

"I'm going to leave a few questions for you to ponder in your mind."

"Why can't I answer them now?"

"I don't want you to .... I want you to think carefully on them."

"I will."

"First," Peter said, "Do you believe in God? Is there a place or state of being called Heaven? Can man black and white, attain this place or state of being called Heaven? Can man, with an impure heart, enter the Kingdom of Heaven?" he walked slowly out of the room. "Think on them," he said, as he assisted Elizabeth on to the buggy. "You have a lifetime to do so."

"Goodbye, Doctor," said Elizabeth, as the buggy rolled away.

"Bye," he returned.

They had only travelled a short distance when Elizabeth took hold of the reins and tugged the animal into a slow, sickly pace. "We don't need to hurry," she said. "The work in the field and in the house will be taken care of. The doctor said I should go easy, don't you remember?"

"The doctor didn't mean this sort of easy," Peter told her. "You are not active in this case."

The sun was hot, and there was little breeze to minimise its burning effect. The clouds, as if to avoid the scorching rays of the sun, had retired to the outer brim of the blue dome of the sky.

"Hey! look you master and missus," said Dorothy. "They like they went out." Irine looked up. She said nothing. She continued with her work.

"I wonder where she went," Dorothy went on. "She mus' be went to de doctor, 'cause she lookin' very pale and tin dese days. This time she wid chile for me master. De only body who en know dat he does live wid she is she husband."

"That red rag you got in your mouth," Irine said warningly, "goin' cause you uh lot uh trouble."

• • •

181

Ellin was standing at the entrance to the driveway when Peter pulled the animal to a halt. Elizabeth stepped down and he drove around to the backyard where the yard-hand took over.

"At least you could have told me that you were going to the doctor," said Ellin.

"I didn't have enough time," said Elizabeth. "I had a very horrible experience last night, so Peter decided to take me to the doctor. This morning Peter made the appointment, and we had only an hour and a half to get there."

"Did....did he give you medicine?"

"Yes. Peter has it."

"Did....did....what did he say was wrong?" Ellin wanted to find out if her friend was pregnant; but she was afraid to ask.

"He didn't say," Elizabeth answered. "After the examination he gave the medicine and told me to take it easy."

As they spoke, they walked slowly and entered the house by way of the back. When they passed the kitchen the cook said: "You didn't tell me what to prepare for lunch, mistress."

"I could chill some butter milk, scramble some eggs and...."

"You fix up something, Cookie," Elizabeth interrupted, "and send in enough for three."

"Very well, mistress."

Minutes later they were served a lunch of buttered bread, scrambled eggs, chilled butter-milk and full ripe bananas.

"You certainly leave things to the discretion of your servants," Ellin said.

"And they prove efficient," Elizabeth returned proudly. "They are the servants you advised me to hire years ago; don't you remember?"

"I do. But I did a better job for you than I did for myself. My servants wouldn't take the slightest bit of liberty on any matter. The furniture would remain in the same order from year to year if I didn't suggest to the maid that the arrangement should be changed. Sometimes it makes me mad like hell."

"You shouldn't be angry with them," Peter said calmly. "Alfred's behaviour to you is not at all pleasant in the presence of the servants; and silly as you may think they are, they very well realise what kind of treatment they would get."

"Peter, I never thought of that," Ellin said genuinely. "You seem to know all the answers."

"Not really," he said.

As prescribed, Elizabeth took the first dose of medicine the following morning. Peter reminded her that the medicine was to be taken first thing in the morning and on retiring; but when night came, he found that he was faced with the task of reminding her again. When three days had passed and her memory showed no sign of improvement, Peter got a notion that it was not a lack of memory on her part, but a scheme to solicit his attention.

"What's the matter with your brains?" Peter asked her on the morning of the fourth day. "The doctor prescribed that medicine for you, can't you remember to take it?" After that, he never had to remind her again.

When Elizabeth had taken three bottles of medicine in a corresponding number of weeks, Dr. Watson said: "Against my better judgment, I was hoping that the medicine would have performed a miracle; it has not been performed, and I'm not surprised."

"Why did you say that?" Peter asked.

"I know that medicine can't cure your wife," Dr. Watson answered calmly. "It has built up her resistance somewhat, but the lack of resistance is not the main factor of her troubles. She is a worried woman. Her mind is upset."

Elizabeth made a sudden gasp. Peter and Watson were

startled by the sound; and she was conscious of her own betrayal. During the silence that followed, they exchanged wondering glances.

"Have I said something wrong?" Dr. Watson asked. There was no reply. "My dear child," he went on in a fatherly tone, "those of us who know will tell you that a disturbed mind is more destructive than tuberculosis. The latter seeps slowly into the body and destroys it; while under normal circumstances, the former does not actually destroy the body, but tortures it until death. I could lecture for the rest of the day on the dangers of a habitual worrier," he said after a pause, "if I didn't have other patients to attend."

"Why do you assume that my mind is upset, Doctor?" Elizabeth asked.

"It is not an assumption," he answered, "you are in perfect health, and you betrayed yourself when I suggested it. My advice is a change of scenery for a couple of weeks of absolute rest; and last but not least, a truthful discussion on the subject that is bothering you."

"Thanks for the advice, Doctor," said Elizabeth, as she went through the door. "I'll try to carry out your instructions as closely as possible."

"If you do," said Dr. Watson, "it will pay off hansomely."

Elizabeth was reading by the light of the setting sun through an opened window when Stephen strode briskly into the room and stood over her.

"That isn't fair," he challenged childishly.

"What isn't fair?" Elizabeth asked, a note of concern in her tone.

"Two days ago you made plans to spend your vacation at the bay house," said he, "and today you've decided to go to France."

"Who told you that already?"

"I heard Mama and Pappa talking about it."

"Alfred and Ellin talk too much."

"Did you intend to keep it a secret from me?"

"Not really."

"Oh! Elizabeth," he cried, "why have you got to go so far? Couldn't you go where you'd formerly planned?"

She stood up; she dropped the book in the chair and took hold of his small hands.

"Stephen," she said sweetly, "I want to see who remains of my family, and I think this is a good opportunity."

"Do you mean that some of them have died since you were here?"

She nodded. "My father is ill," she said softly, "and I'd ever so much like to see him before he dies."

"Ooooh! I'm very sorry," he cried, his shiny, brown eyes dimmed by approaching tears. "I'm going to miss you."

"Much?"

"Very much."

"I'm going to miss you too, Stephen," she said tenderly. The tears rolled down his cheeks and fell onto the long sleeves of his faded, blue shirt.

"There," she said, putting her arms around his shoulders and drawing him close, "you don't need to cry."

He rested his head against her bosom. "I am surprised by your reaction to my going away," she went on. "I didn't know you cared so much. You always showered your attention on Peter. I often...."

"I was attracted to Peter," Stephen interrupted, "his fatherly understanding, his books, and his willingness to explain anything I'd read and did not quite understand; but all along I was secretly adoring you .... your girlish attitude appealed to my childish mind." And while he spoke, the tears rolled down his lean cheeks to mingle with her blouse and caress the softness of her breast. To her, this was the strangest of all sensations.

Never was her bosom chilled by a child's sorrowful tears. They started a revelation in her metabolism, and thereafter her womb yearned to give forth its own fruit.

Stephen's head shot up suddenly. The moisture among his sleek, brown hair told him that he was not alone in his bereavement.

"Why are you crying?" he asked, looking into her tear-filled eyes.

"I can scarcely imagine how the years have flown," she said ignoring his question. "When I came to the island you were just a little boy."

She replaced his head against her bosom and held it there. Stephen was astonished by the quantity of moisture he had deposited on Elizabeth's blouse, and the wide area over which it had spread; but the warm, affectionate hand on the one side of his cheek compensated adequately for the icy, loathful chill on the other. Oddly enough, they blended harmoniously to paint an indelible picture on his mind .... a picture weird, but strangely beautiful.

"When are you leaving?" he asked.

"I don't know," she answered, "I'm going to the shipping office tomorrow and book my passage."

"How long do you plan to remain there?"

"About three months."

"Three months?" Stephen asked. It was almost a shout. "That's awfully long." He added. "Don't you think so?"

"No, Stephen," she answered. She held him by the shoulders at arm's length and looked into his eyes. They were free from tears; and so were her own. "Three months will be gone before you know it," she went on, "and I'll be back to share openly of your secret adoration." She took hold of his wrist and playfully clapped his hands together. It was childish, and they laughed. A warm, and throaty chuckle. "Be a good boy," she said, "and don't cry any more."

"I'll try," he said. He slipped his hands from her gentle grasp and went hastily out of the room.

"I have one week to prepare to catch the boat," Elizabeth explained when she returned from the city. "The sooner the better."

"Why?" Alfred asked eagerly. He was suspicious. It annoyed him. He wanted to find out if Elizabeth was really pregnant; but this was not the occasion to do so. It was not convenient. He watched her closely for a sign of some sort. He got none. This was the first time during the long weeks of her avoiding him that he was able to ask so bold a question, but he got no reply.

"Don't you think so?" she asked.
He did not answer. His mind was too muddled to think of a justifiable reason. To his mind, there was only one. It haunted him.

"I don't see why you should be in such a hurry," Ellin said.

"You don't eh?" Elizabeth asked. "You wouldn't think of it. I'm not taking much clothing," she said quickly. "Just a few dresses to change on the voyage; but I want some rum, and a good collection of souvenirs."

"I'll go to town and help you select some of the things you need," Ellin said.

"That'll be grand," Elizabeth said. "By the way," she went on hurriedly, "where is Stephen?"

"As usual," said Ellin, "when he is away from school he is at your house."

"Good," said Elizabeth, going towards the door, "I can't allow anyone to give him the news. I'll give it to him myself."

Peter and Stephen were sitting in the study when Elizabeth knocked softly and opened the door. "I'm back," she said cheerfully.

Stephen got up and rushed to her. "When are you leaving?" he asked. She told them of the proceedings at the shipping agents and the date she was expected to sail. Stephen suddenly grew sad; but she cheered him with a hug and a pleasant smile. "The sooner I leave," she told them, "the sooner I'll return."

Elizabeth had only a few days to prepare for her trip; but they were cold, listless and devoid of the zestful activity which usually went with the preparation for a long desired visit to the old familiar place of her native land.

In honour of Elizabeth, Alfred held a farewell party on the eve of her departure. He invited a few of their mutual friends. He played gramophone records and they all danced to popular tunes. Ice cream, pudding, sandwiches and a variety of drinks were served regularly. Many glasses were raised and toasts of health, success, bon voyage, and speedy return were said. It was a hectic session which ended at midnight with the group singing: "She's a jolly good fellow."

Elizabeth slept soundly for the rest of the night. When she awoke the sun was high in the sky. She looked to her side for Peter, but his place was vacant. Lying on her back she stared unwinkingly at the tester while her thoughts drifted unrestrainedly. It suddenly occurred to her that she had a very important letter to write. She slid hurriedly out of bed; took from her travelling trunk a pen, ink, writing pad and envelope. Then she briskly scribbled across the page, tore it from the pad, folded it neatly, placed it in the envelope and sealed it. She then replaced everything in the trunk and locked it.

The house was noticeably quiet when she went downstairs. There was death-like stillness about its atmosphere. To her, it was nerve-wracking. She hoped to get away from it soon. Except for an occasional glance at each other, she and Peter ate breakfast silently.

• • •

When the servants were assembled, Elizabeth said: "This is the most decisive moment in my life. As you all know," she went on tonelessly, "I am going away today; but before I go, I have come to say goodbye and to ask you all a favour. It is simple and I hope I will not be denied it."

"No mistress," said the cook. "We will be glad to do anything that will make you happy."

"I know that you are willing," said Elizabeth, "and so are the others, but all you do will not make me happy; it will make me feel less worried, but certainly not happy."

"Tell us what you want, mistress," one servant said.

"I've planned to be away for about three months," said Elizabeth, after a long pause. "While I'm away, I want you all to give the master the best of everything .... not only food and drink, but also care and attention. You have always done your work efficiently; keep things that way so that the master will only miss my presence." She took the three parcels from a nearby chair and gave one to each of the servants. "You have material for two dresses," she went on, "and ten dollars .... not as payment for the favour I've just asked, but as a sign of appreciation for your service during the past years."

"We are going to miss you very badly, mistress," said the cook. "You have been such a nice person." She sniffed softly.

"Now, Cookie, please don't start any crying," Elizabeth said sadly, trying to hold back her own tears. "If you do, you may force me to do a little myself. Take care of yourself .... all of you and be kind to the master .... for my sake."

As the two buggies rolled out of the yard, the servants from the two houses hastened to get a final glimpse of Elizabeth who waved a feeble glove-covered hand.

"I'm going to drive with Peter and you," Stephen said.

"But suppose your Mama and Pappa want you to drive with them?" Elizabeth asked.

"What would you do?"

"They would never insist while I'm seated with you." Stephen replied. He did most of the talking along the way. Many of the things he said were humorous, and provoked much laughter. He was glad to be on holiday from school, or he might not have been allowed to accompany her.

"The city has changed a great deal since I came here," said Elizabeth, as they drove pass the railed Public Gardens which formed a parking stand for a limited number of long buses into which the passengers entered from either side, and a few shorter buses which entrance was by way of the rear. "It is fast changing from a horse cart to a motor transport city."

"You are perfectly right," said Peter, as the wheels of the buggy rolled unevenly over the wooden logs of the Chamberlain Bridge. "When you return we'll buy a car and add to the number."

"That will be grand," said Elizabeth, as the buggy came to a halt outside the customs building.

It was not difficult to get a boatman to row them to the side of the 'S.S. LATHENA', which was gracefully riding her anchor in the harbour. When they got to the deck in safety Ellin said: "I didn't know a ship stood so solidly in the sea."

"It isn't always like this," Elizabeth told her. "There are times when the sea plays over where you are standing almost as easily as it does along the hull."

"It is true that I've never travelled," Ellin said doubtfully, "but don't try to fool me with that."

"She isn't fooling," said Peter, "when the sea is really rough the water bangs along there." He pointed to the ship's lofty bridge. Ellin looked questioningly at him.

"That sounds incredible," Alfred said.

"I was thinking how I'd like to sail one day," said Stephen, "but you have scared me."

"You don't need to be scared," Peter assured him. "I've seen it that way often enough, and I'm still here with you."

"That is true," said Stephen, "but cat luck isn't dog luck."

"I have never heard that one before," Peter laughed.

"It just means that your luck isn't mine," Stephen told him.

Peter asked that he and his friends be allowed to accompany his wife to her cabin. His request was granted, and he led them around explaining things as he went along. When the tour of the ship came to an end and they were all standing on the main deck, Ellin said: "I hadn't the faintest idea that a ship was so magnificently laid out."

"I am thrilled by the experience," said Stephen, taking a deep breath. "Even the air is different .... it seems to have a salty freshness about it."

"You should sail, Stephen," said Elizabeth, "even to one of the neighbouring islands .... have you ever sailed, Alfred?"

He did not answer. He was absorbed in deep thought. During the tour of the ship he made his last effort to find out if she was pregnant, if Peter had found out about their clandestine affair and the true cause of her speedy departure. But he failed in his attempt; and now he stood forlorn and bewildered as he rested against the rails.

"Elizabeth is speaking to you," said Ellin, tugging on his jacket sleeve.

"Wh....what did you say?" he stammered.

"Have you ever sailed?" Elizabeth repeated.

"No," he answered. "I never really cared much about sailing, although I like swimming."

"I'm sorry that Wilfred and Hilda couldn't come to see you off," said Ellin, "they have missed a treat."

The ship's horn sounded its pre-sailing blast, which indicated that all visitors should go ashore. Elizabeth threw her arms around Stephen's shoulders and drew him close. She kissed his forehead and said: "Be a good boy until I return."

"And you," said Stephen, "take care of yourself."

Alfred shook her hand and kissed the back of it. "Be good," he said.

"Thank you."

"Have a good trip," said Ellin, as they hugged and kissed each other's cheeks.

Peter was gazing at the crimson glow of the sinking sun. When he turned around Elizabeth was watching him. For a long time they stared silently at each other. Then, with the swiftness of a flash of lightning they leaped into a vice-like embrace. They buried their faces about the shoulder and neck of each other.

'Oh, my God!' Elizabeth thought to herself, 'why did you allow me to be so unjust to Peter .... a man of such fine qualities .... a man who has trusted me without limitation. The few moments of thrill can in no way compensate for the quality of anguish I am now suffering. If this is the way women must suffer for their unfaithfulness, please, dear God, hear my prayer and show them before they transgress, some visual sign which will remind them of their marriage vow, and their duty to keep it. Peter, I love you .... not now, I have always loved you. You who have always been so kind, noble and understanding. You who have never tried to exercise your authority to restrict my activity, but have always left me to decide for myself what is right from wrong. Peter, why did you leave me to come to this horrible little island?' And while she lamented silently, her tears, as though propelled by some mechanical force, rolled swiftly from her cheeks, to Peter's jacket and onto the ship's deck. With one desperate action Elizabeth tore herself from Peter's embrace and ran unheedingly along the companionway and vanished behind a door. Peter's arms remained outstretched for a brief moment before they fell listlessly to his side. For a fleeting instant, he supported himself against the rails before he turned slowly and led his friends down the gangway and into the waiting rowboat.

'Oh, Liz' Peter said to himself, 'why have you done this terrible thing to me? At least you could have destroyed that letter.'

"Uh hear that you master wife gone 'way today," said Dorothy, "you hear?"

"Yes," Irine replied.

They were journeying wearily homewards after a hard day's work in the field.

"You did hear before today?" Dorothy asked.

"Yes," Irine replied. "I did hear since yesterda'."

"An' you didn't tell me," Dorothy retorted. "You is a fine one .... an' call yourself a friend."

"I en got no time to mind no body business. I does leave it de same place uh hear it."

"She gone 'way very sudden," said Dorothy. "Uh wonder what run she? This time she husband catch she wid she slackness an' now she running 'way."

"You always thinking evil 'bout people," Irine protested. "I can't understand why."

"I know what happen with you," Dorothy said angrily." 'Cause dese people white you think they better than we."

"I don' think so," Irine remonstrated, "but I would like you to mind your own business .... de sun was too hot today," she added quickly, "an' de few cents uh work for does spen' like butter 'gainst de sun."

"Why you don't get a job for your son David?" asked Dorothy. "The few cents 'e work for would help."

"David!" she exclaimed remorsefully. "You would never hear 'e name ring out in no farm ground. David mus' learn a trade, soul."

Alfred was greatly surprised when three months had passed

and no letters or cables were received from Elizabeth. "I believe I'd go crazy," he said one evening while they were all sitting together, "if Ellin had gone away and all this time had passed without a word from her."

"You would, eh?" said Peter, taking from his pocket an envelope. It had neither address nor stamp. He opened the flap and removed the folded sheet of paper. "Do you care to read this?" he asked, extending the note to Alfred, "or should I read it for you?"

"You read it," Alfred replied.

Peter unfolded the paper. To make sure that he was not wasting his time, he looked at Alfred, Ellin, Hilda and Wilfred; they were all looking eagerly at him.

'My Dear Peter,'

he began. *'Words cannot express my suffering since the discovery of my unfaithfulness …. a sin, for which I will never be able to summon enough courage to ask forgiveness. Peter, grievous as it is, I can do nothing but admit your accusation. I have been dishonest. I have fallen from the esteem of a wife; and I now regard myself no more than a servant who does not deserve the hire of a master as virtuous as you are. It was your own friend who contributed to the destruction of your happy home: but he alone should not be blamed. I am equally guilty. My guilt is only a small contribution to my anguish; but to live unnoticed in a house where I was once the idol is more than I can bear. Peter, I am going away and you will never see me again. I know that you are obsessed with the desire to eradicate the practice of a very irrational racial pattern, and therefore you will not follow me. You will not suffer because of your confidence in God's power to sustain you to the last. Peter, I am no good for you; but pray for me, so that I may meet you on the last day. God bless you.*

Elizabeth.'

• • •

"Look! look!" Wilfred shouted. "Uncle has fainted. I'll get the smelling salts."

"Bring the bay rum, too," Hilda said. From Alfred's pocket she yanked his kerchief. She soaked it with bay rum and folded it across his forehead, while Wilfred held the phial of smelling salts to his nostrils. At first he was motionless, but as the strength from the phial assailed his nostrils, his head shifted to avoid it.

"What....what is...what happened?" he stammered faintly. "I remember you were reading the letter."

"Yes," Peter replied, "but we'll talk about it another time."

"Let me sit in the rocker," said Alfred, when he felt able to walk. "I want to be quiet for a while." Supporting him by the arm, Peter and Wilfred led him to the chair.

Ellin was without strength to offer assistance to her weakened husband. Like him, the letter shocked her but to a lesser degree; but his fainting drained her energy. She burst into a frightful fit of perspiration; and Hilda had to give her a kerchief, dampened with bay rum to smell.

"When did you discover this letter?" asked Ellin, when she regained composure and was somewhat refreshed by the breeze through the opened windows.

"On the night Elizabeth sailed," Peter replied calmly. "She had placed it where I was most likely to find it."

"If I may ask," Ellin said cautiously, "where was that?"

"Under the Bible," he replied. "Liz knew that I'd be supposed to find it there because I read my Bible nightly."

"Tell me Peter," said Ellin, "what was your reaction when you read it?"

"Certainly not like ...." he indicated Alfred, who was rocking slowly with his eyes closed and his head resting on the tall back of the chair.

"I was shocked," he went on, "but...."

"But what?"

"I got over it."

Hilda and Wilfred were silent, but they listened attentively.

"Peter, you surprise me," Ellin said.

At another corner of the room Alfred was sitting silently. From his position, he seemed to be utterly relaxed; but he was not. He was thoughtful .... thoughtful of the embarrassing situation in which he now found himself. In his mind, there was an uncontrollable state of chaos .... a state for which Elizabeth was to blame. 'Oh! Elizabeth,' he cried to himself, 'why did you so foolishly admit to our clandestine affair? Was it the pressure Peter exerted against you that drove you to admission? Or was pregnancy responsible? In any case you should have done a better job rather than leave me with my back against the wall. Now that you have admitted, I will have to do the same.' His eyelids felt heavy. 'How can I open them?' he said to himself, 'and look across the room at the man I've grievously wronged .... the man who has trusted me and cared for my child as though it was his own son. What I have done is the most ungrateful act in the world .... an act for which death should be the penalty. I will be a man and admit .... don't be a fool,' he thought after a pause. 'How can you admit to an affair with Elizabeth when such an admission could destroy your own marriage? Have you gone mad? .... but you have destroyed your friend's marriage. Was his marriage any less sacred than your own? .... but you can't deny the affair to which Elizabeth has admitted.' He saw Ellin's contorted features, her hasty movements as she packed her personal belongings in preparation to leave him. Unlike Peter, he saw himself less able to face the problems of life alone, and finally committing suicide. "Peter," he said, interrupting a conversation, "I want to say something to you."

"Then say it," Peter urged.

There was an interval of death-like silence before he said: "I am ever so sorry for what has happened to you .... and the childish way I have reacted .... I couldn't...."

"You don't need to worry," Peter interrupted. "Things like that help to make life interesting. There was ...." Alfred was glad that Peter had taken on an easy side to talking; it relieved him of the responsibility .... a responsibility, for which he now felt mentally and physically inadequate.

"And besides, I don't think you should worry unduly," Peter was saying. "This thing occurred when she was left alone in England."

"In England?" asked Ellin. "I thought ...."

"I discovered an old letter," Peter interrupted.

'And to think that I almost destroyed my marriage and a good friendship,' Alfred said to himself, 'all because of a morbid suspicion.'

"Elizabeth was an asset to my business," said Peter. "She kept books superbly. Now that she is gone, I'm going to need some help."

"What do you intend to do?" Alfred asked.

"When I go to town tomorrow, I'm going to put an ad in the papers."

"That is a splendid idea," said Alfred. "You will get more than enough applicants to choose from."

Before leaving for work, Irine was making her home tidy. She was sweeping the leaves and bits of paper into a heap in front of the door. "Samuel," she called out to her husband, "if yuh want to see uh fly in milk look out hay."

Samuel came hurriedly around the hut and stood next to her. There was a dark skinned, medium built man approaching. He was wearing a suit of white, matching canvas shoes, white shirt, a faded, blue and white tie and a creamy, straw hat.

"Good morning," said the young man, as he drew near.

"Good morning," Irine replied.

"I am looking for a gentleman by the name of Mr. Peter

Barrow," said the young man.

"Can you direct me to his home?"

"Y..e..s," Irine hesitated.

The young man noticed. He said: "I am going to apply for a job."

"Uh job?" Irine asked.

"Yes," replied the young man. "A job as overseer."

"Overseer!" Irine exclaimed. "In all me born days," she went on quickly, "I never hear 'bout a black overseer."

The young man winced. "But yuh don't think it too early to go to de gentleman?"

"I know it is early," replied the young man, "but I want to get there before anyone else."

"Go straight down de road," said Irine, indicating with her makeshift broom of withered, cherry brambles, "and de firs' dwelling house you get to is de one. While you on de way, say a prayer an' ask God to help you get de job."

"Thank you," said the young man, turning away. "I will."

"If God be for yuh no man can be against yuh," Irine told him.

" 'E en so black," said Samuel, when the young man was out of earshot. "It is the lot of white clothes 'e wearing."

"Black people should never wear so much white," said Irine, sweeping the stuff onto a piece of tin and dumping it on the heap to which Samuel had applied a lighted match.

"It make them look too black."

"Good morning, Sir," the young man said politely as he went cautiously up the garden path towards the blonde-haired gentleman who was leisurely shifting his attention from one species of rose to another.

"Good morning, son," said the blonde-haired gentleman, in a soft, fatherly tone. "What can I do for you?"

"Are .... are you Mr. Barrow?" he asked timidly.

"Yes," Peter replied, looking him over. "I am."

"I have come to see you in connection with the job advertised in last Saturday's paper," he said hurriedly. He breathed deeply and tried to calm himself.

"Ooooh!" said Peter. "Have you come about that job? Do you think you are capable? Have you ever worked in that capacity before?"

The young man was defeated. He could answer only one question .... the first; and to his mind, that was not good enough.

"Have you?" Peter repeated.

"No .... no, Sir," he stammered defensively, "but a fellow has got to start with the first. If I get this job I'd be able to say yes the next time I get an interview, Sir." His voice was charged with desperation. Peter heard and liked it; but he gave no visual sign of his recognition.

"Have a seat," said Peter, indicating a chair under the porch. "I'll be with you in a minute."

"Thank you, Sir," he replied. He climbed the steps and sat with his hat in his hand.

Minutes later he was sitting across from Peter who sat at a small desk.

"What is your name?" Peter asked.

"My name is Norman Brandford, Sir."

Peter wrote in his note book. "Where do you live?"

"Ellerton, St. George, Sir."

"Have you got a family?"

"Yes, Sir," Norman replied. "I am married and we have a son, Sir."

"I would like to give you this job," said Peter, "But ...."

"I'd be awfully glad Sir," Norman interrupted. "Excuse me, Sir," he added quickly.

"But what are your qualifications?"

"Sir, I passed from seventh standard at the age of twelve," Norman explained. "I was extremely brilliant, especially in figures, Sir."

"Did you have a secondary education?"

"Me, Sir?" Norman asked in wonder. "Very few people like me get a chance to go to a secondary school, Sir."

"What do you mean, 'like me'?"

"People with dark skins, Sir."

"I see," Peter said disdainfully. "It is necessary to know a good amount of arithmetic for this job," he went on after a pause. "Suppose I tried your ability?"

"I hope you do, Sir," said Norman, his large, black eyes shining with hopeful anticipation.

"Good," said Peter. "I'll get some material."

"This is undoubtedly good," said Peter, when he thoroughly examined Norman's test papers, "but this alone does not qualify you for the job. The qualifications are strictly personal and confidential .... are you willing to hear the terms?"

"Yes, Sir," Norman replied.

When Peter explained all he expected from his employee, he added: "It is a big proposition, I know. One that requires a great deal of consideration; so I am not expecting you to decide anything now. You can talk it over with your wife. Consider the pros and cons and write and let me know your decision."

"Thank you very much, Sir."

The following evening Peter received a letter. It read:

My Dear Sir,

After a very lengthy discussion on the possible prospects your job offers, my wife and I have decided to accept and make a try of your generous proposal
I am,

Respectfully yours,

Norman Brandford

• • •

Peter felt elated. He smiled with himself. His plans were slowly taking shape. He reached for his pen and wrote:

Dear Mr. Brandford,

I am ever so glad that you have found it convenient to accept my offer. The house is already furnished; but if you have anything which you treasure and want to keep, you have my permission to bring it along. You can make all arrangements necessary and prepare to move in on the last day of this month

Yours

P. Barrow

The last rays of the sun were still lingering in the sky when the mule-drawn cart, which bore the Brandfords and the chosen pieces of their personal belongings, rolled to a halt. Attracted by the sound, Peter hastened to snap on the light which lit up the yard.

"I am awfully sorry to be so late, Sir," said Norman apologetically. "We had some difficulty along the way, Sir."

"Son, life is made up of bitter and sweet," said Peter, releasing the bolted half of the door which he threw open. "We should learn to accept both. Put your things here," he added quickly, indicating a place. "You can decide tomorrow where is best suited for them."

"Thank you, Sir."

After the introduction, during which Norman was extremely formal, Peter said: "I am one of the people who like to begin at the beginning. If we are to live in this house like one family, it is absolutely necessary to inculcate a feeling of congeniality. To promote this, we must eradicate the very thought of the inferiority and the superiority complex, and learn to see each other as human beings who possess no more than a greater or lesser degree of ability, which can be used for good or ill. From this very moment," he went on quickly, "I will be calling you Norman, your wife Cecilia and your son Clarence. You all will call me Peter."

Norman was surprised. He said: "But Mr ....."

"But nothing," Peter interrupted. "You have already condescended to a far more unreasonable request; and to this you will. I insist."

"Well," Norman said resignedly, shrugging his broad shoulders, "if this is the way you want it, we'll have to accept."

Peter showed the Brandfords the interior of the house. They were all astonished by his warm hospitality. When the tour ended he said: "I have asked the servants, who are already informed that you will be taking up abode here, to be as co-operative as they have been in the past; a request for which I see no reason to doubt its possibility. But of course, if we're looking for co-operation, we must learn to be equally co-operative."

When they were ready to take breakfast on the following morning, Peter said: "Since I became master of my own home, it has been my custom to sit at the head of the table and say Grace before meals. I will continue to do so while I am able. When I'm not able, please promise that you will do the same."

"I promise," Norman said.

Peter said grace and they ate in pleasant family style. When breakfast was over, Peter told them that it was the coachman's Sunday off, but if they wanted to go to church the buggies were at their disposal.

"Thank you very much," said Norman, "but I had no intention of going to church today. In the first place, I am in a strange district and I don't know my way around; and secondly, our things are all topsy-turvy. Thanks, just the same."

Peter spent the greater part of the day in his room. He left it only when he was summoned to table, where he spoke quite freely during meals and for a short while after.

"In order that you may realise the free access to this house," Peter said on one occasion, "I have absented myself. I don't want you to catch me watching you at any time because you may misunderstand my gaze."

The sun was warm and golden, and the breezes soft and gentle. "I am riding to the field this morning," said Peter, immediately after breakfast. "I won't be gone long. When I return we'll get down to the method of book-keeping."

"Cou .... couldn't I go to the field with you?" Norman asked shyly. "I can ride."

"Sitting on a horse's back isn't riding, son," Peter returned. "I want you to look just right when you go riding. I have a very tame animal ...." He broke off. He was making reference to the animal Elizabeth used to ride. He remembered her. He wondered if she was still alive. Where she was? What she looked like? "I have a very tame animal in the pen," he continued. "You can practise riding all around the yard this evening."

"That is very kind of you," Norman said.

"So you have a new servant," said Alfred humorously. "I saw her in the garden this morning."

"She isn't a servant," Peter replied. "She is the overseer's wife."

"I'm speaking about a black woman," Alfred laughed; "the one I saw picking roses this morning."

"I didn't see her picking any," said Peter, "but I guess it's the same person .... the overseer's wife."

"You don't really mean wife," said Alfred, frowning slightly.

"You mean kept-woman."

"I mean all I've said."

"What colour is the overseer?"

"Black."

"Black?"

"Black."

"I don't believe you."

"Well," said Peter, shrugging his shoulders, "I can tell you the truth, but I can't make you believe it."

Alfred's face twisted into a serious grin. "Ellin," he called. It was almost a shout. She quickly appeared in the doorway.

"What is it?" she asked concernedly.

"This man here seems to be going off his head," Alfred stormed. "He's been telling me the craziest thing I've ever heard."

"What is it?" she asked, taking a seat on the edge of a chair across from Peter. "Is something wrong?"

"Not as much as I know," Peter replied calmly.

"Then why is he so upset?" Ellin asked.

"Because I told him that I have employed a black overseer."

Ellin was silent. She looked at Alfred. His face was red with rage. She, too, was angry; but she didn't think it proper to express her anger. She wanted to say: 'Alfred, that shouldn't worry you. Peter is a man and he can do what he likes with his estate.' But she dared not say it. She knew what was likely to follow.

"I placed an ad in the papers," Peter went on. "This young man applied and I gave him the job. It was not just another job. It had quite a number of obligations."

"What special obligations does an overseer have to subject himself to?" Alfred demanded.

"Oh! Alfred," Ellin managed softly.

"Ellin, I will explain it to you," Peter said calmly. "I'm no woman," he began after a pause. "Seeing about a house and its decoration is a woman's job; so I have asked the overseer to bring his wife to act in that capacity."

"Do you mean that they are living there?" Alfred wailed. Peter nodded.

"I will have no more of it," said Alfred, and he walked hurriedly out of the room.

Undisturbed by his behaviour, Peter said: "I would not have been able to get one from our group to accept such a miserly job, so I had no alternative."

"But surely you could have hired a housekeeper," Ellin said.

"No," said Peter, shaking his head sadly. "The gossip would be that I am living an immoral life."

Cecilia took her son Clarence to the school across from the village where few of the other children were as neatly clad as he; but he was welcomed by all. After the first three evenings of riding practice, Norman was able to sit in the saddle like an experienced rider. But that was not all; he soon learnt the art of book-keeping, and Peter's masterful technique in agriculture. It was not long before he was given full authority to dictate in the field and pay the workers, while Peter lapsed into a state of restfulness.

Within a few weeks at the school across from the village, where junior pupils were expected to pay one penny per week for school fees, Clarence was progressing admirably. Of course, Stephen was largely responsible for the improvement. He assisted Clarence with his home-work and gave him private tuition. For this, Clarence was extremely grateful; and since it gained him special exemption from one class to another, he felt elated.

"You know something, Peter," said Cecilia one day, "it is almost a year since we have been living here."

"Time has flown," Peter chuckled. "I like the company and comfort you have afforded me."

"Thank you," she said sweetly, her shining black eyes gleaming with appreciation, "but ...."

"Come on, say it," Peter urged.

"I can't say you have given us the cold shoulder," she smiled, "but you spend more time in the company of Stephen and Clarence than you do with us."

"I have often felt that way myself," Norman interjected, "but I have never expressed it."

"The answer is simple," Peter smiled warmly. "I still honestly believe in the old Proverb: *'Train up a child in the way he should go: and when he is old, he will not depart from it.'* Quote: Proverbs 22 v.6.

It was inevitable that he would be asked: "Peter, how are you able to tolerate those people who are living in your house?" Alfred asked one day.

"Tolerance is a rare virtue these days," Peter answered politely, "and to develop it to a high standard is one of man's greatest difficulties; but it can be accomplished. We only have to exercise a little within ourselves."

With no regard for the advice, Alfred said: "Those people can't even converse to any particular standard."

"Have you ever spoken with them?"

"No," he replied. "I mean that type of people."

"At least they understand each other," Peter chided. "Isn't that a standard?"

"What I really mean is," Alfred growled, "they can't converse to our standard."

"That may be true," Peter said sadly, "but it is no fault of their own if they can't."

"Whose fault is it?"

"I hate to say this, but it is no fault of mine." Peter said flatly. "People like you are to blame; people who refuse to give them the education and the opportunity to prove themselves; but it can't remain that way forever."

• • •

Stephen and Clarence became fast friends. Together they spent a great deal of time in Peter's study, where they read and discussed books. Stephen soon discovered that he was teaching Clarence from Peter's books, just as he had been taught by Peter. One day Clarence said: "For some time now I wanted to ask you something, but I was afraid you would get vexed."

"Among the many things I've learnt from Peter," said Stephen proudly, "is to be tolerant; so go straight ahead and ask me."

"Sin .... Since I've been living here," Clarence began timidly, "I've never seen any of your family visit Peter, why is it?"

"I was hoping you would never ask that question." Stephen eyed him narrowly. He was four years Stephen's junior, but tall for his years.

"Why were you?"

"Because the answer isn't very pleasant," Stephen replied sadly, "and due to your immaturity, it may damage our friendship."

"Then you better not tell me."

"It may prove more harmful if I don't tell you and you get to find out."

"Why do you think so?"

"Because you will think that I am like my family and distrust me."

There was a long interval of silence. Breaking it, Stephen calmly said: "I'm going to tell you and leave the rest to providence. My family does not like black people. The only one who does is Hilda."

"Ooooh!" Clarence exclaimed. "I didn't know that people disliked you only because of the colour of your skin. Do black people hate white people because they are white?"

"I once asked Peter the same question, and he said, 'Stephen, people hate each other out of ignorance or being taught to. There is no sensible reason for either. Nine out of every ten blacks hate the white for their financial achievement. Finance is usually the trouble. Here is an example: If a garbage collector is thrifty enough to own a spot of land and a furnished house, he does not worry about the white man's achievement. But the slothful fellow who makes nothing out of life is always envious; not only of the white man, but of his own black brothers as well. Both black and white should remember that there was a time in their life when they could not walk; and therefore learn to live comfortably within the realm of their limitation'."

"If I live to be a father," Clarence firmly said, "I would never sow seeds of discord in the minds of my children."

"That is exactly what I told Peter when he explained it to me, but he said: 'Stephen, unless you ask God to give you the strength, and the courage, and the endurance to stand almost alone and fight against a condition under which you could normally live most comfortably, you would fail miserably'."

"Then I'll ask God." Clarence said resolvedly.

"Peter, do you lock the door to your room at night?" asked Alfred.

"Do you mean before I came here?"

"Before you go to bed."

"No, why should I?"

"Do you sleep comfortably?"

"Yes."

"I don't see how you can," said Alfred. A note of surprise in his voice, "with all those black people sleeping in the house with you."

Peter smiled wryly. He said: "I fail to see how people can be anymore dangerous when they are sleeping than when they are awake. Your servants are black and they are allowed to move about your home. And to make matters worse, they deal with your food. Did you ever stop to consider how risky that is? I suppose your mind is too deeply occupied with hatred for them, to realise the danger you could be in if they were to develop the same amount of hatred for you."

When Peter was gone, Alfred said: "Within the last few weeks Peter has been extremely hostile towards me."

"I don't think he has been," said Ellin. "You have expressed your opinion in connection with various matters and he has expressed his. They differ, that's all."

"You make it sound very pleasant," Alfred snarled, "but if I didn't have something in mind, I would have ordered him out of my house long ago."

"Norman, I am not feeling as young as I used to," said Peter one day. "I am going to take you to town on Friday and have things so arranged that you will be able to deputise in my absence."

"That is a helluva responsibility." Norman said proudly. "Do you think I'm capable?"

"Yes," Peter replied confidently. "I know you are. You have proved yourself time and again."

Alfred's worries worsened at the close of each day, when Peter's long desired visit did not materialise. Due to illness, five weeks had gone by since his last visit. He had been confined to bed by the doctor. Alfred learnt all this from Stephen, who resolved not to speak of Peter's condition unless he was questioned. Alfred was too haughty to ask to be allowed to see his friend.

"H..e..l..l..o, Peter," said Alfred, when he went to answer a knock on the front door. "Come right in. I'm ever so glad to see you. Have a seat. What about your estate? Have you any plans? I was wondering a couple of day ago if we could get together about it. My reason for selling it in the first place was due to the trouble I was getting from my overseers, so I kept no more than I could handle myself; but now that Stephen, an energetic young man has left school, I have to think in terms of his security. For his benefit and to keep strangers out, I would like to re-purchase the estate. My next neighbours may not be as appreciable as you are, you know. I was wondering if I could buy the estate; but have a legal order made, agreeing that I will only assume absolute ownership at your death. It could all be arranged," he concluded.

Peter was silent for a long time. He realised that the improvement of his health had not been questioned .... in his health there was no interest; only in his estate. He wondered how long Alfred had been contemplating the deal. Drying his brow, Peter said: "The idea is quite a ...."

"Will you do it?" Alfred interrupted quickly, as he shot forward to the edge of his cane-bottomed chair to lean towards Peter. "I knew you'd do it. I was almost sure. So much goes for knowing a friend."

There was satisfaction in his tone; the gleam in his eyes and in the restful manner with which he relaxed quietly against the curved back of the chair.

"You got me so mixed up," Peter said reluctantly, "that I don't know whether I should reveal the facts now, or later."

"You don't need to say yes, here and now," said Alfred. "We could decide in a day or two; and for your own convenience, I could have our solicitors come here and have things made right."

"But Alfred, it can't be done that way again."

"Why?"

"In the first place," Peter began cautiously, "I didn't think you would want to live, or own an estate over which a black man had so much authority."

"But they wouldn't be there, or have the authority when I'm owner," Alfred chided.

"There is the danger," said Peter. "I didn't think you would want it; and because I have no relatives....I....I....I gave it to the overseer."

"You gave what?" asked Alfred, leaning forward. "You don't mean the estate, do you?"

Peter nodded.

"Do you really mean that?" Alfred asked, grinding his teeth and making little slits of his eyes.

"Yes," Peter answered.

Alfred sprang to his feet. He hurried to the door. He opened it and moved back. "Get out!" he roared, indicating the door. "Gawd blast you! Get out!"

Peter's eyes widened and his face grew pale as he struggled to regain his mental and physical equilibrium. Slowly he rose and moved towards the door. 'What an out-burst of temper,' he thought to himself, 'from a gray-haired man to his contemporary.'

"Never you cross these doors again!" Alfred shouted vehemently as Peter passed him. "Never in life or death."

Outside, Peter turned around to say something, but Alfred slammed the door with such force, that one of the two small glass panes in the upper panels of the door fell out and smashed. Peter looked at the tiny bits of glass. He raised his gaze whence they came, smiled warily and went slowly home.

At breakfast the following morning, Alfred explained to the family what occurred between Peter and himself.

"I don't see why that should affect you," Hilda said reproachfully. "The estate is Peter's and seeing things from where I am, I think he has the right to do what he likes with it."

"Yes," Alfred growled, "the estate is his. He has the right to do what he likes with it. But what about me? My pride? How do I feel? Imagine a black estate owner .... not only an owner, but also one living next to me .... on my own land. Living and enjoying life like me. Can't you see that is an insult to my manhood?"

"Alfred, a manly person does not allow his pride to precede logic," Hilda threw back, and left the table.

Prior to the school-leaving age of fourteen, Peter made special arrangements with the master of the school to take Clarence in private tuition at an advanced level. This was begun, and as time slid by, Peter watched with much satisfaction the steady mental and physical development of the lad.

Again, Peter took ill. This time his illness was of a more serious nature. Two nurses were employed. One to watch over him by day and the other to watch over him by night.

"He is the most pleasant sick person I ever 'tend to," said the middle-aged, dark-skinned nurse who was assuming duty from her brown-skinned colleague.

"That is true," returned the other, "but he didn't sleep so well last night. I think he is getting weaker."

"He is."

Two days later Dr. Watson was called. He came promptly. Dressed in white from head to foot, he strode hurriedly into the room. Since his last visit a week ago, he was astonished at what he now saw lying on the bed.

"What have you brought me now, Doc?" asked Peter. "The solution for the racial cure or something to cure my physical being?" The doctor was silent.

"If it is a cure for the latter," Peter went on, "you will fail."

"You and your racial cure," the doctor said reproachfully, "why don't you concentrate on something more realistic?"

"That is realistic enough," Peter said confidently, "but neither you nor I will live to see it effected."

"Peter is going to give you the surprise of your life," said the doctor to Norman and Cecilia in an adjoining room. "He is going to talk with you almost to the last."

Cecilia was sad. She asked: "Do you mean ....?"

Dr. Watson nodded.

"Isn't there anything you can do?" she asked. Her voice was just above a whisper.

He shook his head.

A few days later Peter beckoned the nurse to his bed-side.

"Please call .... the mistress," he said.

"Very well, Sir," said the nurse, and she hastened to execute the order.

Seconds later Norman, Cecilia and Clarence stood at the side of the bed and looked down on him. So wasted was his body, that its contour was scarcely evident beneath the white bedspread which covered him to his arm-pits. His two, thin, pajama-clad arms rested at his side. The top of his head was bald, and the blonde hairs on either side were unevenly clipped. Beneath the grotesque appearance of large, sunken eyes and a thin chin of stubby, white bristles, there was a faint smile of contentment. Looking at the nurse in her white uniform, Peter said: "Excuse us, please!"

Cecilia looked at her. She bowed understandingly and made her departure.

"Norman, I want you .... to .... make me a .... promise," said Peter, when the door was closed about them. His voice was low, and his words, although broken by his quick, uneven breathing, were well chosen.

"What is the promise you want me to keep?" Norman asked.

"I want you .... to .... continue .... to pay to those .... dismissed .... old workers .... their .... weekly allowance .... pay them until they die."

"I....I will do that for you," Norman said reluctantly. There was a long interval of silence during which Peter scanned their sad faces. In his own subtle way, he felt sorry for them: sorry, because he knew that when he was dead there would be no end to the ridicule and hatred that would be hurled at them.

"What day .... it is?" Peter asked.

"Thursday," Cecilia answered.

"I am going .... to give .... you .... a Sunday .... funeral," said Peter. "Have you got .... things .... ready?"

Cecilia's face suddenly twisted with grief. Tears rushed down her cheeks. She fell on her knees and took his hand in hers. "Oh Peter!" she sobbed, burying her face in the palm of his cold hand. "Why have you got to go?"

"It is not .... my will," he answered peacefully. "But before .... I go .... I must leave .... a message .... with you." He reached out an unsteady hand to Clarence, who was crying and biting on his lower lip. Clarence took the icy, delicate hand. Peter smiled. His face lit up. And with renewed vigour, he said: *"He that dwelleth in the secret place of the most High shall abide under the shadow of the Almighty. I will say of the Lord, He is my refuge and my fortress: my God; in him will I trust. Surely he shall deliver thee from the snare of the fowler, and from the noisome pestilence. He shall cover thee with his feathers, and under his wings shalt thou trust: his truth shall be thy shield and buckler. Thou shalt not be afraid for the terror by night; nor for the arrow that flieth by day; Nor for the pestilence that walketh in darkness; nor for the destruction that wasteth at noonday. A thousand shall fall at thy side, and ten thousand at thy right hand; but it shall not come nigh thee. Only with thine eyes shalt thou behold and see the reward of the wicked. Because thou hast made the Lord, which is my refuge, even the most High, thy habitation; There shall no evil befall thee, neither shall any plague come nigh the dwelling. For he shall give his angels charge over thee, to keep thee in all thy ways. They shall bear thee up in their hands, lest thou dash thy foot against a stone.*

214

Thou shalt tread upon the lion and adder: the young lion and the dragon shalt thou trample under feet. Because he hath set his love upon me, therefore will I deliver him: I will set him on high, because he hath known my name. He shall call upon me, and I will answer him: I will be with him in trouble; I will deliver him, and honour him. With long life will I satisfy him, and show him my salvation." Quote: Psalm 91-1-16.

But while Peter was speaking, Norman was thoughtful .... thoughtful of himself, his achievement and the method he would employ to improve his estate .... his most treasured possession.

"And now for a final word," said Peter after a pause. "Go forward into the unknown, conscious of the living presence of God."

He never spoke again. He was buried on the following Sunday. Disliked for his way of life, few of his contemporary farmers attended the funeral; but many of the villagers had gone to the church where they mourned his loss. Alfred did not go, nor did he allow anyone from his home to attend the funeral. He was standing at the entrance of his drive-way when the carriage which took Norman and his family to the funeral came rolling by.

"Black filth!" Alfred shouted, as the carriage got abreast of him. He spat at them as they passed. "Black filth!"

Chattel House

THE PASSAGE TO EDEN

PART FOUR

Agust of breeze rushed through the trees just as the sun came peeping out of the water .... a token that a new day was born to this rural village and all the sunny world. Birds in the trees, awakened by the breeze, chirped tunes of prayer as they flipped from bough to bough. It was good to be alive. The sun came slowly over the hill stretching its golden rays like hands farther and farther down the hill and through the trees, assuring more and more birds of the new day and of their duty to join their neighbours in chirping prayers; a way of thanking God for life and nature's goodness; and, like an obedient child stirred by the loving hands of its mother, so responded the birds in the trees to the groping hands of the sun's rays. Down, down, still farther down, until the air was filled with the tunes of various birds - one happy family in accord.

At the foot of the hill stood two formidable stone buildings, whose lands were divided by tall, thorny hedges. Like the birds, the occupants of these buildings were stirred by the rays of the sun; but they were less active in response .... night's slumber still rested heavily upon them and no sign of life could be seen from outside. But farther along the foot of the hill, some distance away, life was evident.

"Irine, your house look real good now it done," said Dorothy. "What size it is?"

"The house is eighteen feet long by ten feet wide. The shed is eighteen by seven, kitchen seven by five and the closet and bath is six by four. Come let me show you inside."

They entered by way of the front panel-door. A partition of beaded boards divided the house. There was a small bamboo table in the centre of the colourful grass mat, which almost covered the area of the wooden floor of the room. A vase of withered roses and a few postcards were on the table. Four three-cornered chairs were evenly spaced about the room. In one corner of the house there was a shelf. Its design seemed to suggest that it was destined to serve no other purpose than to bear the large oil lamp which stood firm in its place with its crystal clear chimney.

"What is de meanin' of all them?" asked Dorothy, pointing.

"Those are my son's books," Irine replied.

"What 'e doin' with all them?" asked Dorothy, "he studyin' to be a liar?"

"No. He didn't have a good education as a boy," said Irine, "so he is trying to improve it. He even teaches me .... and sometimes his father."

"Teach you?" Dorothy laughed. "It near time you look for you grave and you talkin' 'bout 'e teachin' you?"

"One is never too old to do a good thing." said Irine. "Come and let me show you over the place."

Dorothy only got a glimpse of the iron bedstead, when David exclaimed: "Mama, the milk is boiling over!"

"Oh father!" cried Irine, rushing out of the room and into the kitchen where she removed from the burning oil stove a small enamel saucepan which she kept only for the purpose of scalding milk. Over the rack in which the dishes were kept, two larger saucepans were hanging.

"Who paint de place for you?" Dorothy asked.

"David."

"David paint the house all through in and out?" Dorothy asked in astonishment. "I don't know how to believe it."

"I sent him to the painter's trade," said Irine. "Have you forgotten?"

"No. But I didn't think 'e could do such a good job .... and who dis bicycle belong to?"

"David bought it to ride to work."

"Good morning," said David, emerging from the division in the shed which was his room.

"Morning," Dorothy returned.

David sat at the table, drank his milk, ate a few slices of buttered bread and then took off on his bicycle.

"Tch, tch, tch," said Dorothy, shaking her head, "fate was good to you all."

"Not fate," Irine chided, "God ..... and not was, He is good. He will be good to you too, if you allow Him."

"How you mean if I allow Him?"

"When you forsake wrong doing."

"What I don't do nobody nothin'."

"That may be true," Irine said sadly, "the wrong you do is to yourself. You will never get God's blessings while you believe in the fortune-teller. Have you ever noticed that week after week more houses like mine are being built? Can't you see that the village is being transformed? How do you feel when you see all of these nice houses. Don't you think it is about time you get out of that hut?"

"Yes. But you different to me," Dorothy protested. "You got

help. You got David. He is uh man working and bringin' in 'e money. Look, he could stop you from working."

"That is true," said Irine, "but there was the time when I had to provide for him. You never had anyone to supply with food and clothes."

"I too old to worry 'bout house now," Dorothy said defeatedly. "I don't got too long to live now."

"Although so many weeks have passed since Peter has gone," said Norman at the breakfast table, "I can still hear the refrain of that repulsive remark said by the man next door." This was the first time he had spoken of the incident. "Did you hear it?" he asked.

"I know he said something," said Cecilia, "but I didn't understand it clearly."

"He spat at us and called us black filth," Norman said.

"Did he really say that?" Cecilia asked Norman nodded.

"Oh, no!" Cecilia exclaimed. "That is terrible."

"I can well imagine that man saying all sorts of evil things against us," Norman said.

"You know Norman," said Cecilia, "I am never willing to jump to hasty conclusions and judge people too harshly; but why do you think Alfred would say things against us?"

"Because that man is a Negro hater."

"Why do you think so?"

"I am going to give it to you straight." He paused for a moment. "Peter bought this estate from that man," Norman began, "and as time went by, they became quite friendly and visited each other regularly. But when we came to live here, he stopped his visits. H ....."

"Why do you think Alfred stopped his visits after we came to live here?" Cecilia interrupted.

"Because he has never been here, although Peter continued to visit him. He never came during Peter's illness."

"That sounds reasonable," Cecilia said.

"And hear is more," Norman went on. "Shortly after Peter gave me the estate he took ill. When he recovered, he went to that man's house. They must have had some argument, because his son Stephen never came again, nor did Peter go there."

"You know you are right." Cecilia said thoughtfully. "You are perfectly right."

"That man hates us," Norman said.

"You seem afraid to call his name," Cecilia chided.

"Not afraid," Norman snorted, "I hate to call it. I hate him .... his family. I even hate to live so near to him." Norman spoke rapidly and loudly.

"The servants will hear you," Cecilia cried warningly.

"But I will live next to him." Norman said. There was desperation in his tone. "Yes, I will live next to him," he repeated, "so that it will haunt him until death."

"But it will haunt you just as much," Cecilia told him.

"I don't mind, so long as it makes him uncomfortable."

"Peter once told me that we should never return evil for evil," Clarence said.

"Peter was a fool," Norman snapped.

Cecilia gasped; and a shaky hand covered her mouth.

"Not really a fool," Norman said apologetically, "but who for a man could love someone who hated him?"

"Somewhere in the Good Book it says that love begets love," Clarence said.

"I like that," Norman chuckled. "If love begets love, is it not conclusive then, that hate begets hate?"

"Yes," said Clarence, "but God did not make us to hate each other. He wants us to love each other."

"Young man, what God wants is only one side of the picture," Norman said flatly. "What I want is the other side."

The following day Norman was riding around the estate when he saw Alfred in the distance.

"So you called me black filth and spat at me?" Norman

asked in an undertone as they approached each other. They drew their animals to a halt when they were abreast. They were a little more than an arm's length away.

"Yes," Alfred replied, "that is what I said. You are filth in my eyes. Not even good filth; because I wouldn't put you to my canes." His face was red with rage. "Do you think I could like you?" Alfred went on. "You thief. Peter made arrangements to sell me the estate, but you cheated him."

"He didn't tell you that, did he?"

"No. But I know you black people."

"From this very minute," Norman hissed spitefully, "you and I are at war."

"Did you say this very minute?" Alfred asked. He chuckled. It was a throaty, cantankerous chuckle. "From the day you came, to live in that house we were at war," Alfred went on, "but this is now a declaration," he ground his teeth.

"I could kill you," Norman growled.

"I would advise you to," said Alfred, his face contorted with irony, "because if I get the chance you are dead."

They rode off and neither looked back.
To the many workers who were on either side, but out of earshot, it had been a casual meeting of their masters who had stopped for a moment to extend the hour's salutation and a brief discussion on the weather.

After dinner, Norman told his wife and son about the incident with Alfred.

"Where did the two of you meet?" Cecilia asked concernedly.

"At the southern end of the land by the little bunch of shrubs. If I had my gun I would have blown his brains out."

"Don't say that," Cecilia protested.

As the weeks sped into months, life became increasingly

intolerable for Hilda and Wilfred. Alfred imposed upon them extravagant fees for board and lodging. He restricted their coming in and their going out. He dictated to whom they should and should not speak. When they could take his dictatorship no longer they left his house and took abode elsewhere.

The domestic servants, yard-hands and farm workers were not exempted from the relentless onslaught of Alfred's ridicule and abuse. He dismissed many of them, and others left in disgust. While those who lived on the segregated section of their master's estate had to endure his treatment. Of course, some of the latter group was cunning enough to secretly make negotiations and remove their homes to other tenantries where they got employment and hoped to be treated more like human beings. As for the villagers, many of them were sending their children after the school-leaving period to become artisans.

Alfred ordered a plough; and when the crop came to an end the plough was ready to go into operation. He concluded that he was not to be out-done, at least, not by a black man.

Taking a stroll a few months later Alfred saw four of his neighbour's cows being led away; and he decided that financial circumstances were responsible for the sale of the animals. His decision was somewhat justified when there was a similar occurrence on the following evening. 'He will soon be bankrupt,' Alfred said to himself, 'and if I don't own the estate one of my white brothers will. At least that will satisfy me.' But when he saw his neighbour's canes being conveyed to the factory by two brand new motor lorries, he queried the ownership; and on learning the facts, he nearly went mad.

"It is all your fault," he stormed, when he returned home. "You are responsible for it."

"Responsible for what?" Ellin asked pensively.

"It was your idea that I should sell part of my estate. You said it was too much for me to handle alone. You are always interfering with my personal affairs."

"What has upset you now?" Ellin asked.

"Norman has two brand new motor lorries," Alfred wailed. "Can you imagine that? Can you imagine that? Answer me!" Ellin was silent. Her body was fast becoming numb and unresponsive to his accusations.

"Papa, you shouldn't shout like that," cried Stephen. "It isn't good for you at your age."

"Now look who's telling me what's good for my age," Alfred said quietly. He nodded slowly. "I wouldn't stand for it," he shouted loudly. He stamped angrily, then tottered uncontrollably across the room before falling to the floor where he remained motionless. Ellin and Stephen hurried to his side. They shouted for the servants who came and assisted in getting his limp body in bed.

When Alfred regained consciousness he discovered that he was being examined by the family doctor. Ellin and Stephen were standing near by. They were crying.

"What happened?" asked Alfred, when the doctor was gone. "I don't remember."

"We'll tell you some other time," Stephen said.

"I want to know now," Alfred demanded.

"Be quiet, please," Ellin implored. "The doctor said you should remain quietly in bed."

"Is he drunk or mad?" Alfred asked. But as he forced himself to a sitting position, his mouth fell open and his brown eyes glared frightfully. His big head fell back on the pile of pillows. He covered his face with his hands and burst into tears. He discovered that his legs were paralysed.

"I sorry the son-of-a-bitch isn't dead," Norman said joyfully, when he heard of Alfred's condition. "He is the worst bastard in all the world."

"You shouldn't say that, Daddy," Clarence said reproachfully. "It isn't right."

"He would have wished the same for me," Norman threw back.

"Maybe," said Clarence, "but you shouldn't return evil for evil."

"What else I shouldn't do? I don't suppose I should be your father, eh?"

Astonished, Clarence retreated a few paces. He looked questioningly at his father.

"What .... what made you say that?" Clarence stammered.

"Well, you have come along with a silver spoon in your mouth," said Norman, "and you ...."

"If I can remember correctly," interrupted Clarence, "I didn't always have it, did I?"

"And you have a good education," Norman went on, ignoring the question. "At least better than I have."

"Who is responsible for it, daddy?"

"Peter."

"But daddy, you don't seem to realise that Peter only got the opportunity because you gave it to him."

"How do you make that?"

"By accepting the job and bringing us here to live," Clarence said flatly. "In any case you are responsible for my being in the world," he went on after a pause, "and most of the things that occurred to me during my youth."

"You should never have spoken to Clarence in that manner," Cecilia cried miserably, when they were alone. "It can give him the impression that you are envious of him; or on the other hand, inferior to him."

When Dorothy took ill, she was taken to the St. Philip's Almshouse where she died without the realization of God's power. And the financial responsibility of her burial was undertaken by the parish authorities.

The rapid deterioration in the production of Alfred's crops made him antagonistic. He refused to relinquish his authority; and from his wheel chair, he dictated the manner in which the land should be cultivated and planted. Stephen, who was by this time an accomplished farmer, remained calm under the tyrannical rule of his crippled father.

"Papa, I want to discuss something with you," Stephen said one evening.

His mother was sitting across from him. It was the third time in two weeks that he had made use of those words without response from his father; but this time he was determined to say it as quickly as possible lest he postpone it again.

"Papa, I am asking your permission to bring here the young lady to whom it is my desire to marry, and introduce her ...."

"Bring her where?" Alfred interrupted.

Stephen was silent. He looked at his mother who was deliberately avoiding his pitiful gaze. The muscles about the left side of her face stood out clearly; an indication of clenched teeth. She felt sorry for her son. She wanted to say: 'Alfred, you are making a fool of yourself. You should be proud of such a son. Many fathers are not treated with that sort of respect these days. You should be glad to listen; and if necessary, offer advice to the youngster. Instead, you have treated him like a schoolboy.' But she said nothing.

"I will meet her on the road when I go wheeling," Alfred said shortly.

"But you wouldn't know her," Stephen said breathlessly.

"Who said I wanted to?" Alfred asked coldly, wheeling himself out of the room. "I don't want to know the whore who is going to squander my hard-earned savings."

• • •

A humiliated Stephen fell on his knees before his mother. He threw his arms about her waist. He buried his face in her lap and burst into tears.

"Oh! mama," he cried in muffled tones, "what an awful thing to say!"

"Never mind, son," she said tenderly, patting his shoulder while the tears rolled down her cheeks. "You'll soon get over it."

"Stephen, my crops are going from bad to worse," said Alfred a few days later.

"It is all your fault," Stephen ventured. "Nobody can successfully supervise the cultivation and planting of a field from a wheel-chair. One has got to see the field."

"That isn't all," Alfred whispered. He looked around to see if there was anyone near by. He wheeled himself next to Stephen.

"There is more to it than seeing the field," Alfred went on. "There is a secret. Yes, a secret; and I will give it to you. You must carry it out if you want to succeed. Will you?"

"I have never openly refused to execute any order given by you, have I?"

"No. Now listen attentively."

When he had thoroughly explained the secret of his success and what measures should be adopted in order to ensure quick and lasting improvement, Stephen rose from his chair. He was thoughtful. With his fingers locked in a firm grasp behind his back, he slowly paced the room. His head was held high and he looked straight ahead. Suddenly, he stopped before his father, whose gaze had followed his every movement and facial expression.

"I'm terribly sorry, Papa, but I will not do it," he said hurriedly. "I will not engage myself with anything of that nature."

"Young man! Are you standing before me, in my house, and telling me that you are not going to do it?" Alfred inquired angrily. His face grew red with rage and his fingers clutched in a vice-like grip on the band of his chair. "Am I hearing right?"

"Yes, Papa," Stephen said calmly. "You are."

Mad with rage, Alfred made an attempt to grab Stephen, but he stepped aside, and Alfred and his chair toppled over. Summoned by the crash, Ellin hurried into the room to find her crippled husband partly buried beneath the chair.

"What have you done, Stephen?" she asked accusingly, glancing at him as he stood motionlessly only a short distance away.

"What is it, Alfred?" she asked helping him to a sitting position.

"That blasted boy ...."

"Don't swear, Alfred, please," Ellin pleaded.

"Don't touch me!" Alfred shouted, as Stephen went to assist his mother.

"Alfred, why don't you learn to accept your fate and act your age?" cried Ellin. "You are making matters worse all the time."

The doctor was called and Alfred was confined to bed. The fall had severely shocked his aging body.

"What is the trouble with you and your father?" Ellin asked, when the doctor was gone.

"He wants to force me into some superstitious practice of his," Stephen answered abruptly.

"It isn't as foolish as you think," she whispered cunningly. "When you have lived as long as I have, you too, will realise the facts of life."

"If that's the way you feel about it," Stephen threw back, "you can do what he wants me to do."

"What is it?"

"You can get the particulars from Papa." When she said

nothing, he added: "Can you imagine that all his life he has been giving a man in the City one hundred dollars every year for a phial of some sort of liquid to throw at the four corners of the estate with the hope of improving the crops? Well, that is what he has been doing, and now that the crops are failing, he is convinced that his former practices were right. Well, I am going to tell you this here and now. Neither you, he, nor anyone else is going to make me superstitious. And last but not least, I don't want to hear any more of it," he concluded angrily.

Two dark-skinned nurses were employed to care for Alfred. In his thoughtful moments he realised all too late that he had allowed his son too much time in the company of Peter Barrow, whose influence was slowly revealing itself. Alfred's disability did not make him any more tolerant than formerly; instead, it seemed to aggravate his anger and intensified his restlessness.

As the days dragged slowly into weeks, Stephen noticed with much concern the tired look on his mother's lean face which was rapidly growing pale for the want of rest and from her husband's constant nagging. The nurses, too, although they worked alternately, looked exhausted, and dissatisfied with Alfred's behaviour. Stephen prayed that relief would come; but when it did, he cried bitterly. He loved his father, but he did not cry because his father was now dead, it was the way he acted before he died that grieved Stephen most.

"I....I....I don't want .... to .... die," Alfred had said, gasping breathlessly. "Not to .... leave my .... estate. That black man .... will rob you. I don't want .... to die. No .... No .... No .... !"

His funeral was well attended, but few of the villagers were there. His attitude towards them in recent years was terrible; and they were for the greater part glad to be rid of him.

• • •

"Your behaviour is the greatest display of ignorance I've seen," Cecilia said sternly. "I see no reason why you should rejoice at Alfred's death. He has not blocked the way. We all must go that side. Today for me, and tomorrow for you."

"I don't care what you say," Norman said hatefully, "I hated the old bastard. I'm glad he is gone, and that is that."

"In some things you're little different from Alfred," Cecilia said angrily.

"In what way?" Norman demanded.

"You think too much of this world and its goods," Cecilia replied calmly. "I heard that Alfred did not want to die. I hope you will let go of your earthly possessions peacefully when you come to die."

"I hope so."

After Alfred's death, Norman's resentment subsided. He had proved to Alfred and to himself that he was able to supervise successfully and get the desired crops; but his resentment did not remain dormant very long. Obsessed with the desire to prove himself, he had lived in seclusion; and now that his greatest enemy was gone, he decided to lead a more sociable life.

"Nobody's talking to you," snapped one of the four men who were standing together discussing the falling rain and its scarcity. His face was red with rage. By their attire, Norman knew that they were managers or estate owners. He knew, too, that the discussion was commonplace; and anyone was entitled to voice his opinion in a conversation of that sort. "By fraud," the man went on angrily, "you have been able to own an estate like us, but you are not like us. Look at the colour of your skin."

Humiliated and numb with rage, Norman walked hurriedly out of the building and into the street where he moved unheedingly onwards.

"Hey you!" shouted a little light-skinned street urchin from the doorway of a City store, "you can' feel de rain fallin'?" Embarrassed, and charged with hatred for those of the other race, Norman took shelter in the next store, where he resolved to associate only with the people of his origin.

"I have not forgotten that first day we met," Norman said.

"Neither have I," Irine returned. "You were seeking the job."

"That's right," said Norman, smiling friendly. "And you were engaged as you are now."

"Is that so?" asked Irine, returning his smile. "I don't remember."

"You have improved your living conditions admirably through the years."

"Thank you."

"You are always making tidy."

"Cleanliness is next to Godliness, you know."

Norman was silent for a moment. He noticed the gray hair beneath her white head-tie. He thought of her seniority and he did not want to offend her. Then he said gently: "I don't seem to understand it."

"Understand what?"

"How poor people like you," Norman said slowly, "can find so much time for God."

Irine looked astonishingly at him.

"You wouldn't understand that," Irine said sadly.

"Why?"

"Because there is little room in man's mind for God and wealth at one and the same time. I don't believe you would have spoken in that vein a few years ago. You were not riding a horse then."

"I don't know," Norman frowned, as he rode off, "but I was always ambitious; and I still have more to achieve. I'll see you around."

"Goodbye!" said Irine, shaking her head sadly, "I'll pray for you."

"Thank you," he returned, and galloped away.

During the years that followed, Norman concerned himself strictly with the hoarding of money. It was now a tidy sum. Cecilia knew that his objection to Clarence's wedding was financial.

"The boy is entitled to a life of his own," Cecilia said, when they were alone.

"And I'm entitled to spend my money the way I think best," Norman threw back.

"Spend?" Cecilia laughed. "It is a long time since you've spent any to speak of."

"What about the car?" Norman snapped angrily. "Haven't I just changed it for a new one?"

"I had completely forgotten that," she laughed.

"You would," he stormed. "It is just like a woman to forget the things she doesn't want to remember."

"Anyway, I don't think you should object to Clarence's marriage. The girl is quite a nice person."

"She may be nice for you, but not for me."

"Where you are concerned, no woman would be right for Clarence."

"Why?"

"Because you would hate to face the financial responsibility of a wedding," Cecilia said heatedly, and left the room.

Obsessed with an insatiable desire to live and amass riches, Norman ignored the advice of the physician who prescribed a diet of high protein, vitamins and calories. But when his body became weakened as the months went slowly by, he resolved to adhere to the doctor's counsel, but it was too late. His system revolted against the treatment; and his long illness filled him with the hope of recovery; and when his family repeatedly implored him to make a writing for the distribution of his estate, he paid no attention to them.

"I don't want to die," Norman said grievously, "not after I've accumulated all this. I .... I am not going to die .... but I'll make a will."

Two days later he lost consciousness and died in his sleep. Mostly because of Norman's wife and son, many of the villagers dressed themselves in their best clothes and went to the funeral service, which was performed during the morning. They said that Norman had been a hard master; but his wife and son were kind and gentle.

A huge, dense cloud rose slowly out of the sea and hovered over the island. The sun that had been shining brightly was now shaded. It was dark. Some people were spending lavishly, while others had nothing to spend. Some were eating and drinking sumptuously, while others were starving. Some were driving and dressing luxuriously, while others were walking in rags. Some were laughing joyfully, while others were crying sorrowfully. Some were giving birth in grandeur, while others gave birth in misery. Some were entombed with pomp, while others were interned with simplicity. Some were talking loudly, while others were silent. These were the best of times; these were the worst of times.

And there was a great storm; not a storm of wind and rain and thunder and lightning and raging seas, but a storm of bottles and stones and bricks and sticks and shells and cans. And people ran madly to and fro shouting and insulting and assaulting others; and looting and smashing shop windows and setting fires and overturning cars.

And martial law was read, and rifles roared. And the guilty fled and the innocent fled. And the guilty were shot dead and the innocent were shot dead. And the guilty were arrested and the innocent were arrested. And the guilty were fined and the innocent were fined. And the guilty were imprisoned and the innocent were imprisoned. And there was a great calm.

And when the dense cloud lifted, there was light. And in the light, there stood a tall, dark figure .... the figure of a man. The man who was to be a leader .... the leader of a very dominant party .... the party that was to decide the destiny of its people, and the destiny of the West Indies and the West Indian Federation.

THE PASSAGE TO EDEN

PART FIVE

A gust of breeze rushed through the trees just as the sun came peeping out of the water .... a token that a new day was born to this rural village and all the sunny world. Birds in the trees awakened by the breeze chirped tunes of prayer as they flipped from bough to bough. It was good to be alive. The sun came slowly over the hill stretching its golden rays like hands farther and farther down the hill and through the trees assuring more and more birds of the new day and of their duty to join their neighbours in chirping prayers; a way of thanking God for life and nature's goodness; and, like an obedient child stirred by the loving hand of its mother, so responded the birds in the trees to the groping hands of the sun's rays. Down, down, still farther down, until the air was filled with tunes of various birds .... one happy family in accord.

At the foot of the hill stood two formidable stone buildings, whose lands were divided by low, green olive trees. Like the birds, the occupants of these buildings were stirred by the rays of the sun, but they were less active in response. Night's slumber still rested heavily upon them and no sign of life could be seen from outside. But farther along the foot of the hill, some distance away, life was evident.

'There is so much to thank God for,' Irine said to herself, as she rose from kneeling and praying beside her bed. 'I never thought I would have lived to enjoy the pleasure of a home with an oil-stove, electric lighting and running water. It is unfortunate that Samuel did not live to share these things with me. But God knows best. To tell the young people of the hardships I have gone through they wouldn't want to believe it. Of course, God is the forerunner of all things; and out of evil cometh good; but I do believe that the riot is responsible for many of the privileges which we now enjoy.'

The trend of her thought was broken by a loud knocking. It was the man who came to deliver the daily newspaper, which she and David read with much interest. She reached for her spectacles, and read the headline aloud. "Labour Party to contest General Elections." She put aside the paper and the spectacles and went about preparing breakfast for David, who had gone to the beach for an early bath. 'The Labour Party is sure doing good work,' she said to herself. 'One cannot fail to see the vast improvement. More schools to meet the need of the increasing population, good roads, street lighting, housing schemes, public baths, public libraries, health clinics and social centres. If it wasn't for that big-head man whose influence has so many coloured men like himself in the House of Assembly, we would still be working year in and year out without vacation with pay. Many of our children would not have been able to see the inside of a Government secondary school; and to be educated there as they are now, would be out of the question.'

"I'll be there in a minute," she said, in response to a knock.

"Good morning," said the dark-skinned young man who was standing under the verandah. "Are you Mrs. Goddard?"

"Yes. I am," she answered politely.

"Is your son's name David?"

"Yes."

"This is the place," said the young man, looking over his shoulder to the two men who were standing next to the small, aluminum-painted van, which was parked at the door.

"Start to work."

"What does all this mean?" Irine asked in surprise.

"We come to install Radio Distribution," said the man. "You sign here."

Irine took from the man the sheet of paper. "I'll do nothing of the sort," she said when she had read it.

"I don't see why you should be afraid to sign it," said the man. "It is for your son."

"I am doubtful."

"Why are you doubtful?"

"Because my son always discusses business matters with me before ...."

"Here I come," said David, arriving just at that moment. He placed his bicycle against the steps and joined the others under the verandah.

"Why didn't you tell me about this?" Irine asked.

"I wanted to surprise you," he smiled, "just this once. Since I am on vacation, I was hoping to be at home when the men arrived; but I got detained at the beach."

Smiling proudly with her handsome, dark-skinned son, Irine returned to the house and to her domestic affairs. When the installation was completed, the man turned on the switch, and there was the blaring sound of organ music accompanying a choir which sang the Twenty-Third Psalm, and while the singing continued, Irine, overwhelmed with joy, lifted her tear-filled eyes in thankfulness to God.

• • •

Stephen, with no one to hinder him, was now happily married to Patsy, the woman of his choice. The woman who had borne him a sturdy, blonde-haired son; who, with a single puff, had blown out the two candles which were placed on his last cake. Stephen was proud of himself and his family. Due to his mother's illness and death, which followed only a few months after her husband was buried, Stephen's wedding had to be postponed until a later date. It had been a quiet wedding, which was performed in the parish church. Except for the best man, only relatives witnessed the ceremony. When it ended, Stephen's car lead the way to his home where the reception was held under the glow of a brilliant sinking sun, whose light about the decorated green lawn afforded the photographer the opportunity to take many intimate pictures. Pictures, whose revelation would unfold the unspoken congeniality of those moments. As the sun slid slowly out of sight and the evening shadows fell, the small number of guests strolled into the house where they spent a few memorable hours.

Within six months of his father's death, Clarence announced his engagement and was married to Diana, the young lady he had chosen. She was now the mother of a little baby girl who was already stepping unsteadily about the house and calling names with her own peculiar pronunciation. Clarence's wedding ceremony was performed in the Cathedral with the full choir in attendance. The organist played with such mastery, that he became the topic of discussion immediately afterwards. On reaching home, Clarence and his many guests were astonished to find that the rain had been falling and the out-door preparation for the reception had to be abandoned; but they took to the house where they enjoyed themselves until well into the night.

Riding his horse leisurely around the estate one bright,

sunny day, Clarence heard a loud, shrieking sound. He looked around to see Stephen, who was also riding, waving a hand and galloping towards him.

"I certainly didn't expect this," said Clarence, as they drew near.

"What?" Stephen asked. There was a note of surprise in the tone of his voice. Clarence noticed. He felt ashamed.

"This sort of salutation," he answered quickly.

"Why?" Stephen asked, looking into his eyes.

"W..e..l..l, a lot of water has flowed under the bridge since then."

"I am equally aware of that," said Stephen, "and it makes no difference to me. Does it mean all that to you?"

"No. It doesn't mean one thing to me either. The truth is," he smiled, "I've wanted it more than anything else in this world; but I didn't know how you felt about it."

"I'll tell you," said Stephen, returning his smile, "ever since we were separated I've looked forward to a re-union."

He offered his hand. Clarence drew his animal near and took the extended hand in a firm grip. "A re-union," he said. There was sincerity in his voice. When they had spoken for some time Stephen suddenly glanced at his wristwatch. "Gee!" he exclaimed. "I didn't realise we've been talking so long. When I saw you I was hurrying into the yard to meet someone; but I was awaiting this opportunity so long that I couldn't afford to miss it. Now I've broken my appointment."

"Which one was hanging longer?"

"This one, of course …. much too long."

"Then there shouldn't be much remorse."

"There isn't much, but I'll see if I can kill two birds with one stone. I'll see you around," he concluded happily, and rode off swiftly towards home.

Clarence turned slowly in the opposite direction; but he had gone only a short distance when he seemed to hear his name called. He looked back. He was alone. He saw only the cluster of shrubs and suddenly realised that he and Stephen became re-united in the area where their fathers had declared open hostility against each other.

'This is a strange occurrence,' said Clarence to himself.

'An occurrence that shouldn't be taken lightly,' came his father's voice echoing from beyond. 'Oddly enough, it occurred there to remind you of the things I told you about him.'

'Surely those things can't be true,' Clarence argued. 'No one could be as treacherous as that.'

And to escape the scene and the man's hateful words, Clarence spurred the animal into a quick trot and rode away.

"I met Stephen this morning while riding around the estate," said Clarence, as soon as he got in the house.

"Where did you see him? Did he speak to you?" Diana asked. Her black eyes were shining hopefully. "Did he?"

Clarence was glad that she spoke so eagerly. It had given him the opportunity to avoid making mention of that dreadful place.

"I didn't even see him until I heard his whistle."

"What did he say, Clarence?" she asked impatiently. "Did he talk to you?"

"Sure. We talked a long time."

"Oh! Clarence," she said sweetly, moving up to him and placing both palms on his shoulders, "tell me about it."

"You seem exceptionally glad," said Clarence, smiling fondly.

"Don't you think I should be?"

Clarence shrugged his shoulders.

"I haven't forgotten our adolescent years," she went on. "Have you?"

"Certainly not."

"It is no secret what God can do," she quoted, as they moved into the lunch-room.

• • •

The sun was high in the sky; but its light was frequently diminished by the thick, dark patches of clouds that were drifting regularly over its face. Stephen, in a rather pensive mood, was inspecting his crops when he suddenly stumbled upon the cluster of shrubs and remembered Clarence and their previous meeting on that spot. He pulled the animal to a halt and looked cheerfully at the insignificant bunch of bushes, which became such a monument in his life. He smiled at the thought. It was pleasant. But he was soon shocked by the recollection of a less recent encounter .... that of Clarence's father and his own. He gazed intently at the shrubs which seemed to reach up to his face and dance mockingly before him.

'Why did I ever come back to this place?' Stephen asked himself.

'To be told the things I've already told you,' came his father's voice from the grave. 'I told you to keep away from Clarence. He is no good for you. He is a thief. Like his father, he will devise means and ways to rob you of your estate. Don't trust him.'

"I will trust him utterly," Stephen stormed. He grew mad with rage as he watched the dancing shrubs. "I am a man, and I'll dictate for myself. All your life you've dominated me. You can't do that any longer."

'I may not be able to dominate your life to the full,' came the voice from the grave, 'but I can influence you negatively, and you will have no peace of mind.'

Engrossed in thought, Stephen did not hear his name called until Clarence was near at hand. He suspected the state of chaos in Stephen's mind; but he did not betray his thoughts. He said: "I just rushed into the yard for this can of diesel oil. The man was ploughing when the tractor ran dry. I was returning with the oil when I saw you and came over. What are you doing this evening?" He spoke rapidly. He was in a hurry.

"Nothing," Stephen replied.

"Then I'll be expecting you and Patsy at my home this evening."

"What time?"

"About six .... Is that a deal?"

"Yes."

"See you at six," he said, and shot down the lane and out of sight.

"I'll bet you saw Clarence again today," said Patsy, as soon as Stephen entered the house. "Did you?"

"Yes," Stephen replied. "How did you know?"

"I can see the joyful expression all over your face."

"Is it as obvious as that?"

"As obvious as that."

"He has invited us over this evening."

"Really! What time?" she asked smiling cheerfully.

He told her and she was glad to know.

Stephen, Patsy and their son were standing under a tree discussing the planting of their newly designed garden-beds when a loud whistling sound filled the air. They looked around to see Clarence, Diana and their little daughter. They were standing in the drive-way.

"What are you waiting for?" Clarence asked.

Stephen looked at his watch. "Six o'clock," he replied smiling.

"The invitation is not as formal as that," said Clarence, looking at his own watch. "We'll utilize the five minutes along the way."

"Alright," said Stephen, and he lead his family down the drive-way.

"You have a sweet little girl," said Patsy, as she took her from Diana.

"Thank you," said Diana, dropping to her heels. "And you have a sturdy little man ..... what's your name?"

"My name is Richard," he replied boldly. "What is hers?" Patsy lowered herself to a squatting position.

"Tell your little friend your name," Diana coaxed.

"My name is Monica," she said softly.

"Let's go," said Clarence, looking down on the four individuals whose heads were clustered in childish chatter, "the drinks are getting hot."

"Hot!" Diana exclaimed. "Has the fridge gone out of order?"

"Anything could have happened since we left home."

"Oh! Clarence," said Diana, "it isn't so long."

Clarence led the way; and as they strolled onward, Stephen was thoughtful of his childhood and the many occasions he saw his parents under similar circumstances strolling the same road with Elizabeth and Peter .... a man who expressed in his way of life, some of the finest qualities to be desired. Stephen was sorry similar qualities could not be found in his own father.

Chatting gaily as they walked along, Clarence kept the lead by a few paces. From within the house as they drew near, soft music floated through the open windows; but as they filed into the room the gruff voice of the announcer through the large radiogram said: "Now we'll play you a brand new tune. It is called: "Our Love Is Here To Stay." The whole party stood motionless and listened attentively to the words of the tune. When it ended, the atmosphere was chilled and devoid of the mirth that was so evident only minutes ago. Breaking the icy quiet, Clarence said: "Since that is true we should be joyful, not sorrowful. Let's have a drink on it."

Clarence returned a few minutes later. He was pushing a trolley. It contained a number of glasses, bottles of liquor, soft drinks and a container of ice.

"You may choose your drinks and help yourselves," he said.

"What are you going to drink, Monica?"

"Coke, daddy."

"And you, Richard .... what do you want?"

"I want a Ju-C, please."

When drinks were served, Clarence held his glass high, "This is to us," he said, making a sweeping motion with both arms, "and may the congeniality of the moment live on until the end of time."

"Thank you," voiced the adults in unison.

After they had a number of drinks Stephen said: "What about the library? Is it still in shape?"

"Still in shape .... want to have a look?"

"Why not?"

"Excuse us for a minute," Clarence said.

"They are just grown boys," Patsy said, when they left the room.

"I don't think we are any better than they are," Diana said.

Inside the library, Stephen closed the door. He rested his back against it. He closed his eyes. Then, with a slow painful motion he passed the back of his right arm across his brow.

"What's the matter?" Clarence asked. "Do you feel bad?"

"No," Stephen whispered. His voice was barely audible. "No. I don't feel bad. I am trying to blot out those horrible years. The years during which I was deprived of the right to this pleasant home, these priceless books and your stimulating company. No one will ever know what those years meant to me." He spoke slowly .... painfully.

"I always like to act and speak in keeping with my age," Clarence said with matching sincerity, "but I feel very silly when I admit that those years were almost intolerable."

Breaking the silence Stephen asked: "What has become of your mother?"

"She is beginning life again."

"Getting married?"

"Got married .... I think Providence has been good to us."

"Do you mean to you and your mother?"

"No .... to you and me." When Stephen said nothing he added, "My mother took up abode in St. Joseph two days before you and I met."

"Your mother is quite a nice person."

"Yes. But she had some fixed ideas about you and me. Ideas that I would never like expressed in Monica's hearing. Of course mother's ideas had their origin in the behaviour of your ...."

"My father. You don't need to be ashamed to voice it. I know he wasn't very pleasant ....especially when colour was involved."

"My father was little different from yours; and things being what they are, we can now pattern our lives to suit ourselves and for the benefit of our children. Once more the doors of this house are open to you and your family with free access to the books."

"You have kept them superbly."

"Yes. I had a very good reason. I knew that you and I would become re-united and the books would be of vital importance."

"It was very thoughtful of you."

"No more than you would have done if the books were in your possession."

"I guess so."

As Stephen returned to the sitting room, Richard ran with out-stretched arms. Lifting him from the floor, Stephen said: "Yes, son. Daddy has been very inconsiderate."

"He and Monica had a fine time together," said Diana, "until she fell asleep on the carpet."

"They had enough for one night," Patsy said.

"I think we all had enough," said Stephen, going through

the door. "The next visit is yours."

"That will be nice," Diana said.

That night Clarence went to bed in the best of moods. 'It is good to be re-united with Stephen.' He thought to himself when the lights were out.

'Did you ever stop to recall the warning I gave you about him?' came his father's voice from beyond. 'I told you he is no good for you. He is going to cheat you out of your estate. His father hated me.'

"But Stephen is different from his father."

'I suppose you are different from me too.'

"In a way, yes."

'Because you are better educated. I was a fool to educate you. I should have known that you would have thought yourself superior.'

"I am not superior. I just think different from you."

'Yes. You got your silly idea about living in unity with the white man from Peter Barrow. I am to blame for that. I left you in his company much too often for any good, and now that you are sitting on a fortune his influence is going to ruin you.'

"Let it ruin me. I will do or say nothing to betray my confidence in Stephen; and no one will know of my inner conflict."

It was well after midnight when Clarence's tossing ended and he fell asleep. But it was not a sound restful sleep. Diana had to shake him several times.

"What's the matter with you?" she asked on one occasion.

"I was dreaming," he replied.

"I know you were," she said, "but what could cause you to make so much noise."

"Bad dreams, I guess." He felt ashamed, but he did not admit it.

• • •

Patsy hurried to answer the door-bell. "Oh! look who's here, Stephen," she exclaimed cheerfully.

He was standing before the large radiogram. In his hands was a pile of records from which he was making his selection and sliding record after record over the slender spindle of the record changer. Looking over his shoulder, he said. "They are overdue by two days."

"That is true," said Clarence. "I was a little busy the past two evenings."

"Never mind," Patsy said pleasantly. "Early or late we are glad to entertain you."

Stephen started the machine. The first record fell. The tune was: 'The Second Time Around.' "Shall we dance?" he asked.

"Why not?" said Diana, embracing him. "The dance tempo has changed greatly since we were young. I can't do many of the latest steps."

"Neither can I," Stephen said.

Clarence and Patsy were dancing in fine style. The children were looking on. Another record fell. It was: 'Love Is A Many-Splendoured Thing,' followed by 'Autumn Leaves.' When the selection ended the atmosphere was charged with a warm friendliness that the house had never known.

At another corner of the house, the children were talking in a friendly mood.

"You want to see my toys?" Richard asked.

"Yes," Monica replied.

"Come," said Richard, taking hold of her hand and leading her away.

"Not so fast," said Patsy, rushing to check his swift movements and assist in supporting Monica. "You are too rough. She is not as strong as you are."

They all entered the toy room. Monica was attracted to the

247

colourful fire-engine with its long ladder and tiny tin men who were stationed to their posts. She went down on her hands and knees for a closer look. Crouched forward as she was, a lock of her kinky, black hair fell over her brow to obstruct her vision; but as she took a hand to remove it, Diana felt about her own head for a hairpin and fastened the unruly plait. After some minutes Monica crawled over to where the teddy-bear stood.

"You want that?" Richard asked, taking the bear from its sitting position and handing it to her. "Take it."

With her little legs buckled under her, Monica sat on her heels and took the toy. She cradled it as a mother would cradle her baby and smiled down on it. Then, looking Richard in the face she returned it to him.

"You don't want it?" he asked.

"No."

"Why?"

"I have one," she replied, crawling over to a fluffy little dog.

"You want that?" he asked. He seemed determined that she should have something. She looked at him and shook her head.

"You have one?"

She nodded. He seemed disappointed.

"You have one of these too?" he asked, reaching for the electric type iron with its long, black rubber cord. She hastened to receive it with outstretched hands. Watching the children, the adults were reminded of their own childhood days, and their willingness to share their joys and sorrows. The thought was pleasant.

"No," she answered, smiling childishly.

"Take it," he said.

"You give me?"

"Yes."

"To take home?"

"Yes."

"True?"

"Yes."

"Thanks .... look Mummy, Richard give me this."

"Did you say thanks for it?"

"Yes, Mummy."

"Richard is a nice boy." Diana said. "Don't you think so?"

"Yes, Mummy."

"What are you going to give him in return?"

"A doll."

Diana laughed. "Boys don't play with dolls," she said.

"I don't know what to give him, Mummy."

"All right, when we go home we will see what we can find."

"Come and go now."

"Not yet, honey," Clarence said fatherly. "You can play a little first."

The day Richard was sent to kindergarten was the most disastrous thing that could have happened to Monica. She cried to break her little heart. She had become so accustomed to Richard, that to be alone was more than she could bear. She ate very little that day. Clarence and Diana felt sorry for her. They tried to coax her, but it was fruitless. Richard, too, had been reluctant to leave. He had always said that he wanted to go to school; but now that the time had come, he was hesitant. When he returned from school that evening Monica asked: "You going to school tomorrow?" Richard did not reply. He did not know. He looked at his parents for assurance.

"Yes," Patsy answered, "but he will be home with you in the evening."

"I want to go too," Monica said.

"You are not old enough," said Diana. "You will go next year."

"Please! Mummy," she pleaded, "I want to go tomorrow."

Realising that they were all faced with a great difficulty, the

Queen's College

Harrison College

adults looked questioningly at each other for a solution to the problem; but neither seemed to know the answer. And when one week passed with no progressive change, Stephen said "The best thing to do is send her to school. If we don't it may destroy her zeal and retard Richard's progress."

"I think I see your point," Clarence said. "I'll take her in the morning and explain to the mistress."

After that day the children went to school together until Richard gained entry to Harrison College and Monica to Queen's College. During the years that followed, life was extremely pleasant for Richard and Monica's parents who gloated over their children's academic success, and finally their graduation. But when Richard ignored his literary ability which got him much credit at school to take a job in the commercial field, and Monica became employed as a stenotypist in the Government Service, Diana's dreams became a nightmare.

"I hate to think of what is likely to happen to those children," Diana said one evening just as Monica had driven off with Richard in his new car. "It frightens me."

"There is no need to be afraid," Clarence said, "Richard is not a reckless driver."

"It is not his driving that scares me," Diana said.

"Is it sex?" Stephen asked.

"No," Diana replied.

"Then what is it?" Patsy asked.

"Don't let us fool ourselves," Diana began, "we all know that sooner or later, colour is bound to come up before those children."

"What happens when it does?" Clarence asked.

"That is what worries me," Diana said. "I don't know what to expect."

"I'm not afraid," Clarence said. "Are you?" he looked at Stephen and Patsy.

"No," Stephen replied. "But I should like to hear your reason." He gazed challengingly at Clarence.

"By virtue of their training ..... in the first place," Clarence said with some assurance, "our children have stronger characters than we; and the genes we have implanted in them are no less strong than those in us. If our parents failed to influence us against each other, how can outside influence affect our offspring?"

"I think your explanation is reassuring," Stephen said quickly. His voice was charged with sincere admiration. "I couldn't have done as good in so few words," he went on proudly. "You have certainly made an intimate study of human nature."

"Are you still afraid?" Clarence asked.

Diana shook her head. She smiled. The tension was gone. "No," she replied. "I am not afraid ... not any more."

"Prepared as they are," Stephen said assuringly, "our children can face the difficulties of this world with confidence; and instead of being inveigled by its vice, they can assist in converting others as the years go by."

"Did you hear that sarcastic remark from the blonde-haired young man sitting at the table behind us?" Monica asked, as she slid into the car in the parking lot across from the restaurant, which was aglow with fluorescent lighting.

"About you and me?" Richard asked.

"Yes."

"I did."

"I've heard it many times."

"You've never told me about it before."

"And I only mentioned it now because I thought you heard."

"I see."

"When we were at college I used to hear it occasionally; but I hear it more frequently since we're grown."

"I see."

"On one occasion I was actually told ...."

"Say it," Richard urged.

"That I should not allow a white man to wash over me."
Richard felt sick in the stomach. He sighed loudly.

"Surprised?"

"At least that you never mentioned it."

"Why should I? I know you to be a fine person."

After a pause Richard said: "Among other things, I've been
told I should not go around with you in public .... all this talk
about colour, and never once have I heard my parents with it."

"Neither have I."

"Does this racial talk embarrass you?"

"Not in the least," Monica replied. Her voice was like music,
and as the car glided away, she added, "I know what to expect
from a community as lopsided as the one in which we live."

"Then, are you prepared for what is to come?"

"Of course I am."

"It is not as easy as you think," Richard told her. "My father
once said: " 'Richard, unless you ask God to give you the
strength and the courage and the endurance to stand almost
alone and fight against a condition under which you could
normally live most comfortably, you would fail miserably.' "

"On whose power do you think I depend?" she asked sweetly.
He could not answer.

"I'm very proud of you .... and the way you think," he said.

"I'm proud of you too," she said, switching on the radio.

"Here comes a beautiful song," said the announcer. "It is
called 'Mr. Wonderful.' " "Listen to the lyrics," said Monica,
turning up the volume. When the tune ended, she touched his
shoulder and said: "That is you."

"Is there a song called 'Miss Wonderful'?"

"I don't know."

"Then I'll substitute Miss for Mr. and sing it all over
again."

"You're not being very original ," she said teasingly.

"Do you ever make an allowance?"

"Not often," she replied. "But I'll do so now because it is appropriate."

Quite unlike former times when at the foot of the hill the lands were divided by low, green hedges, tall thorny hedges or low, green olive trees, today, the lands are undivided and so is the attention of the occupants of the two plantation buildings who are together planning a wedding - a wedding at which old friends of Stephen and Patsy, old friends of Clarence and Diana, as well as the young acquaintance of Richard and Monica who would be married in a few days' time.

And as the date of the most unusual wedding of the century, the first inter-racial marriage in Barbados drew near, there was some gossip among the village people, and indeed, almost everywhere else. Then, suddenly, the day was upon them, when Stephen and Patsy were at the home of Clarence and Diana where they could all join to welcome and introduce the guests as they arrived for the wedding.

Monica was radiant in her white, flower-patterned knee-length, lace frock which was v-shaped at the throat with elbow-length, leg-o-mutton sleeves over a rose-pink petticoat. The narrow brimmed white hat was draped with matching lace; short at the front and shoulder length at the back. Her ears were adorned with pearl-like bobbs. She wore off-white, high-heeled shoes and in her hands, she carried a small bouquet. Her lips were slightly smeared with island plum lipstick.

Accompanied by her father, they were greeted with loud shouts of Cheese! Cheese! Cheese! From the already seated guests under the shade of the huge canvas which comfortably covered the lawn. Stephen and Richard (Bridegroom and Best man) were already waiting when Clarence and Monica took their places besides them. The men wore double-breasted, parson grey suits, suitable shirts and ties and black, patent leather shoes. In the buttonhole of the left lapel, they wore a leaf of fern and a red carnation.

"Dearly beloved," said the prune-faced minister in a British accent, "we are gathered together here in the sight of God, and in the face of this congregation, to join together this man and this woman in holy matrimony; which is an honourable estate, instituted of God in the time of man's innocence, signifying unto us the mystical union that is betwixt Christ and his Church; which holy estate Christ-adorned and beautified with His presence, and the first miracle that he wrought, in Cana of Galilee; and is commended of Saint Paul to be honourable among all men...."

Richard vowed his faithfulness to Monica and Monica vowed her faithfulness to Richard. They exchanged rings and were pronounced man and wife.

Then Richard, on behalf of himself and his wife, expressed gratitude to the many guests who had taken time out from their busy schedules to attend the wedding. He also showered thanks upon those who had, in any small way, helped to make the occasion a success. He explained that chairs and tables were already arranged in the house, and soon the same would be arranged here. "There is plenty, and a wide variety of food and drinks. Feel free to enjoy yourselves," he invited.

The place was a hive of activity. Men, women and children were moving freely back and forth with food and drinks. Sitting wherever space was available and taking part in discussions of every sort. And when the multi-coloured lights came on and the dancing got under way, it was difficult to determine who was dancing with whom. Encouraged by the guests, who were passing around food and drinks

the peasants, they were also dancing respectfully on the
erimeter of the lawn.

Suddenly the music stopped; and Richard, with his hand
esting upon Monica's shoulder, said: "Ladies and gentlemen,
we are overwhelmed by what we have experienced here today.
hope that the togetherness does not stop here tonight; that
ll of you take this spirit with you and exercise it at home.
Our parents told us of an Englishman, Peter Barrow, who
ad this house built and was the owner of this section of
he estate. He defied all social and economic customs of that
lay and employed my wife's grandfather as an accountant;
f course, Peter taught him most of the work. Peter was
ruly a philanthropist. He argued that if you teach people to
late, they will teach others to hate, which is destructive; only
unconditional love will cure man's dilemma. I sincerely hope
hat this day remains in your mind for as long as you live. God
bless and take you all safely home."

"Thank you, thank you," they shouted, "for he's a jolly good
ellow ...." The music started and so did the dancing.

Richard and his bride slipped out the back, into his car and
drove into the moon-lit night towards their newly-designed
bungalow between the two weather-beaten buildings, and
turned slowly onto the red-tiled drive way which led to the
bungalow that was painted in pearl white and trimmed with
green, where the fragrance from a variety of flowers filled the
air. At the door, Richard unlocked it, stretched an arm around
the doorpost, flicked a switch and the room was aglow with
electricity - which was powered from the Electric Company in
the vicinity of the City, which had not yet expanded its service
sufficiently for the parents of Monica and Richard to enjoy the
luxury of multi-coloured lighting at their wedding reception.

Lifting his wife over the threshold, Richard kissed her

passionately before gently setting her down to close the door. They hastily removed their wedding garments to leisurely consummate their marriage.

Agust of breeze rushed through the trees just as the sun came peeping out of the water .... a token that a new day was born to this rural village and all the sunny world. Birds in the trees awakened by the breeze chirped tunes of prayer as they flipped from bough to bough. It was good to be alive. The sun came slowly over the hill stretching its golden rays like hands farther and farther down the hill and through the trees assuring more and more birds of the new day and of their duty to join their neighbours in chirping of prayers; a way of thanking God for life and nature's goodness; and like an obedient child stirred by the loving hand of its mother, so responded the birds in the trees to the groping hands of the sun's rays. Down, down still farther down, until the air was filled with tunes of various birds .... one happy family in accord.

And like the birds stirred by the rays of the sun, so too did the rays of the sun stir Richard and Monica to be up and kneeling beside the bed to offer their share of thanksgiving, by reading the prayer they had together written: "Almighty God, we come before You at the dawning of a new day to start a new life as man and wife. Bless us, we beseech You; and if it is Your will that we should have children, let the examples we set before them be no less lofty than those that were set by our parents, who emulated their own parents, whose spiritual domain was greatly enhanced by Peter Barrow's philosophical input. However, some folks have said abroad that our marriage will fail because the yoke is uneven. Nevertheless, we will continue to be obedient to the teaching of Jesus who said: *"I am the true vine, and my Father is the husbandman. Every branch in me that beareth not fruit he taketh away: and every branch that beareth fruit, he purgeth it, that it may bring forth more fruit. Now ye are clean through the word which I have spoken unto you. Abide in me, and I in you. As the branch cannot bear fruit of itself, except it abide in the vine; no more can ye, except ye abide in me. I am the vine, ye are the branches: He that abideth in me, and I in him, the same bringeth forth much fruit: for without me ye can do nothing. If a man abide not in me, he is cast forth as a branch, and is withered; and men gather them, and cast them into the fire, and they are burned. If ye abide in me, and my words abide in you, ye shall ask what ye will, and it shall be done unto you. Herein is my Father glorified, that ye bear much fruit; so shall ye be my disciples. As the Father hath loved me, so have I loved you: continue ye in my love."* Quote: St. John 15-1-9 But in the darkness of its own making, the race continues to teach separation: religious, economic, scientific, political, social, national, international, regional, intellectual etc. etc. Nevertheless, from the east of the globe to the west of the globe; and from the north of the globe to the south of the globe; within that vast circle of darkness they are the seekers of TRUTH; and as these persons evolve more, and more, moving towards the LIGHT, they will in the fullness of time find LOVE - which is, in Eden."

F. Ellerton wrote:-
Oh how fair that morning broke
When in Eden Man awoke!
Beast and bird and insect bright
Revell'd in the gladsome light;
God looked down from Heav'n above
All was life and joy and love ...."

(Hymn 533 Ancient & Modern Version)

THE END